Traveling Abroad
Without A Camel

A Novel

By

Charles Wapner

Cover art and design: Coverabook

Book Formatting by: ibookboy.com

Write: charles.wapner@yahoo.com

ISBN: 978-1-7331029-2-6

To My Children Elena, Paul, and Jude

Special thanks to Beverly Wapner Robinovitz, Linda Mead,

Ira L. Feinberg, and Natasha Wapner.

Table Of Contents

INTRODUCTION

Adam was a smart kid who grew up in an upper middle-class family in New Jersey. His father was a successful medical doctor. He wanted Adam to be a medical doctor, and from an early age, he educated Adam to be an expert in human anatomy. By the age of 15, he was as knowledgeable about the subject as any first-year medical student who had completed gross anatomy.

At age fourteen, his mother died from a ruptured blood vessel. He became depressed and began to have headaches. When he was nineteen, his obese, cigarette smoking, workaholic dad died of a heart attack. He and his younger sister moved into a modern-day castle on the other side of his home town, where his mother's brother, Uncle Rick, a wealthy international furniture manufacturer, lived alone.

In 1965, with the Vietnam War raging, Adam went off to college. During his third year at university, the war got to him in a bad way. His depression became worse. His headaches were mild but began to occur more often. Because he was healthy enough to be drafted into the American military upon graduation, he became an angry, depressed young man.

In the late winter of 1968, Adam bought an airline ticket to London with a return ticket three-months later. He was going abroad for the summer, traveling alone. The big question was whether he would return...

TRAVELING ABROAD WITHOUT A CAMEL

PROLOGUE

"In Israel, in order to be a realist, you must believe in miracles."

–David Ben-Gurion, the first Prime Minister of Israel

Ein Gev Militarized Zone, Israel – September, 1968

I could still see the military patrol truck parked down below with its constant and unnerving vigilance, and it slowly dawned on me: my plan was blown. I had hoped to make a run for the lake, drink all the water I could and fill my small water bottle, before climbing back up the mountain. But would it have made a difference? Here I lay, no longer able to stand or climb, let alone run.

When I finally stopped crying, I turned my attention to the stars overhead. I gazed out to sea when, out of nowhere, a row of angels appeared to my right, sitting on the mountain crest with their short, chubby legs dangling over the side. I could not believe it. They were dressed in linen and appeared to be identical to the paintings of angels I had seen in Rome. I tried not to stare, until another row of angels appeared, this time to my left. They sat naked on the mountain top with their little legs dangling. These angels appeared to be identical to the ones I had seen in Greek paintings. I didn't speak to them, and they didn't speak to me.

After all, there was nothing left to say…

TRAVELING ABROAD WITHOUT A CAMEL

CHAPTER 1

From Oslo, I traveled farther north by train. When the rails came to an end, I continued in a modern bus with large windows. It allowed us passengers to see the beautiful countryside and the sea. The crowning attraction was Norway's fiords. My bus crisscrossed them several times on a series of ferry boats.

The driver pulled over to the side of the road after we passed Trondheim, but not yet to Narvik. He personally handed each of us a small, colorful card. It said, "I have crossed the Arctic Circle in Norway." It was just before the sun set, not many minutes past midnight, the red sun never sank from sight. Instead, as if by magic, sunset turned into sunrise. The red sun simply rose back up. Who would have thought it could happen? We certainly were in the land of the midnight sun. Not sure which direction the sun set or rose, I guessed North. It was a hell of a time to be without a compass.

The bus made its last stop at Narvik's train station, a short distance from the Norwegian Sea. The Atlantic Ocean ends at the Arctic Circle, not far below Narvik. I never would have guessed the Atlantic Ocean ended there. I guessed there were probably no signs warning swimmers and boaters: "Warning: Danger! Ocean ends ahead. Beware of Norwegian Sea and sudden drop of water temperature."

When the bus unloaded its passengers, sometime before 3 a.m., several lucky passengers already had a place to go. Some walked away to their homes. Others were picked up by family or friends in cars. Soon, I guessed, they would enjoy food, water, booze, warmth, and a clean bathroom. But for me and three others, the only homeless passengers hanging around the front of the train station on June 20th, 1968, the humid air was cold enough to freeze the balls off a bull.

I wasn't dressed for the weather. I wore a shirt, sweatshirt, sports jacket, long green Levi jeans, undershorts, socks, and my Florsheim shoes. I could only dream wearing a thick winter coat, a knit skiing hat, and fur-lined leather gloves. And there was no shelter from the damp cold: the train station was tightly locked up. Three of us tried at different times to open the door! We didn't know it wouldn't be unlocked until 6 a.m.

We waited apart from each other. No one spoke. One of the strangers was a middle-aged woman, dressed in black. She wore a winter coat. When I couldn't bear another minute of the cold, I walked up to her and asked if she spoke English. "No," she said abruptly and turned her back. I walked away disappointed. She killed the only survival plan I could muster: open her coat, open my sports jacket, and hug her tightly for dear life. Just because she wasn't freezing to death wasn't an excuse to turn her back on me. I saw James Bond do it in one of his movies. Saved his life and the woman's. Mine was a good idea.

Five thousand moments later, just before death by cold finally did me in, I nearly jumped for joy when a loud creaking sound came from the large train station door. The station master held open the door. I didn't jump for joy. I held back. If I had jumped, my frozen toes would have broken off into little pieces.

Four strangers walked briskly toward the door. The station master waved us in like a preacher welcoming his congregants. I wondered if he welcomed frozen passengers this way every day? The four of us quickly made our way to a giant, roaring fireplace. We stood close, careful not to be very close to each other. God forbid we touch. We rubbed hands— our own, of course. And I made a gentle prayer to the God of Fire for saving my life.

When the stationmaster eventually opened up his ticket window, I asked when the next train to Stockholm would arrive. He looked at me as if I should have known better, and said, "The train is already here. I'll announce when to board. You will change trains in Boden." The train was very close to the station. I don't know how I missed seeing it. Perhaps my upper eyelid icicles hadn't completely melted.

Having traveled through the scenic fiords of Norway, the northern Swedish countryside quickly became monotonous. Monotony became an opportunity to nap and recover from the sleepless, freezing night. Or was it a freezing morning? Without darkness, I was confused. But I did nap. And it did make a difference. I felt much better.

When I reached Boden, I switched trains and made myself comfortable on a vacant three-seater. Although I had paid 180 dollars for a Europass—a pass for first-class train travel for three months in some fifteen countries—this train had no first-class seating. If it had, I never would have met Olof.

The train stopped, and young male Swedish soldiers trickled into my passenger car, each carried an identical carry-on bags. They carried their bags in one hand and six-packs of beer in the other.

Once again, our coach rolled down the track headed southward. Wheels and rails soon settled into their own rhythm. To make myself more comfortable, I removed my Florsheim shoes. I nodded off again. During an open eye moment, I caught a soldier peering down at my Florsheim shoes. We made eye contact. I was about to have a new best friend.

"American?" the soldier asked loudly. Everyone in the train car heard.

"Yes, I am," I quietly answered. I hadn't wanted everyone in this train car to know my nationality, although I thought somehow people could probably just look at me and tell. Being an American during the unpopular Vietnam War was best kept secret. "Canadian," I should have said. I blew my cover. I was not a good liar.

"My name is Olof. Yours is?"

"Adam."

He sat down across from me and offered me a cold beer. I accepted the beer graciously.

"I like your shoes," he said, smiling, and in perfect English with a Swedish accent. His accent was more foreign than a British accent, but not as unusual as Scottish or Irish. My shoes *were* nice. I paid thirty-five dollars for them back in North Carolina. They were the most comfortable shoes I could find for the trip.

"Thank you, I like them too." I put my shoes back on and buckled them up. I didn't want to wear them, but I thought it was the only way to prevent them from disappearing should I fall back asleep.

The soldier was an athletic, good-looking guy, about my age: twenty-one. He had light brown hair and bedroom blue eyes. He told me he and his fellow soldiers were homesick and couldn't wait to get back to their parents' homes just outside of Stockholm.

"How long has it been since you were home?" I inquired.

"Three weeks," he answered. "We have mandatory one-year military training. We have just completed our first stage." I kept a straight face, but inside I was laughing. *Only three weeks?* I would have guessed much longer.

Sweden's military was not at war, so there was no hurry to ready them for combat. The country hadn't seen military action for a long time. The Congo Crisis had been by far the most serious international operation the Swedish Armed Forces had faced during the Cold War. It had been the first time in 147 years Swedish forces had been forced into battle. A total of 6,334 Swedes had served in the Congo between 1960 and 1964. A total of forty Swedish soldiers had been injured and nineteen killed.

CHAPTER 2

"I have an unbelievable story to tell you," confided Olof. "It happened recently, when my family was on holiday at our country home. We have a farmhouse, a large greenhouse for flowers, and a hay barn. Our fields produce hay for local dairy farmers.

"One afternoon, some friends of my parents came to visit. They brought their fifteen-year-old daughter with them. Cute girl. I was eighteen-years-old. My father told me to give her a tour of the greenhouse. I showed her the flowers and plants. Then I showed her the barn. She saw the tractor and asked for a ride on it. I drove her around the farm. It was a nice ride on a warm sunny day. She seemed to be a nice girl.

"When we got back to the barn, she jumped down from the tractor and wandered off. I left her alone and went off to return the tractor key to the lock box. But when I returned, she wasn't there. I called her, 'Annika. Where are you?' She didn't answer. 'Annika, this isn't funny.' I shouted.

"'Here I am,' she called out to me and I saw her head stick out from behind a wall. I went over there and found her naked, lying on her clothes laid out over the hay.

"I didn't shout at her, and I didn't panic. I asked her in a calm voice, 'What do you think you are doing? Get dressed.'

"She said I was to have sex with her, or else she would tell her parents I forced her to have sex with me.

"What could I do? I was speechless. But I had no choice, and I had no protection. So, I had sex with her. Guess what happened?"

"She told her parents you raped her? You had to join the army to escape her? She is pregnant? You are on your way home to marry her?" They all were reasonable answers.

"I got an STD from her: Annika, a fifteen-year-old girl. The doctor gave me medicine to take for ten days." I wasn't close. "What would you have done, Adam?"

I wished he hadn't asked. My very first thought was to kill myself and the girl, an unreasonable answer I held back from him. "I never knew of a situation like this one. Olof, if a fifteen-year-old threatened me, this is what I would have done. I would have started to unbutton my shirt. I would have told her I had an active case of venereal disease, and asked her to give me a rubber, protection. I would start to cry if she didn't believe me. Crying almost always makes a man was incapable of sex. Under no circumstance would I have had sex with her. Better my word against hers than her presenting herself to a doctor to prove intercourse. Don't you have laws against having sex with a fifteen-year-old in your country?"

"She was in my care. When in care of someone fifteen or younger, sex is not permitted."

"And if she was not in your care, and the two of you mutually agreed to sex, it's perfectly permissible to have sex with a fifteen-year-old?"

"I think so. But she was an alluring girl. I saw her naked body and I got stupid."

Poor Olof. She was dangerous. *I'll be on my guard when I get to Stockholm, just in case I bump into Annika. It's an unusual name. Maybe she is the only one in Stockholm… If I hear that name, I'll just be sure to run like hell!*

CHAPTER 3

We pulled into Stockholm's train station at 8 a.m. Olof and I traded goodbyes and a manly hug, and we went off in opposite directions. I checked my baggage at the train station and hiked out to explore the city.

I walked eastward, passed through a beautiful park, and kept walking until I found myself on an island. In front of me was the Moderna Museet, a museum of modern art. It was a beautiful morning. I decided to wait around until 10 a.m. for it to open. I took a seat on a bench across from two women. I opened my book and began reading *The Canterbury Tales*. The weather was perfect for being outdoors.

The two women were waiting for the same reason. The younger woman, maybe in her late twenties, attractive, greeted me and introduced herself and her aunt. Her name was Gunnel and she was a nurse. She was there with her aunt to see a new exhibit. She was interested in knowing about me, America, and what I saw and thought about the people and places I had visited this summer. My longest answer to a what-did-you-see question, was watching a Volkswagen Beetle convertible sink in an Amsterdam canal. As soon as I finished answering one question, she fired off another. I graciously answered. We didn't discuss art, and I was thankful she didn't ask about the Vietnam War. I learned nothing about her, except for a vague idea of her interests based on the questions she asked me. I did learn her name: Gunnel. It was a nice name.

At 10 a.m., the three of us entered the museum. We said goodbye. I walked off alone, down a hallway to the left. They disappeared in a hallway to the right. I didn't know anything about modern artwork or the amazing artists who created them. The exception was a Remington statue. When I returned to America, I vowed to go to the Guggenheim Museum in New York City, a gallery of famous contemporary and modern art.

While I was admiring the Remington sculpture, Gunnel came up to me. She had a warm smile. If I were a hospital patient, I would want her to be my nurse. She was well-groomed and fashionably dressed. Any chance I could spend the day sightseeing with her? I could only dream.

"Are you familiar with American modern artists?" she asked.

I was truthful. "Hi. Sadly, only one: Remington." I pointed to his sculpture, or was it a copy? It was a cowboy riding a bucking horse. "He is famous for his artworks and stories he wrote about the Old West, the American frontier." I still had not seen another American artist I recognized.

To my surprise, Gunnel decided to spend a few minutes with me. She pointed out one art piece after another, and told me the name of the artists. She reached into her purse and pulled out a card with her name, phone number, and address on the front. "I have to go. My aunt is waiting for me. But I'll be home this evening. Call me if you have any questions about the art or artists.

I am very knowledgeable. I do volunteer work here and I often come here to browse just as you are now."

I told her, "I am sure I will have some questions for you by this evening. I'll try to call you. You know I just arrived, so I don't know anyone. I don't know how to use the phones yet. I haven't seen Swedish money. I don't even know where I will stay tonight! But I would hate not to talk with you again before I leave tomorrow." I don't know why I told her I would leave tomorrow. I hadn't given it thought.

She appeared to be studying my face before she spoke. "I understand how such things can be a problem for you." Maybe she didn't see it as a problem, and was being polite. "I suggest you take a taxi to my home." Both my socks dropped down to my ankles. "Give my card to the driver. Arrive around eight p.m. But don't bring wine. I hate wine. I have vodka. Bring flowers or dessert, but only if you must. I will have dinner ready for us." *Man alive, I think I am going to have an interesting dinner.* "Bring your luggage. I have many friends in my apartment building. Someone will have a place for you to stay the night. I know you'll come. I will be sad if you don't. I have never had an American in my home for dinner. One more thing: my aunt likes you. Bye."

"See you tonight." I waved to her aunt who I could see waiting for her farther down the exhibit hall. She waved back. I watched Gunnel walk away.

I thought about tonight, constantly. It was a welcome distraction as I explored the beautiful city. I paid serious attention when I cross streets like never before! I didn't have time to be hit by a car. There would be time tomorrow. Perhaps I read too much into her invitation. But with my luck, her aunt and friends would hang out with us all evening. After, I would be packed off to spend the night at a beatnik's apartment across the hall. No doubt he would look exactly like Maynard G. Krebs.

I arrived on time with flowers in one hand and my belongings in the other. She took the flowers from me and gave me a warm, close, full-body hug. I must have looked surprised, because she said, "Did you expect something else?" I think she was pulling my leg. "Don't you enjoy hugs?" she asked.

"Yes, I do. But I had forgotten. My last hug was a long time ago."

"Oh dear. I get hugged all the time. Here, I'll give you another." She hugged me again, but held me close longer. It was wonderful.

Her perfume was intoxicating. After she put my flowers in a vase and filled it with water, she gave me a tour. Her home had a large eat-in kitchen, a laundry room, a small bathroom behind the kitchen, a large living room, a large bedroom, and a full en suite bathroom. What stood out were the paintings in the kitchen, living room, and bedroom walls. There were also many art pieces, some modern, some not, in the living room and her bedroom.

Her aunt wasn't there. Neither was anyone else. And I didn't see any signs of a man living there, as both toilet seats were in the down position, and I didn't see men's shoes by the front door. The closet doors were closed, so I couldn't tell if men's clothing was hanging inside.

We sat down at the kitchen table to eat. She carved meat from a leg of cold lamb. Her aunt's cook had roasted the lamb earlier and had her manservant deliver it. I asked her about her aunt. She told me her aunt was wealthy and owned five hundred apartments, including those in this very building. And all of the apartments were free of debt. I couldn't even imagine. "She is very generous to me. She buys me all these expensive art pieces. I am her favorite relative. Aunt was married, but her husband died six years ago and they had no children. She is good company. Actually, she is my best friend. Apart from my inability to choose acceptable boyfriends, she thinks I am perfect."

Gunnel cooked a pot load of dumplings. On the dinner table were apples, pickled onions, cheeses, a bottle of vodka, and two beautiful glasses. She called the vodka "snaps." We ate and talked as if we were old friends who hadn't seen each other in a long time. I helped her with the dishes. We passed on coffee. She carried our glasses and a bottle to the living room coffee table and told me to sit on the couch. She pulled out a book on modern art from her tall, wide bookcase. She thought I might be interested. She sat close to me. Our knees touched. She pointed out one American artist after another. She got quiet. Then, with a serious face, and said, "My favorite artist is not in this book. Keep your eyes open for him. He is an American artist named Roy Lichtenstein. His name doesn't sound American, does it? You will be impressed with his work. His paintings will be very valuable someday." I didn't tell her Roy Lichtenstein had once lived in my hometown when he taught art at Douglass College, a part of Rutgers University, in New Brunswick, New Jersey.

When I tired of the book, she closed it. Maybe she read my mind. I was interested to know if she had a boyfriend or husband, but I was hesitant to ask. Then she said, "You are wondering if I have a boyfriend." *I'm looking at a mind reader.* I cleared my mind, just in case. There was a lot going on up there. I was unwilling to share with her. "He is out of town. If he does come to my door, he is not coming inside. He is a boring, bossy, moody artist." She told me she didn't want to think about him and only wanted to have a fun evening. She also said she called the hospital where she works, and told them she was unavailable to cover for other nurses tonight or in the morning because she would be "out of touch." Those last words were code for, "Drinking quantities of alcoholic beverages tonight."

She asked me if I had a girlfriend back home. I said "no" because it was complicated. She asked if I liked her given name. I told her I did: she was the first Gunnel I had ever met. She smiled and stood up, swallowed her vodka, and walked over to the turntable to play a slow dance record. I asked her if she was expecting a visit from her aunt tonight. "Hell, no. Why do you ask?" *Uh oh.* "Um, because I don't want to drink too much if she is to join us."

"She is not to come. She knows I invited you. She likes you. You made a good impression on her by how you answered my questions. She thought I was nosey. She also liked you because you weren't an artist or a doctor. She wished you lived in Stockholm, so she could fix you up with pretty girls. Wait until I tell her you brought me flowers, expensive ones too. My aunt hates the men I date. Drink as much as you want. I have plenty of vodka. It's so good you won't have a headache tomorrow. Just don't get your stomach sick."

She asked me to dance. I stood and said, "I would love to." To make more room for dancing, she grabbed hold of my luggage and moved it into her bedroom without discussion. Things were looking up.

Gunnel changed the record for another slow dance one. She turned off the brightest lights in the room. The atmosphere was now romantic. She signaled me with outstretched arms. When I walked up to her, she put her arms around my neck and laid her head on my shoulder. We danced close. I kept thinking about firetrucks, hoses, and fire hydrants to avoid the embarrassment of stimulation. I felt a strong attraction for her. I wouldn't trade the world for how this evening was progressing.

"I like you," Gunnel said. "I feel extremely comfortable with you. I don't know why. I am usually a very cautious woman. But tonight, my guard is down." I had to take her word for it. We danced until the music ended. She left me to put on another slow dance record. She returned and poured us each another drink. She drank down hers and waited for me to finish mine. We danced again. She stopped and kissed me. "Adam, tonight feels special."

"You are just a sucker for expensive flowers and men who show up with their luggage." I smiled. She kissed me again, this time an open-mouth kiss. I told her, "I like you. And I like being here with you. But you have to tell me something, and be honest. When you hugged me earlier at the door, was it a dinner guest hug as you said?"

"Yes. It was. If it had been a boyfriend hug, a boyfriend who I wanted for him to make love to me that evening, it would have been very different. Can I show you?" I nodded. She brought my face to hers and we kissed. We kept kissing as she gently took hold of my backside with both her hands.

When she finally let go, I asked her, "Do you do it often?"

She laughed. "Actually, I have never done it before. I swear to you. I made it up. Did you enjoy it?"

"Best hug ever."

"It could have been better. We could have been naked."

"You have a good imagination."

"Do you like me, Adam?" she asked seductively.

I grinned back, "Yes I do. Can I show you how much I do?"

"Yes, please." I hugged her, and took hold of her firm backside.

"If you agree," she said with her nose about six inches from mine and still holding her backside, "we will go to bed later. I promise. But first, sit down on the couch with me."

She said, "Would you let me show you my idea of a romantic evening? We will pretend to be lovers who haven't seen each other for a long time. I have been waiting for this night my whole adult life. I had no idea it would be tonight, or it would be with you. Can we? Can I be your good time tonight? I would be very grateful if you would say yes."

Thrilled, I said, "You're going to be my good time?"

"Actually, I will try to be your best time. And what is only fair, you will be my best time. I have had many good times, but never a best time. Hopefully tonight… Let's dance. I will explain." She put on another slow dance record. "I need you to hold me. I am not confident speaking about intimate sex with a man, even a man I have known for a long time." She put both her arms around my neck. "My men perform sex the way they want to do it. I choose boyfriends who are imaginative artists, but have no imagination or flexibility in bed. I've had the same bad luck with doctors. Doctors are actually worse because they don't want to change their boring sex routine. And doctors go to bed early, and hurry up to finish because there isn't enough time. They don't care if I finish. A boyfriend finished quickly one night, and then he blamed me. He said I was very sexy. He blamed me for his problem! I told him we could do it again later when he was ready. But he refused and went to sleep."

"Adam, I watch television, I watch movies in the theater, I read popular novels, and I read magazines. Sex, sex, sex. Men and women have wonderful sex. I have missed best times because it seems men get what they want, but not me. So tonight, I want to be the one who gets what I want. You will have the best time, I promise. Let me explore. I hope not to embarrass you or me. When I am finished with what I want, then it will be your turn. Don't worry. If you finish, we will wait and continue later. We have the whole evening and night. You are to stay here tonight with me. You saw my big bed."

"I was worried I would stay in a neighbor's apartment or your aunt's home tonight."

"She would have liked having you. At fifty-five-years-old, she would enjoy a young man, especially you. But you are mine. And I am not sharing you, not even with my dear aunt."

I kissed her. She kissed me back and poured us drinks. We drank up. She poured again and quickly downed hers.

"I'm excited for us. I'll be right back." She went into the kitchen, came back with a straight chair, and placed it in the middle of the living room. "Sit here, please." She put on a romantic record. "I'll be right back. I'm drunk. Are you drunk?"

I swallowed all of my drink. "Yes, I am drunk." I was definitely half drunk.

"Good. Keep drinking. It is very important that you do." She ran to her room and turned on the light. She came out wearing pink baby doll pajamas, a loose top, and a loose-fitting pair of short bloomer bottoms. She was excited, bouncy as hell, and poured herself another vodka. She downed her drink in one swallow. I sipped mine. I didn't want to get sick. "Please sit on your hands and do not touch me." She put on the record "*Respect*" by Aretha Franklin. With the lights still low, she did the most amazing thing. She began dancing around me, kissing me, and touching me. She danced unrepressed. I had never seen or experienced anything like it.

When the music stopped, she said, "Please stand up. Did you like my dancing?"

"Very much."

"My first time. I've never practiced! Maybe next time I'll play music with a different beat."

"Don't change a thing. You, the dancing, everything was perfect." It was perfect.

"Let's have one more drink." She handed me mine and raised her glass. "To you, Adam. And to our best time."

I said, "Bottoms up."

She quickly drank hers and led me to her bedroom.

After hours of fun, while I held her in my arms, she announced, "Adam, I made up my mind. I am finished with my boyfriend. No more artists, doctors, or married men. I am serious." She turned around and kissed me. She was the happiest, most sexually liberated Swedish woman in Sweden tonight.

I told her not to tell her boyfriend about me until my train left the station tomorrow. I don't know if Swedes get violent. She said she would never tell.

I held her in my arms the entire night. From our necks to our knees, you could not slip a twenty-dollar bill between us. We were one.

Morning followed 'best time' night, and with it came a soft voice: "Adam, wake up. Good morning. I'll make coffee." Gunnel jumped off the bed after laying a slew of kisses across my face and chest, and ran off to the kitchen. I sat up in time to see her skipping.

I brushed my teeth and jumped back into the bed. I was overflowing with joy because last night hadn't just been a dream. I heard Gunnel banging around in the kitchen. Now in the living room, she turned on her turntable and played the soundtrack of "A Man and A Woman." She returned with two cups of hot coffee. I needed the coffee. We had gotten maybe five hours of sleep.

The coffee was good and hot. I told her, "I want to continue, but my way this time." She nodded yes. We made love once more, not the mechanical kind we did last night. This time it came from a place of pure passion.

"That was wonderful." She pulled my face closer and we kissed. "What just happened? It was so special. It felt as if we were madly in love with each other."

"Passion, Gunnel, it was passion. I made love to you with all the love and warm feelings I had. I knew it would be our last. I was able to show you how much I care for you. I adore you. You are so damn special, so desirable."

She kissed me. "Thank you. But was last night terrific?"

"It was. But just now was heavenly for me. Sex doesn't have to be passionate every time. But it needs to be there when you need it. But don't you and your boyfriend make love passionately?

She didn't answer. "If not, you haven't found the right man. Any straight guy in his right mind would love having you. But if he loves you, you should feel his passion. And incidentally, maybe you should avoid any boyfriend your aunt doesn't approve of." She laughed. I held her tight.

I was surprised she patiently listened to me. I didn't dare go any further. I hoped I hadn't crossed the line telling her what I thought. If I thought she would appreciate the advice—and I wasn't so sure she would—I would have told her a story from Chaucer's *The Canterbury Tales*. Chaucer listed qualities women want of a man: courage, intelligence, wealth, generosity, kindness, and lust in bed, the writings found in "The Sea Captain's Tale." But lust is not the same as passion. Lust means being strong, vigorous, robust, and energetic. I was somewhat surprised passion didn't make Chaucer's list.

She pulled my face closer to hers and kissed my face over and over again. When she finished kissing me, I said, "I need to get going."

"Will you take a bubble bath with me?"

How could I say no? I was going to miss her something awful…

It was painfully difficult to say goodbye. She teared up. Neither of us spoke about seeing each other again. It was an unspoken understanding we had from the beginning. Our relationship had been fast-tracked from the start, and now the time had come for an abrupt ending. Besides, she was nine years older than me, and I was just passing through from another world. We kissed, we hugged, we said goodbye.

I sat in the train station waiting for the express train to Copenhagen to be announced. I was sad. I was happy. I was exhausted. Having been intimate with Gunnel for hours and hours, it would take me hours and hours to reach full recovery. There was no rush. So fantastic a time, and nothing I could write home about.

The train boarding announcement came none too soon. I didn't want to leave, but I had to. I stood up and looked all around one last time. I didn't see Gunnel. She hadn't rushed to the train station at the last minute and begged me not to leave her. "I can't live without you Adam," she didn't say. It was not going to happen. I can't imagine a woman demeaning herself by chasing a man all the way to a train station.

I handed my Eurail train ticket to the conductor. He took my bag from me and I followed him to my train car and then to my seat. I found it difficult to walk. I had some strength and balance issues resulting from excessive alcohol, exhausting fooling around, sleep deprivation, and sadness at having left Gunnel behind.

When I stopped feeling sorry for myself, I noticed a pleasant-looking female, about my age, sitting across the aisle from me. She was studying from *Grant's Atlas of Anatomy* and marking up one of the pages with a yellow highlight marker. I cringed. Some books are sacred and shouldn't be used as a coloring book.

An hour's train ride passed. It was time to get up and find a hot cup of coffee. I noticed she spent too much time studying one page of her book. I was very familiar with the page. Some kids grow up learning how to play tennis, golf, and volleyball. I grew up studying anatomy, running track, and riding the waves into shore in Belmar, New Jersey, on a light blue canvas raft, in sight of my grandfather's property on Ocean Avenue.

When I could wait no longer, I asked "Miss Grant?" I didn't know her name. "I'm Adam. Is it time for your study break? Would you care to join me for a hot beverage or Coke and a sweet bun in the club car?" She was reluctant. I explained to her there were better pages to study in Grant's. I had her turn to a different page number as proof. It had the same structures, but better presentation. She accepted my study break offer.

I left Geoffrey Chaucer on my seat. There was no need to take Chaucer for coffee, as I now had human companionship. Books can't compete with women, with few exceptions. My book was safe. Only a lunatic would steal it. And I doubted any were on this train.

Studying anatomy had paid off. I wouldn't be drinking coffee alone, and I got to take a break from thinking about Gunnel. I missed her smiling face, along with her other parts. Some lucky guy out there would happily marry her someday. *I hope she chooses well. I already hate him. He's not good enough for her.*

Traveling Abroad Without A Camel

CHAPTER 4

I arrived in Rome mid morning. I decided to check my luggage in at the train station, instead of dragging it around the city. Joan, my high school girlfriend, and I had planned to meet at the Piazza di Spagna, also known as the 'Spanish Steps,' at 4 p.m. Joan had been traveling in Europe since early June. She was tall, beautiful, and smart. And I was still deeply attracted to her. We had never made love, but I was hoping to change my luck in Rome. Maybe we would start our relationship anew? I cut short sightseeing in Vienna and bypassed Venice just so I could be there at the appointed hour.

From the station, I went from hotel to hotel, *Europe on 5 Dollars a Day* in hand, a book by Arthur Frommer, but there were no vacant rooms. The hotels not listed in the book didn't have any rooms to rent either. I hope Joan had a room reservation for tonight and she would share the room with me. I was prepared to beg if I had to.

I sat on the Spanish Steps and waited. The Steps rose up from the Piazza di Spagna. All the piazzas I came across in Rome had fountains, and this one was no exception. At the base of the Steps was Fontana della Barcaccia, "Fountain of the Ugly Boat," built between 1627 and 1629. It is credited to Pietro Bernini, who fathered the famous Gian Bernini, who is said to have worked with his dad. To my mind, it seemed unimpressive. Not ugly. Just unimpressive.

The American Express office was up the street, on the same side as the Steps. I had passed it earlier. I needed to stop in there to check for mail, but I didn't have the time. I was just very excited. What if she was already in Rome? While I sat, I was hard at work watching for Joan, checking out the motor scooters, and all the women who were walking past. There were too many of them, for they made it difficult for me to identify her.

It was still early. I would have time to stop in at the American Express office, after all. I reluctantly gave up my seat. I walked over to the American Express office and lined-up behind a large crowd of people who had lost their American Express checks, needed to cash a check, or hoped to receive mail. Those who were lucky enough to have received mail, consciously or not, held their mail high above their heads as they exited. How bastardly of them, showing off their mail. Some left empty handed and, of course, disappointed. Maybe they were expecting money? Maybe they were homesick and were desperate for mail from Mom? Maybe it was a guy or gal hoping for good news from their lover.

I rubbed shoulders with many young people until I finally made it to the front of the line. I showed my passport and was happy to receive a letter from my family. I stashed it in my pants pocket. I thought better than to wave it above my head. I stopped in front of the last building before the Steps and read the sign. It was the Keats-Shelly Memorial House. Keats died in Rome in 1821 and his grave overlooked the Tiber River. The "house" was small but loaded with books by Keats and his friends Percy Shelly, Lord Byron, William Wordsworth, Oscar Wilde,

Eliza Browning, and Robert Browning. How could there be so many books written by these authors? The answer: there were many identical books, the same writing in different sizes, different covers, different languages, different editions, and so forth. There were exceptional books because of hand-written notes and author signatures, or because they were first editions. It was an impressive collection.

I returned to the Steps about 3 p.m. and luckily found a place to sit. The place was packed. I sat for a while, then stood, searching through all the faces on the street and the backs of the heads of the hundreds sitting between me and the fountain. "Joan, where the hell are you?"

It was 4 p.m. Joan was due now. I kept checking my Timex. At 4:30, I was calm. At 5 p.m., I was antsy. At 5:30, I asked an older man sitting nearby for the time, just to make sure my Timex was accurate. Our watch times matched perfectly. I felt depressed. Depression was not a good place for me to be. I had made sacrifices to be here on time! My heart was now aching for Joan. Why was she running late?

It was now 6 p.m. I sat with my head in my hands, elbows on my thighs, looking down towards the fountain, when I mumbled, "Holy Crap!" I said out loud. I snapped to attention as she walked by. But it wasn't Joan. It wasn't Sophia Loren, either. But this face was very familiar. I stood-up and squinted. I could swear it was Laura, a school classmate, strolling by, conversing with another female. I grabbed my things and quickly worked my way down the steps through a mass of humanity.

Thankfully, I didn't lose sight of her in the crowd. I didn't want to be made a fool. So, I walked past her, turned around, and before I could get a good look at her, she called out my name, "Adam, is that you?"

I nodded.

"I didn't know you were in Europe." How could she? I hadn't seen her in three years. She was astonished to see me. And I was thrilled to see her.

"Great to see you," I said. "It's been a while."

Before I could tell her how nice she looked, and she did, she said, "Adam, where did you come from?" She didn't wait for an answer. She gave me a warm hug. Though I had experienced warmer hugs than hers not long ago, in all the years I had known her, I had never received a hug from her.

"Vienna." I stepped forward and she introduced me to her cute friend. "Hi, I'm Adam. And you are?" She looked to Laura.

"Adam, this is my college roommate Jackie. Jackie, Adam. Adam is a friend from high school, and before high school." Jackie was cute, and just as attractive as Laura. Laura had a lighter complexion than Jackie.

"Hi," she said, smiling while making direct eye contact.

Laura asked, "What are you doing here? Sightseeing?"

"I'm here for the same reasons you are here: eat spaghetti, see the sights, have a good time, and get drunk." She wasn't the type to ever get drunk.

"And meet up with Joan. She was my reason to be here, except I think I've been stood up."

"I can't believe you are here," said Laura.

"Me, neither," I told her about the plan of meeting up with Joan. Laura had been a close friend of hers in high school, but had no idea Joan was in Europe.

"Are you going to stay here and wait for her, or do you want to join us?" asked Laura.

"She didn't show-up, so there's nothing for me here. I'll check in with American Express tomorrow and find out if she left a message. Do you guys have a room by any chance?"

"Yes. Where are you staying?"

"On the sidewalk, at the moment." I was going to play this up big for pity. Pity was the only way I would get a room for tonight. "I haven't found a vacant room. I tried several hotels, but there were no vacancies. Apparently, this is the height of their season, and I would be lucky to find a room."

"Come stay with us. We have plenty of room," said Laura. Jackie nodded her head yes. "The *pensione* is near the train station."

I smiled and bowed my head. "Thank you both." It was settled. Maybe it was out of pity. But I didn't care.

Laura spoke. "Where is your luggage?"

"At the train station."

"Come with us. We are going there now to rest and we'll go out for dinner later. We'll get your bag on the way. We leave Rome early tomorrow morning. We fly to Paris, change planes there, and then fly back to New York. This is the last full day of our three-week vacation." Theirs was a vacation. Mine wasn't. I didn't know what mine was! I have been on vacations. But this was different. This was special to the nth power.

We took a bus to the train station and collected my bag. From there we walked to the *pensione*. When we arrived, Laura knocked on the manager's door, located behind a front desk. Out came an elderly lady, who needed to approve Laura's generous room offer. No approval would mean no room for tonight. I was introduced. Laura kept talking. The old lady inspected me. Finally, she extended her hand out for my passport. Before she opened it, she said yes. I was now an official guest! No sidewalk for me tonight.

Our room—amazing how comfortable I already felt calling it *our* room—was actually a good-size living room with one narrow bed, a bedroom in the rear I didn't get to see, and a private bath off of the living room. Oil paintings decorated the walls. One was of Mary holding baby Jesus. A large cross was hung on the wall above my bed. It was a reminder to me: it wasn't my bed. We washed and drank a glass of red wine. We napped in preparation for an evening out, their idea, not mine. Until now, I had only napped on trains. Normally, I'm out and about all day long. Naptime in a bed felt odd, but I slept deeply. In fact, the girls had to wake me. I recovered quickly. It made a difference: I was wide awake and full of energy.

Well-rested, washed, and dressed in fresh clothing, we hit the big town. The word "hit" was overly stated. None of us were particularly cool. We were good looking, but not cool. We didn't dress cool, walk cool, sleep in a fancy hotel, or frequent night clubs or discos. We were young people behaving like old people. My parents, may they rest in peace, would have done just what we were doing: strolling, talking, window-shopping, visiting the Fountain of Trevi, and looking for a bistro to have a meal. Afterward, we would probably go back to the hotel and retire early rather than later.

We enjoyed ourselves. Back and forth went the conversation. Words flowed so easily about Europe, college, and high school. We did consume large quantities of red wine and ate delicious food. Dishes were shared because, "You just have to taste this." For me, this dinner was a special evening. Eating dinner alone sucked. Most of my meals for the past five weeks had been eaten alone aside from one special dinner in Stockholm with a woman I would never forget. Tonight, we were all having fun.

It was late when we returned to the hotel. The girls had to get up early to catch their plane. But I could sleep in, as check-out time was 10 a.m. I got a goodbye wave from Jackie and a hug from Laura before they retired to the back bedroom. I wasn't tired, thanks to my nap, so I decided to stay up longer. My stomach was full of wine and food. I turned on the lamp light since the overhead light was very bright, and I sat up against the headboard and did some reading.

To my surprise, Laura reappeared in her nightgown and sat on the edge of my bed to talk. With light behind her, I could see one breast through her sheer night gown. She was unaware of it. I kept quiet about it so not to embarrass her. If she had known, I am sure she would have covered up. She was a fine-looking girl and a fine person. One day, she would marry some lucky guy. The scent of her perfume was delightful. I had rarely spoken to her at school, just a few words and smiles when passing each other in the high school hallways. Some of her female friends were my friends. Laura was the quiet type. Seeing her breast was comforting, arousing, and made for a nice ending to a wonderful evening out. She talked. I listened. Her three-week European trip was a graduation gift from her folks. She managed to graduate university in three years. Unheard of! Impressive. Finally, she said, "Good night, have fun," and leaned over and gave me a kiss on my cheek. Then she disappeared into the back bedroom. I turned off the light and immediately dropped off to sleep.

Sometime later, I don't know when, I wasn't alone. She returned in the dark. She pulled back my sheet and climbed on top of me. I put my hands on her hips. I was trying to be polite. I was not prepared for this situation. She leaned forward and kissed my face, shoulders, and neck. I let loose of her hips and put my hands on both sides of her face, then gently pulled it close to mine. I couldn't see her face. I kissed her eyes and nose. I asked her, "Are you sure about this?" She didn't say a word. She was sure because we went all the way.

She climbed off me and ran to the bedroom. I whispered into the dark, "Laura, you were wonderful." But she didn't respond. If the cross above my head was there to discourage single people from having sex in this bed, it hadn't worked.

Early the next morning, Laura woke me just as she and Jackie were about to leave for the airport. I never heard them up and about. Laura whispered, "Adam, good morning. It was good to see you."

"Good to see you too," I mumbled. I turned to see Jackie who was straightening her clothes. Laura continued, "The room is paid for. Check-out is 10 a.m. So, no rush. Enjoy your summer, and safe travels! We need to run right now." She gave no hint of what had happened last night.

"Thank you," I said. Laura bent over and gave me a kiss on my forehead. As she stood up, I smiled from ear to ear. She walked away in the direction of the door.

Still laying there, I said, "I enjoyed meeting you, Jackie."

"Me too." She walked over to me and kissed me on the cheek. She turned her head and saw Laura with her back to us. She quickly kissed me on the lips, while she swept the back of her hand along the entire width of my lap. I was nearly in shock, again.

"Goodbye," she said, and scooted off to meet Laura, who was holding open the door from the hallway side.

"Goodbye."

I had been played. It was obvious. Laura was in on it. *Bait and Switch*! Laura came to my bed. I saw her breast. Her breast was the man bait. Then came the switch. Jackie showed up in the dark, wearing Laura's perfume. It had to be her.

I jumped out of bed, went to the open window, and pulled the curtains apart. They were on the sidewalk out front, very busy hailing a taxi to notice me.

Jackie asked, "How long have you wanted him?"

"Since the ninth grade."

I was played! What they did to me was "*Bait and Bait Catches Fish With Impressive Cover-up.*" It wasn't "*Bait and Switch*" at all. I give them credit: it was cleverly planned with terrific execution. Aside from the after-the-fact revelation, I rated it *the best.*

CHAPTER 5

I met late afternoon with a male student from Michigan while sightseeing on my second day in Rome. It was nighttime when we arrived at Trevi Fountain. Lighting brought out its beauty.

My face and body perspired. My new friend's shirt was wet with perspiration, but there was not a drop of sweat on his face. Neither of us had been drinking. We stood back from the fountain, leaning against a storefront wall. Above us was the store's awning. It offered protection from bird droppings and strong moonlight.

The evening had a surreal feel to it. We had nothing special to be doing. Boredom set-in. So, I came up with a plan. I said to my new friend, "It's hot as hell. What if we partly undressed, put our stuff to the right of the fountain, we walk past the crowd to the left, and jump into the fountain? We run, we swim, whatever it takes to cross the fountain. We grab our stuff and run like hell. Interested?"

He thought about it for one second. "Ok, I'll do it. By the way, can you run fast and swim fast?"

"This is a good time to find out."

Before we took one step, a young, long-haired college-aged male, sitting on the front fountain wall, spun around and submerging one foot into the fountain. Within seconds, a Roman policeman and policewoman appeared from nowhere, grabbed hold of the guy, lifted him up and out from the fountain, and hustled off with him. It was obvious fountain-time was over for him.

I said to my new friend, "Holy shit. The plan would have been a disaster!"

"No kidding. I think we should go it alone. Together we are dangerous." Without another word, we walked away in different directions.

I no longer wanted to hang-out with men. I'll keep my eyes open for a woman traveling companion.

CHAPTER 6

It was my third day in Rome. Having had a good night's sleep, I was energized and took a long walk to visit Capitoline Hill in Rome. I strolled up Michelangelo's staircase. It opened up to the Piazza del Campiglio. In the piazza stood the Equestrian Statue of Marcus Aurelius. It was an ancient Roman statue. It survived nearly two thousand years of weather and Christian Crusaders who probably would have done it harm if they hadn't been confused as to who the rider was. It was the only fully surviving bronze statue of a pre-Christian Roman emperor. This magnificent statue stood thirteen-feet-tall and depicted the emperor seated on his horse. It was apparent the statue had taken a beating from the elements. It needed better conservation. Either a roof needed to be built over the statue, or the statue needed to be moved indoors.

After a short struggle to find the entrance, I entered the Capitoline Museum. Inside, the Capitoline Wolf display contained busts of well-known Roman Emperors, celebrities, and everyday people, as well as some interesting mosaics from Hadrian's Villa. Hadrian's Villa was in Tivoli, an ancient Italian town in Lazio, about thirty kilometers east northeast of Rome, at the foot of the Aniene River. The city offered a wide view over Ro, a small town outside of Rome, as one traveled towards the mountains.

The museum led first into a courtyard. The Head of Constantine the Great stood in the corner and towered over visitors who stood next to it. Some remaining pieces of his body were arranged next to his head so visitors could get an understanding of how enormous this statue had been when it was intact. I walked up a staircase through an underground tunnel to Palazzo Nuovo on the other side of the piazza. I soon realized the actual museum is much bigger than it appears from the outside.

As I wandered my way around Palazzo Nuovo, I stumbled across what was one of my favorite pieces, *The Dying Gaul*. This Roman replica of a Greek original depicted a man in defeat. This life-size statue showed a man who had fallen to the ground with his hands tirelessly keeping his upper body off the ground and his head cast toward the ground hopelessly. It drew my sympathy and gave me a humanistic understanding of the statue.

In the Palazzo del Conservatori, away from the core of the museum, were rooms full of statues and paintings. The one statue stood out. It was the infamous symbol of Rome, called the *Capitoline Wolf.* It was a bronze sculpture of a she-wolf suckling twin human infants, inspired by the legend of the founding of Rome. I would read about the legend when I got home: how the twins Romulus and Remus were cast into the Tiber River, how they were rescued by a she-wolf who cared for them, and how a herdsman found and raised them.

When I had my fill of the Capitoline, and it didn't take very long, I walked down to the street to explore a metal construction I noticed among shrubbery and trees, a short distance left of Michelangelo's staircase.

I walked along the sidewalk until I found a dirt trail near the entrance to a municipal park. From there, it was a very short walk to what turned out to be a cage. To my near shock, inside the cage was a she-wolf, a real live female wolf. I guessed she was caged there in honor of the legendary wolf who had nursed Romulus and Remus, a lesson learned twenty minutes ago. But it was clearly no honor for her to be here. From her appearance, she was poorly cared for. She was thin and scroungy. There was no excuse for this animal to be so badly neglected. I watched her as she swayed from side to side, pacing back and forth from one end of the cage to the other. The cage was very small for her. She should have been in a large enclosure with other wolves.

I love animals. It hurt to see her in this condition. If she was a tourist attraction, why was the cage so hidden away? The person responsible for her care should be severely punished.

When the she-wolf noticed me, she acted as if I was her long-lost friend. She pressed her body against the bars so I could pet her. It was shameful the symbol of Rome would be kept in this condition. I rubbed her back and decided the only thing I could do for her was to feed her.

I left the wolf behind, promising to return soon. Beyond the shaded park, I made my way along Rome's scorching sidewalks until I found a grocery store with a butcher working in the back.

I had to wait my turn for service because the short, stocky butcher behind the counter was engaged in a heated conversation with some college-aged students. Nobody was smiling. When the butcher spoke, each verbal statement was followed by a slam of his meat clever into red meat laying on a wooden chopping block. They might have been discussing student unrest and strikes.

There were many strikes and occupations in Italian factories and universities during the 1960s. At the forefront were the university students. The quality of university education was not as good as it could have been. Fees and expenses were unreasonably high. The winter of 1967-68 saw a series of rebellions in northern universities had led to major changes. Many workers would receive job security, the right to strike, and some degree of industrial democracy. There would be, for the first-time, discussions about the environment and feminism. The quality of education finally rose an acceptable level.

The butcher handed them their wrapped meat package and looked at me as if I might be the next troublemaker. "Beef Steak," I said as I pointed to beef in the curved glass refrigeration case.

"Kilo?"

"No." I used hand movements hoping he would understand half a kilo. He understood. Then he mimed cutting the steak into small cubes. I nodded. He silently went to work. He handed me the package of bite-size steak and the bill. Maybe he knew I was going to feed the wolf. Perhaps a half-dozen tourists had been here already today to buy meat for the wolf. Maybe the wolf was his cash cow. I paid the clerk at the front of the shop.

Outside, it was mid-day and the heat was baking me alive. Never would I come back here in July! I went to see my new friend. She was happy to see me. She probably was happy to see anyone. I was taking a chance steak was good for her. They may have had her on a pasta diet for a medical condition. I didn't know the condition of her teeth. Could she chew the steak? It turned out not to be an issue. I tossed the cut-up pieces of steak through the cage bars, one at a time. Quickly, she gobbled down every piece. After she made the last piece disappear, she came to me and leaned her side and head against the bars in front of me so I could pet her again. I focused closely on the location of her head and the location of my fingers, and I only rubbed her with fingers I was willing to lose.

She was excited to have me pet her, grateful for her steak lunch. She was very excited and she peed. Her urine raced downhill, under the cage, and made contact with my beautiful left Florsheim shoe. I should have been wearing my sandals. I could have washed my foot and trashed the sandals. They could easily have been replaced. You don't throw away thirty-five-dollar Florsheim shoes!

If this was her way of marking what was hers, then she and I were now a happy couple. If not, maybe she wanted me to adopt her. I tried to imagine traveling through Europe with my wolf on a leash, but failed horribly.

Even though I felt bad for her, I declared a urine emergency for my Florsheim shoe and hurriedly said goodbye to my new lady friend, or wife. Off I went in search of water. I wasn't stupid enough to stop at a fountain to wash my shoe, and instead bought a bottle of water for me and one for my shoe. Can you picture the Italians looking at me and saying, "Stupido Americano"?

Stupid? No. Smart? Yes.

CHAPTER 7

It was my fourth day in Rome. I entered the Sistine Chapel in the Apostolic Palace located in the Vatican. This was the site of the papal conclave where they made black smoke or white smoke to signal whether a new pope had been chosen. The ceiling frescos were breathtaking. They were based on stories from the Old Testament. I had hoped Pope Paul VI might drop in and shake hands with the crowd and pass out candy to the kids. But he didn't show. Something must have come up.

After the chapel, I toured the main floor of St. Peter's Basilica. I had nearly completed a long loop when I stopped at the last alter. Large Latin words stood out from all the others. I had seen those words several times already today. A nice-looking girl about my age was also looking at the altar. I walked over to her. I read the Latin out loud in a low voice. "Excuse me," I said not looking directly at her. "Do you know what those Latin words mean in English? I only know English."

"It means 'God is Great'." Nice. She spoke American English, and with a Midwest accent.

"Thank you. You know Latin?"

"No. I asked the priest over there what it meant."

I laughed. "I didn't know you could speak to the priests. They all appear to be busy. I'm Adam from New Jersey."

"I'm Christine from Missouri."

"Are you here on business?"

She laughed. "No. I am visiting my Italian relatives for the first time. Any chance you have finished sightseeing here?"

"As a matter of fact, I have." I was finished. Damn if I was going to risk my life walking around the goat trail way up in the dome. It would scare the fool out of me. I am not brave. I play life safe.

"Coffee?" she suggested.

"Let's go before I get weak and give a donation. I'm Jewish."

"Jews can't give donations?"

"We don't donate because my people can't be sure if the church is collecting donations to finance the next crusade to wage war on the Jews and Moslems and reclaim the Holy Land. There is a lot of demand for land in the Holy Land these days. Jewish people and Moslems fought a war over it just last year. It's just a matter of time before the pope's army, led by the Swiss Guards and Cossacks, head off to Israel, weapons in hand. And those Swiss Guards sure seem tough. You're about to ditch me now, aren't you Christine?"

"No. Why? You're funny. I'm Protestant, not Catholic. My relatives here in Rome are Catholic." I wondered why she told me she was a Protestant. My Baptist and Methodist friends never refer to themselves as Protestants. If I called them Protestants, they probably wouldn't know what I was talking about.

We found a small table at a bistro in Vatican City near the main entrance. The coffee was good: the company was better. We talked and shared stories about our experience in Rome and everything else under the sun. When the check arrived, she offered to pay half, but I refused her offer. "I bought you a cup of coffee. I got away cheap. How about I buy you dinner tonight? My treat."

"Thank you. But I can't make it tonight. I'm expected for dinner with the relatives. Tomorrow night?"

"Certainly."

"8 p.m. Be in front of the store that sells bus tickets at the bus stop on Provolone Street and Chester Street." Many of the bus stop locations had a nearby shop selling bus tickets. You couldn't buy a ticket on the bus. "See you there."

I met Christina the next evening. I was on time. She arrived dressed in a cute white blouse, with a wide black belt and a red skirt. She seemed very happy to see me.

This was Rome. Maybe romance was in the air for us. Why not? "Let's walk this way," she said. We walked and talked through quiet streets until we came to a very quiet piazza with no motor vehicles in sight. Yellow street lighting gave it a magical appearance, a feeling of tranquility. There was a small bistro at one end of the piazza, with four tables for two along the narrow front porch. A table at the end was vacant. We stepped onto the porch as a waiter came through the front door. I pointed to the empty table. The waiter nodded yes and pointed to the table. Table location is very important for a romantic evening. Best not to sit near the restrooms.

We talked, drank red wine, and finally got to the menu. I ordered lasagna. She ordered pasta with meatballs. We sat there enjoying each other's company. She told me she was nearing the end of her two-week holiday in Rome. At her relative's house, she wasn't comfortable with her room because it was decorated with religious paintings and statutes of Virgin Mary. She was amazed by all the religious items in their home.

When our dinner arrived, I was surprised my lasagna wasn't a precooked square and had been reheated before being served. This was different. It was fresh. The sauce was creamy and white. The wide lasagna noodles were layered in all directions and stacked very tall in the center of the plate. It was to die for. But I had this uncomfortable feeling the lasagna would slide off my plate at any moment. Luckily, neither a cement truck nor a fire truck passed by. The vibrations would have caused an avalanche on and beyond my plate.

Christina's dish appeared ordinary, basic meatballs and spaghetti. But she loved it. "It's the sauce," she said. "The sauce is from heaven. Try it." I tried it and agreed. But it wasn't as good as my dinner. We drank a liter of wine, ate our salads and bread, and skipped dessert. When the check arrived, I picked it up. The bill was for 1,400 lire, or $2.25 with service charges. I was amazed at how inexpensive it was.

When it was time to leave, Christina leaned forward in her chair and signaled me to do the same. I thought she was going to lay a kiss on me as a thank you for dinner. Instead, she whispered, "I think I am the only person in my relative's house who uses toilet paper. Honest." What an ending to a perfectly delightful meal! I forced myself to ask her how she knew. I didn't want her to think I wasn't listening or interested. "I made tiny tears in the paper, and the tears were always there. I just had to tell someone." I wish she had told someone else. I was able to stop before I pictured the subject. It wasn't like she would make up this story. I couldn't have. Bathroom talk on a first date? You'd have to be married for years and be suffering from the Hong Kong flu coupled with dementia before it could be an appropriate dinner table conversation.

We walked to her bus stop. Her plan, not mine. Mine was more interesting. But she wasn't interested in seeing my hotel. We could have spent the night in my bed reading *The Canterbury Tales*. Her loss, not mine. When her bus arrived, I got a quick goodbye and no kiss on the cheek. I watched her bus until it was out of sight. I don't know why I did. I wasn't a sad puppy.

It had been an interesting evening. I decided to take a long walk back to my hotel to clear my head with the cooler evening air. Either cooler air or a cleared head triggered a nightmare of an intense, deadly firefight in Vietnam poured into my head. I was firing a machine gun into the dark, and there was screaming.

Deep down, I was still a mess. I thought I had left my problems back in America. I was wrong. Wherever I went, they went too. I showered and was asleep moments after my head hit the pillow. Did I get killed? Did I kill someone? I never knew.

CHAPTER 8

It was my eighth day in Rome and once again it was as hot as hell. My eyes never tired of the women I passed along the Roman streets, but I did tire of art, architecture, fountains, and history, whether it be modern, renaissance, medieval, or ancient. For a change of pace, I decided to take the day off from sightseeing. Using public transportation, I arrived at Rome's Olympic pool. This was the pool built for the 1960 Summer Olympics. It was the first time Rome had hosted the Olympics. They had been scheduled to host the 1908 Olympics, but the eruption of Mount Vesuvius in 1906 had forced them to decline, and the honor went to London. Who could have imagined such an event and the disruption the volcano must have caused southern Italy? Mount Vesuvius kept erupting for thirty-eight years. It killed more than one hundred people. The eruptions ended in 1944, after a major eruption destroyed several villages and melted parts of Naples.

The pool and the Olympic Swimming Stadium were fairly empty. I tried to swim one fast lap down the length of it. I swam the American crawl, the tired American crawl, back stroke, side stroke, and breast stroke. Obviously, I wasn't a long-distance swimmer, but I did finish the lap. I hung onto the side of the pool to rest, and thought about past Olympics.

I am a big fan of the summer Olympics, but not the winter Olympics. Maybe it's because I don't like snow, ice, or cold weather. Or maybe it's because I can't ski, luge, bobsled, or ice skate.

One of my favorite Olympic stories is embarrassing for the athlete involved. He was competing in the 1960 Rome Olympics. The Scandinavian man's name was Vilho. He was a field shooter who shot a target and scored a bullseye. Unfortunately, he hit the bullseye of someone else's target. In so doing, he dropped from second place to fourth place, just missing out on a medal. Since the Olympics is all about gold medals, and less about silver medals and bronze medals—and even less about sportsmanship, despite what Olympic athletes tell everyone—Vilho screwed up. He did not receive a medal. But those who know him said he was a good sport.

Another favorite story of mine begins with the 1960 Rome Olympics. The Soviet Union team won the most gold medals in Rome in 1960. They also won the most silver and bronze medals. The Americans finished second overall: they were embarrassed. They swore there would be revenge for their second-place finish. Nikita Khrushchev, First Secretary of the Central Committee of the Communist Party of the Soviet Union, laughed at America's revenge talk and swore his Soviet athletes would again kick American asses in the 1964 Olympics in Tokyo.

Khrushchev had a problem: the Soviets were not up to the task in the 1964 games. The Americans entered with muscle, skill, and determination. As a result, the Americans won the most gold medals. The Soviets came in second place. Very early on in the games, when it became apparent the Soviets were going to get their backsides kicked by the Americans, Soviet leader Nikita Khrushchev was deposed from his position.

Historians wrote about the issues causing Mr. Khrushchev's removal from office: failed policies, economic and agriculture failures, failures in international relations, and so forth. Those issues were significant. I won't argue those points. He was barely hanging onto his job. And then came the American Olympians, who outperformed the Soviets. It was this reason alone, I truly believe, Khrushchev was sacked during the first week of competition.

I delayed the return lap as long as I could. I was as determined as those 1964 Olympic swimmers, Susan Pitt and Donna de Varona, to make the return lap. The lap wasn't going as planned about halfway back. I struggled to move forward. A young woman swimming her laps near me stopped to check on me. She became concerned about my progress, or lack of such.

She asked, "Do you need help?" I was insulted, but I was polite.

I told her, "I am Canadian and I can swim much faster when there is a thin layer of ice on the water's surface. The pool water is too warm for me, and it's making it difficult for me to swim."

A moment later, a teenager at the end of the pool threw a cup of ice into the pool. Call it a coincidence, but I immediately caught a chill. My right leg cramped, ruining my strokes. The woman screamed for help. Four lifeguards jumped into the pool. One rescued me. Three rescued her. No surprises there.

When more help arrived, they pulled me out of the pool. One lifeguard told me, "You and the woman are the best customers we had all day.

Come back anytime." As for me, I wasn't about to return. Interestingly enough, I was much more comfortable swimming in the ocean than in this gigantic swimming pool.

Later, I did my daily routine of visiting the American Express office to check for mail. Good news. A letter was waiting for me from my sister and Uncle Rick. Good news. I got a letter from Joan. Bad news. She was delayed because she was shacked up with some German guy in France. I was not angry because I cut short my stay in Vienna, or because I missed seeing Venice. I was angry because I wasn't going to share a room with her, or spend time hanging out with her. If I ever wind up in a psychiatric ward, I am certain it will have something to do with a woman.

For dinner, I ate mediocre pizza and drank cheap red wine. I didn't know if it was the news about Joan or the wine I drank, but something gave me a headache.

Back in my room, I pulled out my *Europe on 5 Dollars a Day*, checked out the European map, and read up on some other countries to visit. After careful study, I couldn't decide on my next step. Should I travel to the South of France and westward to Spain, and then continue from there to Paris? Or should I travel to Brindisi, Italy, take a ship across to Greece, from there travel north into Yugoslavia, and eventually make my way to Paris. I flipped a coin high in the air. It landed face side up. The back side would have been the South of France and Spain.

CHAPTER 9

I left Rome in the midst of a bout of diarrhea. I had drunk from a water fountain. "It's clean water," they said. "No problem." It was a problem. The hotel manager told me to continue taking my Pepto-Bismol. I brought it from home just in case I drank from a Roman fountain.

I left Rome on an early morning train, my destination Brindisi. I sat in a first-class compartment with an Italian family. They were enjoying a five-course picnic breakfast which included a ton of food and wine, glasses, plates, silverware, and cloth napkins. The meal was underway before my arrival. It would be another thirty minutes before the train would leave the station. The father insisted I eat with them. I couldn't refuse. Soon, I was one of their picnic guests. It was very nice of them. Never on an American train, nor on Western European trains I had ridden these past five weeks, had a family picnicked. It was surprising.

From gazing out the windows, the countryside in southern Italy was equally as beautiful as the Netherlands countryside. The fields of flowers and windmills in the Netherlands were beautiful, but just as beautiful were Italy's orchards, vineyards, structures, and mountains.

I arrived in Brindisi two hours before the last ship of the day would sail to Greece. But within minutes of purchasing a ticket from a shack next to the docked ship, I was in trouble. I asked the ticket agent to direct me to the nearest toilet. The curse of Rome's fountain had followed me to Brindisi.

The bathroom was the only structure on what appeared to be an abandoned ship pier. It was large enough to accommodate me and my baggage. After finishing my business, I grabbed the doorknob and gave it a tug to open the door. Next thing I know, I am standing there holding the doorknob. I made many attempts to reconnect the knob, but I couldn't make it work. Out of frustration, I kicked the heavy wooden door many times without success. I shouted for help, over and over again, but no one heard me.

I wasn't panicked at first. Anger was my initial emotion. Disbelief followed shortly. I was worried about missing my ship. I pushed against the building side walls, hoping a board would come loose. No luck. Then I got lucky. High above the door, I spotted a transom. The height frightened me. How the hell could I get up there and squeeze through without getting killed? I was also concerned about my luggage. If I pushed my luggage through the transom to the dock below, would the baggage still be there if and when I managed to escape?

I had no choice. I stood on the toilet with a shit load of doubt that I could pull this off. But after several failed attempts, all my belongings were lying unguarded on the pier in front of the door. Now, everything I owned, with the exception of my passport and traveler's checks, had passed through the transom, I had no choice but to follow. The lowest part of the transom stood more than ten feet high. I stood on the toilet and raised my arms. This was going to be close. I would not have bet on my pulling this off. I bent my legs and leaped for my life, figuratively speaking. On my first try, I caught hold of the transom. But my fingertips slipped off. I fell back down, landed on my feet, then slammed my buttock down on the toilet seat cover. It was a big ouch, but the fall could have been much worse. I caught my breath, calmed my nerves, and stepped up on the toilet seat again. Thank god it was solid and secure. I focused and leaped again. This time I caught the transom with both hands, held on, and pulled up, supporting my weight on my forearms and shoulder joints. I lost weight and narrowed my waistline since leaving home because of a lighter diet, increased exercise, and no refrigerator nearby when I needed one. The problem was, could my chest squeeze through the transom? My chest was the thickest part of my body. I hung there, waiting. I was concerned I might end up spending the night in a hospital instead of on a ship.

I let out my breath and pulled upward and outward with my head and upper chest hanging out above the door. I took a last look around the area. Once again, there were no people in sight. I saw my luggage at the foot of the door. It was a long way down. There was a problem: if I pushed forward and my body slid past the transom, would I land on my head? I hoped not. The best landing would be a feet-first one, hoping not to sprain an ankle or break a leg when I landed on my luggage.

The opening was too narrow to turn around to let my feet out first. But I had to get the hell out. I pulled myself through quickly. My adrenaline was flowing. I started down head first. A survival reflex forced me to reach back to the transom. I caught hold of it with one hand. I spun to a nearly upright position before I crashed down on the luggage. The uneven surface sent me flying off to the side. I hit my head, shoulder, rib cage, and hip hard. My eye glasses flew from my face, slid along the dock, and stopped just before the dock drop off. A submerged pair of glasses would have been a disaster. I sat up and took inventory. I hurt in all the places where I had made crash contact. A headache was on its way. My shoulder hurt the most. I was fairly certain I had escaped serious injury. I stood up and retrieved my eye glasses. I could have survived the loss of my luggage, but I couldn't function without my eyeglasses. The lenses hadn't broken. The frame was significantly damaged. My first concern was to get my frame repaired or replaced.

I decided I didn't need to see a doctor. There wasn't time to be examined *and* get my frame repaired before the ship sailed. I would deal with the headache and other pains later. Luckily, I found an optician only a few blocks away. I waited impatiently for the shop to open. They had closed from 12 noon to 4 p.m. for lunch, or maybe for a game of 'bocce.' I could only guess. My ship would sail at 5 p.m. At 4 p.m., the shop reopened, and I handed my glasses to the optometrist. He started working on the frame immediately. I held my breath figuratively, hoping they were repairable. Within a few minutes, he repaired the frame. They were as good as new. He was a craftsman. But he wouldn't take my money. It probably had something to do with me being bruised and in pain. I guess he felt sorry for me. The ship, an auto-ferry, left port on time with me onboard.

CHAPTER 10

The weather was great. Not a drop of rain. I made no friends because I didn't try. Peering out to sea, watching people, reading Chaucer, napping, and thinking about everything important, passed the time quickly. It was a pleasant voyage, a nice change, for the cruise was uneventful: no one fell overboard, and the ship didn't hit anything it wasn't supposed to.

I left the ship in Patras, located on Greece's west coast. Several buses were waiting to transport passengers to Athens. I found a comfortable window seat. I wasn't able to keep my belongings with me. They insisted I stow my baggage in a compartment at the bottom of the bus. I wanted to have my bags easily at hand, safe from thieves. But it wasn't to be.

It was a dark night when the buses got moving. It wasn't possible to see out the windows unless we passed the inland streetlights or campfires roaring along the shoreline. The road followed the Gulf of Corinth. I was thrilled to see horses and horse-drawn wagons lit by firelight with the glistening gulf behind them. Some of the wagons looked like America's Conestoga wagons, the ones pioneers used to open up the American West.

Halfway to Athens, the bus stopped along the road side for refreshments and toilets. Men were selling skewers of shish kebabs, hot from the grill.

At a bargain price of three for less than a dollar, they were affordable and scrumptious.

We continued on. Our next stop was Athens. The driver let us off in the center of the city. Before I decided upon a direction to walk in search of a hotel, one of three Canadians who came in on the same bus asked me if I wanted to share a hotel room with them and split the cost four ways. I don't know why they chose me or why it was important for them to save a few coins. But it worked out for me. It cost me one dollar. We had four beds in one room. They were nice guys from Toronto.

The four of us talked for a while. Mike and I were wide awake. Mike suggested we go for a walk, find a bar, and have a cold beer. I agreed to go, even though I had vowed not to hang out with men after the Trevi Fountain incident. The other two decided to stay put.

The bar Mike chose was across the street from the hotel. We could see our room window from the entrance. We walked in, sat at the bar, and asked the bartender for two beers. There were two women customers seated at one table near the bar. On the far side, the band quickly assembled and began playing Greek tunes. A minute later, the two ladies got up and joined us at the bar. It was now obvious: they were not customers. Although uninvited, the older ladies split up and seated themselves on bar stools on either side of us. I didn't know what to expect, but I was curious about what would happen next. Neither of us made any effort to chase the ladies away, or leave the bar, which was what we should have done. If we had been with female friends, there would have been no ladies.

The ladies began with greetings. "Where are you from?" Next came, "Will you buy us a drink?" Mike ordered beers for them, but the bartender popped open two bottles of champagne.

Mike said, "I didn't order champagne. And certainly not two bottles. How much for a bottle?"

"Twenty American dollars each," said the bartender.

"I am not paying for it," said Mike. The band stop playing, put their instruments down, and scurried to block the bar entrance.

With our escape blocked, I said, "Call the police." Mike agreed. It was the only reasonable thing to do. The bartender called the police. Two policemen arrived two minutes later. One policeman instructed us to follow him with hand signals.

The bartender yelled out to the policeman in Greek. I could only guess that he said, "What took you so long to get here?"

If true, the policeman answered back in Greek, "Did you want us to arrive before you poured the champagne?"

We followed the policeman outside and up the street. We were followed by the second policeman, properly positioned in case we tried to escape. There was no police car out front. How the hell had they arrived so fast?

Behind the second policeman came the bartender, and two guys from the band, and the parade was underway. The parade grew, as young neighborhood children joined in the rear, Others walked ahead of the policeman, just in case he forgot where the station was located. They laughed hysterically and pointed their fingers at us, made fun of us. Why were these kids on the streets at 1 a.m.? The only things missing from the parade were the balloon men, venders selling t-shirts with our pictures on the front, fire trucks, and a herd of unsheared sheep.

The parade marched five blocks, maybe six, until we reached a flight of cement steps leading up to the police station. We paraded through the station to a back area where we were seated in a hallway. I didn't see any jail cells or torture equipment along the route. Maybe they didn't have any. We sat for a couple minutes before being directed into the office of an important-looking policeman. He signaled for us to be seated on the two chairs in front of his desk.

The officer questioned the bartender first, in Greek, of course. The bartender had a lot to say to the officer. I guessed what he said, "Cousin Panos, good to see you! Sorry to bother you with this small matter. Oh, we are having a few guests over at my home at 8 p.m. tomorrow night for drinks and hors d'oeuvres. Please, you and your wife, do join us. We are celebrating my daughter's report card. All A's this time. God is great." Then, he told the cop his version of what happened.

The cop then spoke in Greek to us. When he stopped talking, I asked him if I could use the telephone to call the American embassy. The policeman turned the phone around and pushed it toward me. My uncle Rick had given me two embassy numbers to call in case of emergency, Rome and Athens. I opened my wallet and, to everyone's surprise, pulled out a scrap of paper and dialed the number for the American embassy here in Athens.

Everyone stopped talking. The phone rang twice.

"American embassy. Can I help you?"

"Yes. I am an American and I am in a police station in Athens. I need to speak to Mr. Edward Miller."

"He's not here. Hold on."

A man picked up the phone. I could hear background noise of people talking and music playing. I guessed a late-night party was in progress.

"Yes, how can I help you?" a man said in English.

"Hello. I am in trouble here in Athens and I called to speak to Mr. Edward Miller, who is a friend of my uncle's back in New Jersey." If the man had asked me how my uncle and Mr. Miller knew each other, I couldn't say. I didn't know. But he didn't ask.

"He's not here. What's going on?"

I explained everything to him, mentioning the twenty dollars the bartender wanted from me. The man said to me, "Let me speak to the policeman."

I said, "But he doesn't speak English," before I realized my mistake. "Oh, sorry. Here he is." I handed the phone to the cop and, in two minutes, the cop handed the phone back to me.

"Hello," I said.

"Here's the situation. The policeman isn't angry. It's Friday night. It's very late. And you have a choice. You can go to jail. You will see a judge

Monday morning. You can tell your story to him. Or, you can give them ten dollars and walk out, no questions asked. Do it. Chalk this up to experience. Pay the ten dollars and get the hell out of there."

"Thank you. I'll pay the ten dollars. Regards to Mr. Miller from me, Adam Haisenberger." The phone went dead before I finished speaking. I guess he was in a hurry to get to his wife or girlfriend. I hung up the receiver, opened my wallet, and laid ten dollars on the policeman's desk. I turned to Mike and said, "Are you going to make a call?"

"Forget it," he said. He didn't have a phone number to call, and he just wanted to get out of there. He pulled out an American twenty-dollar bill and laid it on the desk next to my ten. We stood and walked out quickly before someone changed their mind.

There was no parade waiting for us outside, but one of our roommates, a law student, was anxiously waiting for us. From our hotel window he had seen us in the parade. He only caught up with the parade after we had entered the police station. We told him the story. He shook his head and smiled, "Anyone for a cold beer?" Mike punched him in the shoulder. I could tell it hurt from the thud.

Back at the hotel room, we settled in for the night. Lights were about to be turned off when Mike asked me where I would travel next. I told him I planned to travel north through Yugoslavia and make my way back to Italy. From there, I would continue westward to the south of France and eventually arrive in Spain. Finally, I would travel to Paris.

"Whoa," Do you have a visa to travel through Yugoslavia?"

I said, "No. Do I need one?"

Yugoslavia, an Eastern European communist country, consisted of six republics: Serbia, Croatia, Bosnia and Herzegovina, Macedonia, Montenegro, and Slovenia. Yugoslavia never joined the Soviet Union or the Warsaw Pact. In 1968, it was held together by Josip Tito, its powerful leader. Tito turned the country from an agricultural state into an industrial one. Without Tito, a violent breakup of Yugoslavia into smaller nations seemed very possible due to bickering between ethnic groups and the rise of nationalist sentiment.

"Yes, you need one."

"Is there a problem? Can I get a visa at the border?"

"Yes, it's a problem. No, you can't get one at the border. You can't get in there as a tourist. It's a communist country. No chance. Good night."

The fourth roommate spoke up. "He's right. You can't go there. Consider going to Israel. You can take an auto-ferry from here to Israel, if you have the time."

I hadn't considered Israel. It hadn't crossed my mind. It wasn't mentioned anywhere in Frommer's book and was not on my Frommer's maps. If I went, I could fly back to Rome and continue westward by train. But Israel? I had the time, and I had the money. The idea excited me. Before I fell asleep, I made up my mind: I'm going to Israel. I don't know anyone who lives there or had been there. Wait 'til the family finds out! Unreal.

The next day, I saw the sights and bought a passenger ticket on an auto-ferry. It would set sail for Israel in three days. I saw the ancient sights, such as the Acropolis and the Parthenon. One evening, I attended the Acropolis sound and light show. It was wonderful. I felt apprehensive with the armed soldiers, not just police, stationed at major street intersections. Georgios Papadopoulos was the head of a military junta. He ruled Greece following a Greek coup d'état led by a group of colonels on April 21, 1967. I found it hard to believe Greece, the birthplace of democracy, was now undemocratic and ruled by the military. How strange and different from America.

Not willing to make the same mistake twice, I avoided Athens' bars. But I did find the street prostitutes entertaining. On one particularly wide, busy street, men would fish, so to speak, for prostitutes by standing on the sidewalk and jingling and twirling their keys. The prostitute would come up to the gentleman and negotiate with him. I did not partake in such an activity. It never crossed my mind.

On the fourth day, I appeared at the docks, without a police escort, and presented my ticket and passport to one of several men standing watch at the gangway. The ship left on-time with me happily aboard.

CHAPTER 11

Our destination was Haifa, Israel. I could have afforded first class, but I refused to travel differently from the other students. The ship would stop in Cypress before it reached Haifa. I paid the student fare of forty-eight dollars. It seemed to me to be very cheap passage.

The upper deck was for first-class passengers, with cabins and access to showers. The lower deck was loaded with motor vehicles. The canteen was located in a stagnant room below deck somewhere in the ship's bowels. It was like a hot oven. At the swimming pool located on the main deck, my favorite place to spend time outdoors, the air was fresh as the ship cruised onward to the Middle East. While the sun beat down on those who chose to sit in direct sunlight, I found comfort in a shady place over-looking the pool. I worked on some wallpaper designs, read *The Canterbury Tales*, daydreamed, and observed the other passengers. A New York City wallpaper company was paying me fifty dollars for every acceptable wallpaper design I sent them. I sketched bathroom wallpaper from my head. I was highly motivated, for I missed clean, attractive bathrooms. The ship's toilets and sinks left a lot to be desired. There were no showers for us. The bathroom sufficed only for washing faces, hands, pits, buns and balls. But the outdoor swimming pool was a decent substitute for a shower and constituted the only ship amenity. The pool warning sign did say, "No Diving, No Use of Soap." I could picture some fool taking a pool bath with soap.

I watched the young women enjoying themselves in the pool. Some were wearing small two-piece bathing suits. How courageous were these women for making the giant leap from bra and panties to acceptable public bathing attire? Maybe it wasn't a giant leap. Maybe it was evolution, like ape to man. Or a miracle, like Adam's rib to Eve. I didn't intend to make this complicated. I was just a young thinking man.

Since I didn't have a cabin, my personal space was located on a short indoor deck above pool level on the starboard side of the ship. I pushed three deck chairs together to sleep on and managed to sleep well. Atop and beneath those chairs lay my belongings. Although my possessions were unguarded, I had confidence no one would steal.

On the first night out at sea, I stood at the port side railing, gazing northward. Occasionally, we passed large islands silhouetted against the night sky. I didn't know the island names. I couldn't make out any details. I thought about what I would do after the ship arrived in Israel. I didn't have a guidebook to study. Frommer's *Europe on 5 Dollars a Day* was a guide for European travel, not for Middle East travel. But I wasn't worried. I would go with the flow and see what others were doing. I guessed that the roads would be lined with taxi cabs waiting to meet the ship's passengers, and one would take me to a hotel or youth hostel. The following morning, I would buy a map, and with a cup of coffee in hand, I would develop a travel plan. Maybe a waitress or a fellow traveler would give me some advice. I knew some famous places to visit in Jerusalem. But where the hell was Haifa? On the coast, obviously. But where on the coast?

From the beginning, I noticed a group of students who kept to themselves. They spoke French. France French? Canadian French? Belgian French? I had no way to know. But there was a girl who was petite and foxy looking. She could have been a ballet dancer. She sat in the middle of the group. Her hair was long, chestnut in color, pulled back from her face and tied in a single ponytail. She had smooth skin and her eyes were brown, but not as dark as cow eyes. Her nose was perfect for her face. I thought she was fantastic.

The students dressed in swimsuits most of the day. By late afternoon, wardrobe had changed to tee-shirts, shorts, and sandals. The cooler evenings were a welcome change from the hot, sunny days. What was nice about being outdoors the whole day was this that by midevening, most of us had gone off to bed.

On the morning of the third day, 185 miles from Haifa, our ship arrived in Cyprus. I knew of Cyprus and was able to find it on a world map. It was occupied by both Turks and Greeks. They had last fought against each other in 1964. It wasn't a small island. Six hundred thousand people lived here.

The ship docked at the far end of the longest pier I had ever seen. As soon as the ship was secured and the docking ramp set in place, a few passengers disembarked. I left the ship with twenty or thirty students, mostly males. I wasn't about to stay on board. It was Cyprus—another country to visit. Not a country you run into every day. No one back home said, "We're vacationing in Cyprus this summer." Spain? Yes. France? Yes. Cyprus? No.

It was comforting to walk on land again. A general merchandize store was conveniently located a short distance from the end of the pier. I bought cookies, a postcard, and a Cyprus postage stamp. I sat on the front step and wrote to my sister and Uncle Rick. "Hi. Having fun. Guess where I am? You guessed right. Cyprus. I am on my way to Israel. Would you believe it? Love, Adam." I went back in the store and handed over the card for mailing.

I started the walk back to the ship but stopped when I noticed a huge pile of watermelons outside the store, off to the side, under a tree. I went back into the store and bought one. I picked out the biggest. It was heavy as hell, but I was determined to bring it back to the ship. I had no idea at the time this watermelon would change my life.

Picking out the largest one had been a mistake. From the start, the sweat poured from me as I struggled under the hot Cyprus sun. It was a very long walk back to the ship. If there were no other ships in sight, why did the captain pick the farthest parking space and not the closest? Maybe it was cheap parking space.

I was a third of the way back to the ship when I saw that the guys stopped at a truck parked on the pier loaded to the top with boxes of grapes. The truck wasn't there earlier. While they were admiring the grapes, the most amazing thing happened. A man walked out of a small building on the far side of the truck and shouted, "OK!" We, I should say everyone but me, pounced on the truck and grabbed grapes. My watermelon was a full load. I couldn't join in. But not ten seconds later, another man came out of the building screaming at the grape grabbers. Apparently, the grapes did not belong to the first man. We ran: the guys with the grapes, me with the melon. I kept up with them, struggling every step of the way. When we were nearly at the ship's gangway, we slowed down and burst into laughter. We laughed all the way up the ship's gangplank. Soon after, the ship's horn sounded the final boarding call, and the ship was underway. I was glad to be back on board.

I kept the watermelon pool-side while I went off to change. When I returned, I jumped into the pool with it. I tried to use it as a volley ball, but it was much too heavy. Someone would have gotten hurt in no time. I climbed out, and found a good place to slice it. I borrowed a knife and offered the first slice to the knife owner. He shyly accepted.

It was fun slicing up the watermelon and giving it out to strangers. Halfway through my generous give-away, I searched about to see who would get the next slice. I spotted the foxy dark-haired girl who I had been keeping an eye on. She was alone, standing beside the ship's port side railing, peering out to sea, just like in the movies. What an opportunity! I quickly sliced a piece, stuck the knife deep into the rind, walked across the deck to the far railing, and offered it to her with my outstretched arms. "Please, for you," I said. She didn't accept until after I said *please* a second time. She smiled at me and said *thank you* in English. I smiled at her, returned to the watermelon. I cut a thick slice for myself and handed the knife back to the knife owner. *"Please,"* I said, pointing to the watermelon, "for everybody." He nodded "yes."

I returned to the port side railing and stood next to the girl. I guessed she was a college student who was maybe eighteen, nineteen, or possibly twenty years old. Her long chestnut ponytail fluttered in the wind. I couldn't tell if her beauty was equal to those women who long ago had Shakespearian sonnets written to celebrate their existence. I did know she was a darling, a true head-turner.

"Hi. Pretty views," I said. I was looking at two pretty views.

"Yes, the sea is very pretty." She took a bite.

Fantastic, she spoke English. "I'm Adam." I waited patiently for her to spit out the seeds.

"Colette. I like your watermelon," she answered, smiling. It was sweet and perfect, like her.

"I'm glad to meet you, Colette."

I hadn't felt this much attraction for a female since my nurse friend Gunnel back in Stockholm. Although it had been weeks ago, somehow I had moved on and no longer felt strong emotions for her. Of course, strong emotions are different from strong memories.

"I was surprised to see a watermelon. I saw you carry it while you were still on the dock. I wondered what you would do with it," she said.

"I wanted a slice of watermelon. But when I realized everyone was looking at me, and some people were licking their lips," I licked my own lips to illustrate my point, "I made a decision to share before a fight started. I saw you standing here, alone, as if you were an actress in a movie. The truth is, this is the first time I've seen you when you were not surrounded by your friends."

Colette laughed. "So, you have been watching me, and you think they try to protect me?"

"No. I wasn't thinking protection. I think you use them to keep men away. You are very attractive."

"Thank you." She didn't blush. "I admit, I do feel safe in the middle. I'm not always in the middle. As far as keeping men away from me, only one man I am aware of has been interested in me since we boarded the ship. You."

"I was obvious?" She nodded her head. I'm surprised she noticed me watching her. It was a delightful way for me to pass the time.

"Where are you from?"

"Paris. Have you been to Paris?"

"Not yet. At the end of the summer I will be there. And if you are there and accept my invitation, I will take you out for dinner."

"Where will you go in Israel?" She ignored my dinner invitation. She probably noticed my rejection face. But I quickly recovered.

"I don't know. I planned to visit Yugoslavia, but I was mistaken about visiting there without having a visa. Israel was a last-minute plan. So here I am without an itinerary. But I'm not worried about it. I'll figure out where to visit when I get there. I always do."

"You are a university student?"

"Yes. I just completed my third year. And you?"

"My exams are in September." I didn't know what she meant, but I didn't pursue it.

"Where are you going when we reach Israel?"

"To a kibbutz. I'm a volunteer. I will pick fruit. But they will give me time off to travel."

I knew what a kibbutz was. Here was a girl with a plan.

"Where is this kibbutz?"

"It is located in the Upper Galilee, the northern part of Israel. A kibbutz bus will meet us at the ship and take us there. It shouldn't be very far from Haifa."

As unbelievable as one could imagine, when I left the railing, I wasn't alone. For the rest of the voyage, we spent most of our time together. The one time I wish I could have followed her was when she charmed a guard who let her pass to the top deck to use the shower. It's hard to say *no* to her.

We sat by ourselves, or with the French group. She never sat in the group's middle when I was with her. There was no need when she had me by her side. I didn't understand the French group's conversations, except for the word, "*Merde.*" Occasionally, Colette interpreted for me. I learned this group hated Charles De Gaulle, the president of France. I didn't learn much else. At meal times, we ate and sweated together. We spent most of our time at the pool. There was nothing else to do but to read or nap. But almost no one napped. I think the young passengers were too excited.

Colette kissed me lightly now and then, for no reason in particular. She couldn't understand why I read Chaucer when I didn't have to. I didn't tell her I also enjoyed reading Ralph Waldo Emerson. Reading Emerson was a challenge. Sentences were long and complex, and his religious writings were of no interest to me. But his essays, "The American Scholar," and "Self-Reliance," were worth the time and effort. This world needed more American scholars.

I hated the thought of saying goodbye to Colette in Haifa. Apparently, Colette didn't want to say goodbye either. But I had no plan to keep us together. Lucky for me, Colette had a plan. Several hours before the ship reached Haifa, Colette came to me, sat me down, held both my hands, and said, "I asked our group leader, Benoit, if he would give his permission for you to come with us to the kibbutz. Benoit said yes. But the kibbutz director, who will meet us in Haifa, is the person who will actually decide yes or no. If the director says yes, will you please come with me? We will be together. You will have a place to go. It will be fun."

What a surprise. "Kiss me," I said. She kissed me on the lips. "Hug me." She hugged me. I answered "yes" while we hugged. I was beyond happy. It would have broken my heart to lose her just after finding her.

Late that night, with a billion stars above and a billion reflections of light sparkling in the sea below, from out of nowhere appeared the lights on

Mount Carmel. I knew the ship's destination was Haifa. It said so on my ticket. But I was not expecting to see beautiful Mount Carmel with all its lights ablaze. My emotions were already on my sleeve, worried about what the kibbutz director would say. I was truly emotionally unprepared. It wasn't just me. All the passengers grew silent and stayed silent until just before we docked. My emotions swelled and tears flowed from my eyes. It was nearly identical to a scene from the 1960 movie *Exodus*. I wiped away the tears and held Colette close. This was one of the happiest and most emotional moments of my life.

Passports were returned to us before we disembarked. I packed up my belongings, but my *The Canterbury Tales* book was missing. It wasn't with the rest of my things. I could only imagine how that happened: there must be a lunatic onboard.

As we walked down the gangway, I was now pumped with excitement. Colette stayed close. Not far past the end of the gangway, we were met by the kibbutz director. This meeting was critical. Benoit introduced me and Colette to the director, and in seconds he had presented our case. The director and I shook hands. I maintained good eye contact, told him my Jewish and American names. Colette held me close to her. It would have been heartbreaking if he would say no. The director sized up the situation quickly. "You can join us, but not just for one day. You must agree to work for several days. Will you agree?" I quickly realized the director had no choice but to say yes. He couldn't say no to her and this group the first minute they met.

"Yes, I agree." It was settled. I felt great. Colette was all smiles. I had never picked fruit before, but I would learn and work hard. I wouldn't want to disappoint Colette.

CHAPTER 12

With big smiles and not a moment to celebrate, we grabbed our belongings and followed the director. A monster-sized baggage cart awaited us. The kibbutz director ordered, "Load all your belongings on here, and then help push the cart through a large gate." We had avoided the long lines of passengers cued up for immigration, security, and customs. I was impressed.

When we reached the security gate, the kibbutz truck crew helped push the cart. The truck was parked close by. We loaded the truck with all our possessions and climbed on for a warm summer's night ride. Excluding the cab, the rest of the truck was open to the elements. It had no roof, and three sides had alternating wood and open spaces.

Off we went snuggled close as the truck roared through Haifa. I was hungry and thirsty, but I didn't mention it to the others, as I didn't want to stand out as a complainer. I hadn't eaten for several hours. The driver must have read my mind though. Within minutes, he stopped at a small storefront grocery. We were told to stay in the truck. Soon, the kibbutz men came out of the shop with bags full of bottled drinks and submarine sandwiches. I was surprised and thrilled. It was a fine example of Israeli hospitality, and a very nice change from spaghetti.

We hadn't finished our food and drink when the truck sped off. I rushed to finish. From the first shifting of gears, it was obvious the driver was in a hurry. Speed was no friend to those who rode in the back. I felt every bump in the road. And there were many. But it was a pleasant, warm evening to be riding in an open-air truck at sea-level. Unfortunately, the coastal flat roads soon gave way to inclined roads. The kibbutz was located more than two thousand feet above sea-level. As late-night temperatures dropped, and increased elevation had the same effect on temperature, warm air gave way to cool. The speeding truck created an even colder environment due to the windchill. And the colder it got, the more I thought back to Narvik. *"Not again,"* I thought. This time it was my head, neck, and upper body that were uncomfortably cold.

The roads were unusual. We drove on mountains roads that had switchbacks. The driver had to slow the truck to almost stopped to make the 180-degree turn. Then he would speed off before having to nearly stop at the next one. I never experienced anything like it. Were there steep drop-offs along the sides of the roads? I couldn't tell in the dark. I thought it was better not to know.

Just when I thought it was impossible to get any colder, the truck slowed down and turned off the road onto the kibbutz driveway. It stopped in front of an area of large tents and an unglamorous limestone building. We all climbed down and unloaded our baggage. Colette quickly grabbed her bag, jumped off the truck, and made her way ahead of the others. She entered the building. She passed through the first poorly lit room and decided that the back room with five beds scattered about was where she wanted to stay. It also was poorly lit. She quickly picked out her bed and was in the process of pushing a second bed against hers when I walked into the room. "That works for me," I told her. The guitar player and his girlfriend saw what Colette was doing and immediately pushed two beds together across from us. They were Gerard and Cat. A single fellow, Raymond, wandered in a few minutes later and secured the last bed for himself along a sidewall away from the four of us. How odd. I wouldn't want to be him. I would have chosen a bed elsewhere because I would have been envious of the others. After a wash at the shower-house, we all went to bed.

The Israelis let us sleep late. They woke us up at 7:30 a.m. Before I could get out of bed, Colette rolled toward me, gave me a big hug, and rolled away again. She reached down for her shorts and shirt, and dressed under the covers. All the males slept in boxer shorts and dressed outside the covers. We all made quick use of the shower house building. Despite a short night's sleep, I wasn't tired. I was simply very excited to be here.

Benoit and an Israeli named Yaakov walked into our house with piles of kibbutz work clothes. We were given kibbutz hats, kibbutz shirts, and some very short kibbutz shorts. The shorts were too short: the front pockets hung below the bottom of the short fronts. And it wasn't because the pockets were made ridiculously long.

Once we had changed into our kibbutz uniforms, Yaakov spoke. "Welcome to Kibbutz Yir'on. I am Yaakov. I am your work supervisor. I don't speak French. Benoit will translate. I hope you like the clothes we have provided for you. These clothes are what we expect you to wear when you work. We will walk to the dining hall for breakfast.

Immediately after breakfast, I will speak to you about your work. But for now, come with me. I have something else to show you."

He stopped the group when we reached the top of the kibbutz driveway. "At the end of this driveway is the road you traveled down last night. It is the main east-west road for this part of Israel. Down there, on the far side of the road, is a fence. On the other side of the fence is Lebanon. Stay away from there. It is a bad place. There is a shepherd who lives nearby, and he will shoot you if he finds you on his side of the fence."

"Interesting neighborhood," I thought.

"It is very safe here. We can easily protect all of you. Also, the Israeli Defense Forces are nearby. So, don't worry. We will take good care of you."

At 8 a.m., we followed Yaakov to the dining hall. But before I reached the entrance, I noticed there were several military tank traps along the dining hall wall. I recognized them because I had seen them in the movies. *"Tank traps? Sure. No one wants a military tank to drive through the dining room wall and interrupt breakfast."*

We walked into the main dining room. The entrance to a smaller dining room was off to the right as we entered. It was filled with small tables. It was nicely decorated.

Volunteers and a number of Israelis sat in the no-frills main dining hall, filled with long wooden tables. For me, kibbutz life was similar to my summer camp days in the Pocono Mountains of Pennsylvania when I was a kid, except here you had to work all morning instead of play, and the lucky guys got to sleep next to their girlfriends. Besides me and the French group, there was a male volunteer from New Zealand. Introductions were made.

There was plenty of food on the table. Before I could swallow my first mouthful, Yaakov came to our table and told us breakfast was served at 8 a.m. every day. Breakfast ended shortly before 9 a.m. Breakfast broke up the morning's work into two three-hour segments.

Breakfast consisted of eggs, sour cream, fresh fruit, cereal, bread, milk, and a hot beverage. All the food was self-serve from the table, except for the eggs and sour cream. A server gave everyone a choice of two eggs, or one egg and a yogurt. If you were a two-hundred-pound man or a one-hundred-pound woman, it didn't matter. There was plenty of food and time to eat. There was no reason rush or leave the table hungry.

At 9 a.m., orchard workers, both volunteers and Israelis, assembled for work in an area close to the dining hall. There, two large tractors were hooked up to two large wagons. Yaakov spoke to the new volunteers in fluent English with a heavy accent. He told us that he would be our leader for picking fruit. Benoit interpreted for the French, since the best I knew, most of them spoke little or no English.

Yaakov ordered, "The French, the American, and the New Zealander go with Marc on the wagon with the green tractor. The Israelis go with Dovid." Dovid drove a red tractor that was more modern and larger than the green tractor. The Israeli fruit pickers were already on the red tractor's wagon. The Israelis were older and more earthy in appearance than us volunteers. Clearly this land was their land, and we were the here today, gone soon volunteers.

We sat with feet dangling from the wagon, except for Colette, who sat with bent knees and her arms wrapped around them. I stared at her. She turned, looked at me with her million-dollar smile, and turned back again. She made me happy.

The morning air was comfortably warm. The tractor stopped at the edge of a beautiful peach orchard, the trees laden with fruit. Yaakov gave us a brief lesson on their method of picking peaches. Within minutes, we were trained. We each took our baskets and gear. I was assigned a very tall, lightweight aluminum pole ladder. I chose to work on the sunny side of the trees. Colette worked at ground level, protected from the sun by the shadow of the trees.

I worked as if I got paid by the peach and needed the money. Climb up, pick, climb down, walk to the collection bin, gently unload, secure the basket bottom, return to the ladder, climb back up or move to a different location. It was not difficult work. No special skills were needed. What did make the job difficult was the heat and the itchy rash on my lower forearms, caused by an allergic reaction to the peach fuzz or pollen. I had seen a television show where scientists observed that peach fuzz impedes some insects from attacking peaches, and the fuzz protects peaches from damage caused by excessive moisture. Rainfall, and even heavy dew, could easily saturate thin peach skin, weakening it, and allowing bacteria to cause the fruit to rot. Peach fuzz helps to collect water droplets, keeping them away from the skin.

At 10:30 a.m., a man on a small tractor arrived with lemonade. I was thirsty to the bone. At the end of the five-minute break, Yaakov shouted, "Time to work!"

Just before noon, it was time to quit work, and go for lunch. Yaakov told us our work was finished for the day. We climbed back on the wagon for the short ride back to the dining hall. We washed in sinks just inside the entrance. Our table decor, soup, noodles, bread, fresh fruit, and vegetables, I called it that since it was more attractive than the hall's furnishings and decorations, if there were decorations, was pleasing to the eye. We were served portions of beef. I wanted a larger portion, but only one size was allotted to each of us. There was plenty of food to eat. I skipped the peaches, though: had my fill in the orchard. I was still hungry near the end of the meal, so I poured soup over a large bowl of noodles. It was delicious and filling.

The table talk was in French. I only spoke with Colette and Benoit. Only when Colette would translate could I communicate with the others. Those conversations were very brief.

Following lunch, the Israelis climbed onto their wagon and went back to work in the peach orchard. The volunteers' wagon stood empty. Yaakov saw me.

"Your work is finished for today," Yaakov said.

"I know. But I am surprised. There are lots of peaches to be picked and I'm not tired."

"You do not work after lunch." He turned and walked away without explanation.

I returned to the house and grabbed what I needed to take a shower. I showered and washed clothes I had last worn on the ship, and hung them outside on a clothes line. I went inside and found my roommates resting and napping.

Although it was raging hot outside, the house, with its thick walls, held back enough heat to make conditions bearable inside. There was no indoor plumbing, no windows, and limited electrical capacity. In my room and the front room, there were single light-bulb fixtures overhead, the kind you see in a storage shed or closet, that produced inadequate lighting.

I thought about taking a nap, but I was very excited about the kibbutz and wanted to explore. I dressed and wandered off. First I walk down the driveway to the main road. In the distance, I saw several mountain peaks. I picked up a stone and threw it against the border fence. Now I could tell friends back home about living and working only a stone's throw away from Lebanon. Literally.

Of those nearby mountains, two of the mountaintops were in Israel, and both were topped with military installations, equipped with radar and signal towers. The other four were located in Lebanon. A truck and a small white foreign car passed me. I raised my hand to signal hello as each passed. A child in the back seat of the white car raised his hand.

I walked back and continued walking until I came upon an unusual structure. On the back side of it, a man was busy caring for two adult cows. He seemed glad to see me. He spoke to me in Hebrew. He needed help, or at least made me believe he needed help. He wanted me to hose off one cow's udders before he could attach the milking apparatus. He handed me the hose and showed me what to do. While I was hosing the cow's udders, the cow-man hooked up a second cow to a milking apparatus. It was a new experience for me. I was enjoying everything I encountered. The cow-man thanked me for my help and I continued my walk.

I came to a small fruit-packing operation. The peaches were machine-sorted. A conveyor belt moved them along a board with holes. The small peaches dropped through first, and larger ones farther along. Women packed the peaches into boxes, and men carried the boxes to a truck, the same truck I had arrived in last night. I had no idea where the peaches would be taken.

At 4 p.m., I walked to the dining hall for fresh, cold milk and cookies. As I drank the delicious milk, I couldn't help think about those two cows I had seen earlier. Was it milk from those two cows? I had to assume it was. Where was the milk processed? Was the milk pasteurized? I wasn't worried. I was confident about this place, milk and all, was a safe place to be.

I returned to the house. My roommates were asleep. They missed cows and snack time. I lay down to rest my eyes and woke at 5:30 p.m. Colette was sitting up on her bed speaking to the guitar player's girlfriend. I wanted to understand what they were saying, especially if it was about me. I was happy to be with them, even if I wasn't one of them. It was the same way with the Israelis. I didn't have to understand Hebrew. I was comfortable with them and I learnt it wasn't always important to know what was being said. At least it worked out that way today.

Outside, a ball bounced on the volleyball court. I put on a shirt and sandals and walked over to where the game was being played. The volunteers and four other Israelis were playing. I joined a team. It was a lot of fun. Just before 7 p.m., we ended the game and went off to get ready for supper. This would be our first supper. I didn't know what to expect. I brought a good appetite just in case. I washed, brushed my hair, changed my shirt, collected Colette, and we were off to dinner.

At 7 p.m., dinner was served. It was a dairy-based meal, meaning no meat. We each had a portion of fish. There was plenty of bread, butter, fruit, vegetables, and dairy products. An excellent soup was perfect when poured over a bowl of noodles. Yaakov dropped in to tell us additional do's and don'ts on the kibbutz, such as, "Stay in the lit areas at night" and "Be careful with your cigarettes" and "Disco starts at 10 p.m." I smiled. He must have been kidding, but I didn't say a word. We will wake up tomorrow at 4:45 a.m. But first we are going to a disco at 10 p.m. tonight. What an amazing place.

After dinner, the French gathered in the library for discussions. Since the discussion was in French, I left Colette at the library and went back to the house. I read Frommer's in preparation for my travels in France. Paris would be the last city I would visit before crossing the English

Channel to England. Colette returned early. She hadn't enjoyed the discussion group. She lay down next to me and scratched my back. "You have three hours to cut that out," I told her.

Not long after, the other French roommates appeared. They spoke in French until 10 p.m., when it was time to go to the disco. "We'll go," said Colette, "but we won't stay long. I'm tired."

We entered the dark disco room. A flashing strobe light put off just enough for all of us to dance. The music was loud but not loud enough to give you a headache. The volunteers, single Israelis, and a handful of young Israeli couples were dancing. It was crowded; everyone was on the dance floor. Colette and I danced several times but only twice with each other. At 11:45 p.m., the overhead lights were turned on and the music turned off. It was bed-time. We were careful to follow the lighted walkways past the tank traps back to our sleeping quarters. We had to sleep fast, for the 4:45 a.m. wake-up call was fast approaching.

CHAPTER 13

After a one hour nap on Wednesday afternoon, I was restless and needed something to do. I knew Benoit had a fishing line and a hook, and by putting a piece of red fabric on the hook, he would catch frogs. I already knew that the French ate frogs. But there would be no reason to capture one here. Catch and release only. It wasn't possible to have a frog in the kibbutz kitchen. The kitchen and dining hall were for kosher cooking and eating. According to Jewish dietary laws, reptiles and amphibians were considered unclean animals. Frog was not to be eaten.

I found Benoit in his tent, reading. I asked him where he had come across the frogs and if I could borrow his fishing line and hook. Benoit agreed to loan me his line, hook, and a small piece of red fabric. He directed me to a place I had not yet explored. It was a short walk from our limestone house to the swampy area surrounded with tall swamp reeds and cattails. Lilypads covered half the water surface. I threw out the line into a patch of water lilypads.

There was no place to sit comfortably, so I stood. I couldn't locate a water source. Since it rarely if ever rained in summer, my guess was that it was fed by a spring. If I was correct, someday they could dig out this wetland and make a pond for swimming and fishing.

When I wasn't paying attention to the line, I felt a tug. I pulled on the line and my mouth dropped open. *Oh my God*. It wasn't a frog. I had a snake on the line. It had a triangular head and oval eyes. I didn't know if it was poisonous or not, but it didn't matter. I feared snakes and would deal with this one as if it were dangerous. I pulled it closer and dragged it out of the water. I wrapped the line around a rock to hold it taut. Grabbing hold of a big rock with two hands, I threw the rock down, crushing the snake's head. I salvaged what fishing line I could but gave no consideration to free the hook and red fabric. I wasn't brave enough. Or perhaps not stupid. I left the snake where I killed it and hoped no snake predator would be in danger of the hook. I wouldn't have minded if another snake ate this one. Hopefully the kibbutzniks would exterminate all the snakes before creating a pond. I returned the fishing line to Benoit with apologies and an explanation about the hook and red fabric. Benoit looked unhappy. I felt bad and quickly retreated to the house.

At 6 p.m. Colette found me stretched out on our bed. "You are needed, right now. We need more players at the volleyball court." Not ten minutes into playing volleyball, the kibbutz received visitors. A military truck patrolling on Lebanese border road turned up the driveway. The truck drove up to the court, and the game stopped. The truck backed up and out jumped a group of soldiers. One stayed behind and kept two hands on a mounted machine gun pointing away from us. The soldiers took over one side of the court.

The volunteers were many; the soldiers were few. The volunteers were dressed in lightweight clothes; the soldiers were dressed in combat boots, serious uniforms, and carrying equipment on their belts. I thought we had a reasonable chance to beat them. I was wrong. The soldiers beat the crap out of us. My team failed to score one point.

Just when I had enough of losing, a Hebrew command was given, and quickly the soldiers boarded the truck and sped off. It was a comfort to have them nearby. Nevertheless, it would be just as comforting to beat the crap out of them on the volley ball court. Next time. But I wouldn't hold my breath about that happening.

It was 7 a.m. the next morning. I had finished picking peaches high up on an unusually tall peach tree. I climbed down to empty my basket. I picked all I could safely reach. That's when Yaakov came up to me. He spotted two peaches high up in the tree I had missed. I had left them there intentionally because they were out of my reach. I would have had to stand perched on the very top of the ladder to pick them. No way would I do something so foolish. Yaakov thought differently. He told me to go back up the ladder and pick those last two peaches. I didn't want to say no to Yaakov, so I did the foolish thing. I climbed back up the ladder. When I got near the top, I reached up to show him that they were beyond my reach. "Best to leave them there. Maybe feed the birds," I said.

Yaakov shouted and pointed at them. "Pick them." After saying a short prayer, I stepped onto the very top of the ladder and reached out for the first peach. As I feared, I lost my balance. The ladder swung out from under me when I was ten or twelve feet above the ground. I was about to fall on my head when I reached out and grabbed a passing tree branch. I partially righted myself and hit the ground on my right side with a mighty thud. My head hit my outstretched arm, and not the ground. I was lucky to not have fallen on my fruit-collecting basket.

Yaakov reached me quickly. "Are you hurt?"

"I'll know in a minute." I rolled onto my back so I could catch my breath and assess my injuries, if any. A broken peach tree branch lay beside me. Colette came to my side. Before she could speak, Yaakov arrived and bent over me looking concerned. "Are you hurt?" he wanted to know. If I was, he might be in trouble.

"I don't think so." I sat up. "I don't think anything is broken."

He asked, "Are you sure?"

I stood up. "I'm sure."

Now certain I wasn't hurt, he said, "You broke the tree." He had re-set the ladder and picked the last two peaches himself.

Damn, I thought. *He's upset about the tree branch? Upset that the volunteers would have maybe seven fewer peaches to pick next year?* I hurt, but minute by minute I felt better. I felt no sharp pains. I didn't know if I was bleeding internally, but I wasn't dizzy or nauseous, and my vision was fine. I did have a headache. For sure, I will have bruises. I went back to picking, but for the rest of the morning, I stayed off ladders.

Yaakov was angry about his broken tree branch. I was angry at Yaakov for sending me up the ladder after I told him I couldn't do it safely. And that broken tree branch? I am sure it will grow back.

CHAPTER 14

That afternoon, I woke from my afternoon nap and needed to use the toilet. The couple across from us was sleeping. Colette and Robert were reading. I stood up and felt the pain in my bruised body. "How are you feeling?" asked Colette.

"I hurt. I feel stiff." I bent over and gave her a kiss just to prove to her that I could bend. I stepped into my sandals, grabbed my toiletries, and walked off to the shower house.

I walked up the steps to the men's side of the shower-house, and pushed on the closed door. It didn't swing open. I had to push harder because there was something heavy behind it. It turned out to be a very large rock. I didn't give any thought to the rock being there, though I probably should have. I left the door open. Now a cooler breeze passed through the building as I went in to do my business. Water was running in one shower. The breeze was moving the shower curtain to flap open and close at one end, the end through which I could see as I walked past to the toilets. *Oh crap*, I thought. What I saw was the French girl, Dominique, and the New Zealander having sex. I turned around and made a fast exit. I couldn't slide the rock back in place from the outside. I returned to the house and sat on my bed to wait. *Lucky New Zealander.* I could clearly picture them. *I hope I get that lucky with Colette. But when? So far, nothing. But I am patient. I love where I am and what I'm doing. Sex could wait*, a day or two more I should think.

When I couldn't wait any longer to pee, I went back to the shower house. The door was open. The New Zealander was shaving. "Lovely day," he said, looking at me in the mirror as I walked by.

"Just lovely," I answered back. I didn't see Eve. I couldn't help but wonder what I was doing wrong regarding Colette. *She's French. She's beautiful. She more or less shares her bed with me, our beds touch and we share blankets, but no sex. I must be the unluckiest American in Israel!"*

Later that evening on the walk to dinner, Colette told me that the New Zealander would be leaving tomorrow and wasn't expected to return. Dominique sat next to her New Zealander boyfriend. She looked sad. She barely ate anything. Neither participated in the table conversation. They sat there looking from one person to another. My thoughts were that the rock that kept the door shut had been moved, and therefore, they suspected someone entered and may have seen them having sex. When both of them focused on me, I said to the New Zealander, "I am sorry to hear you are leaving us. Dominique seems to be very fond of you." I gave no "gives" that I was the intruder.

CHAPTER 15

The next day, I worked with my feet on the ground. It was a lot easier, safer, and less painful for me to keep working. I didn't see a lot of Colette during work because she chose to work in the shade. We sometimes met while emptying our baskets, but not that often. I noticed more than once that she was taking unscheduled breaks, sitting under trees while the rest of the group were working. That only made me work harder to make up for her laziness. Amazingly, I don't think Yaakov ever gave Colette a hard time about it.

Today's lemonade break was memorable. At 10:30 a.m., his usual time, the lemonade man arrived. It was wonderful to see him. I was so hot and so thirsty. The lemonade man handed me a drink and asked, "The work is good?"

"Yes, except the peach fuzz makes my arms itchy and turns my wrists pink." I didn't know it, but I had just screwed up, big-time. The lemonade man heard me. Yaakov had to have heard what I said. Someone should have said, "Adam, here we do not complain."

"Thou Shall Not Complain," was either a written or unwritten kibbutz rule. "Complaining disrupts harmony, and harmony is the fabric of the kibbutz." That's what I was soon to learn. No one had explained to me or the other volunteers the importance of harmony and that complaints were strictly prohibited. Or maybe that was explained to the French and wasn't passed on to me. The kibbutz community was intolerant of complainers, whether they were volunteers or otherwise. Because the lemonade man had witnessed the event, Yaakov had to report the incident to the director.

That afternoon, I washed my clothes. Afterwards, I had a hard time falling asleep. Colette was reading, and I interrupted her. "Colette, you know there's a good chance that I'm in trouble."

She closed her book. "I'm worried. My friends are talking about you. They know that you have upset the kibbutz members by complaining about the peaches. I didn't want you to worry, so I didn't say anything. But if they make you leave, I will make a scene until they change their mind. I won't work. I'll walk around naked all day long."

"I would like to see that."

"Sure you would. What do you think will happen?"

"Nothing. I barely said a thing. If it was important, I would have been informed by now. If not, then certainly by dinner time. We will stay together the rest of the day. If you want to go to the disco, we will go to the disco."

"And tomorrow?"

"They won't waste time tomorrow if there's a problem. Surely I will know by breakfast."

The next morning, the fruit pickers assembled at the wagon loading area at 5 a.m. and Yaakov called out the assignments. "The French go with Marc, the Israelis go with Dovid, and the American go with Daniel."

Now I knew something was up. I walked right up to Colette and touched her knee and said, "Don't worry. This will have a happy outcome. I love being here with you."

Daniel was seated on a very small tractor, so small that it could have been mistaken for a toy. It was hitched to a wagon not much bigger than the tractor. I took a seat on the wagon and kept my eyes on Colette as long as I could. I tried hard not to show any signs of fear.

Off went the three tractors. Daniel's tractor took a different dirt road than the others. The area was all new to me. *What did they have in mind?* I wondered. Time passed. Daniel finally stopped the tractor just inside a huge field of rocks. Daniel dismounted. He was bigger and stronger than me and nearly twice my age. He had a tattoo number on his lower right arm. It was the first time I had seen one. Daniel had survived a concentration camp. The tattoo humbled me. I decided to try and get along with Daniel and accept him just as I accepted Yaakov as my work supervisor.

Daniel pulled out a pair of gloves from his back pocket, put them on, bent over, and picked up a large rock, and dropped it on the wagon. I did the same, only bare-handed. I asked him for a pair of gloves, but he didn't answer.

From the very beginning, I couldn't keep up with Daniel's pace. When I sped up, Daniel did the same, only faster. He lifted heavier, larger rocks, and loaded more rocks than I did. When the wagon was fully loaded, Daniel drove the tractor to the edge of the field, where both of us tossed the rocks off to the side. No attempt was made to place them in an orderly fashion.

When the last rock was unloaded, I asked Daniel, "This is about the peach fuzz, right? My complaining about the peach fuzz?" Daniel did not answer. I assumed he didn't speak English, but that didn't stop me from apologizing. "Daniel, I apologize for complaining about the peach fuzz. If this is where I'm supposed to be working today because of it, no problem. This is good work, Daniel. Now I can say that I helped create a new orchard. That is very different from picking peaches today that would grow back again next year." Again, Daniel did not answer.

Load, unload, it was all we did for three hours. That was a lot of time to let my mind wander.

I worked hard and sweated like a pig. There was no shade. I wasn't happy about David wearing gloves while I went gloveless, but I wasn't going to complain. No way. Perhaps that was the trap: complain about not having gloves and that would end me. Wagon after wagon we loaded and unloaded. It was disheartening that there were so many rocks remaining on the field that it was hard to tell that we had removed any.

A few minutes before 8 a.m., we finished unloading the wagon. Daniel removed his gloves, shoved them in his back pocket, climbed on the tractor. He didn't have to signal that it was time to go. We slowly made our way back to the dining hall.

I took my time washing my hands. There was no room to sit next to Colette, but I was able to sit across from her. I sat there focused on her instead of eating. The server asked for my choice for breakfast. I wasn't listening. I was exhausted.

"Eggs for him," ordered Colette. To me she said, "Eat something." She pushed the bread and fruit plates closer to me, and I picked up a peach and smiled when I thought about scratching my arms. I didn't dare. Instead, I bit into it, and felt the juice trickle down my chin. Colette shook her head and smiled. I wiped my face dry just before the juice reached my clothing. I drank water like it was going out of style.

Yaakov wandered over to the table and asked me how I was feeling. "I'm alright. You won't believe this but Colette just agreed to marry me. I couldn't be happier."

"Congratulations. Maybe I can be your best man," said Yaakov, raising an eyebrow.

Colette said, "We will probably marry here next year." There was laughter around the table.

I was certain that Yaakov's visit to see how I was feeling was more than a courtesy visit. I watched him walk over to Daniel. It was then that I realized they weren't done with me.

I said to Colette, "I'm fine. Really. Daniel and I picked rocks out of a new orchard. The work is good. I don't need a ladder, and there isn't a crowd of people watching me to see if I was doing it correctly. The rocks are heavier than peaches, but not that much heavier," I lied. "At least they don't make my arms itch. I'm sure I'll be working with the rocks again after breakfast. But don't worry. I'm not going anywhere. We're staying together. I enjoy Daniel's company." I lied again. "He's an interesting man. I'll tell you about him later. The work isn't that bad." I didn't tell her that the rocks were hurting my hands, and that I desperately wished for a pair of gloves. She could see for herself that my hands were red and still dirty in places even though I had washed them.

When the one-hour breakfast break was over, we assembled once again outside by the wagons. The Israelis had climbed onto their wagon before Yaakov announced the next assignment. I saw the small tractor with Daniel in the driver's seat. When Yaakov called out, "The American goes with Daniel," I was already seated on the little wagon. I could tell most of the workers were staring at me.

The sun beat down on us. We followed the same routine as earlier: load, follow the wagon, unload, repeat. By 10 a.m., I was bored. The novelty had worn off, and the work seemed endless. An incredible number of rocks needed to be removed if our work was to be noticeable. I kept working. I self-entertained by thinking about poor Sisyphus.

Work stopped mid-morning when we received a welcome visit from the lemonade man. I was very glad to see him, despite the shit he caused me. But, I was extremely thirsty.

The lemonade never tasted better, and the lemonade man waited around until he got his cups back. I said thank you to him and was careful not to say one word more. As I drank and marveled over the landscape, I couldn't picture a new orchard. Instead, I visualized row after row of posts and wires, with vines climbing up and traversing the top wires. The vines were loaded with clusters of grapes. It could have been Italy: vineyards and fruit orchards, side by side. I didn't know if conditions here were suitable for table grape or wine grape cultivation, but that was what I imagined. My thinking was interrupted by Daniel who dropped a large rock on the wagon. Break-time was over.

At 11 a.m., with only one more hour to go, Daniel said to me in a low voice, "Watch out for the scorpions." I dropped the rock I was lifting. It narrowly missed my feet. I stood straight up, dumbfounded. "Scorpions?"

"Five kinds."

"You speak English?"

"Lived in Britain before immigrating to here."

I was livid. "Now you tell me about the scorpions. Why didn't you tell me earlier? Why didn't you give me a pair of gloves? You have gloves."

Daniel didn't answer.

"What if I got stung? Would I die?"

"You won't die. But big yellow ones are tricky." And that was the last time Daniel spoke to me.

There was an immediate change of plan. I adjusted for scorpions. My productivity suffered significantly thereafter, for I refused to insert my fingers under a rock without first seeing under it. The heaviest rocks were now very difficult to maneuver. I was determined not to be stung by a scorpion whatever its color or size. Maybe there were no scorpions. Maybe I was being tricked by Daniel intentionally just to slow me down. But I couldn't take the chance, and continued protecting my hands from a sting.

When the rock pickers returned for lunch, Yaakov was waiting for me. He announced, "Adam, you will be picking peaches tomorrow."

"Sounds great."

He asked, "How did it go?"

"Good. Better than I thought. I got along with Daniel. He's a nice man."

"No problems?"

"No problems."

We went inside to wash and eat lunch. Colette was overjoyed to see me. I sat across from her and asked her to pass the noodles. "I'm starved." I was a survivor, not a quitter, and that made me feel special. Colette smiled at me. Instead of passing the noodles, she reached across the table and grabbed hold of my hands, and said nothing.

CHAPTER 16

One day at dinner, an Israeli who I didn't know by name, called to me, and asked me to sit at his table. He introduced himself as Joseph. He told me that David, who sat at the table facing us, wanted to tell me a story, even though he didn't speak English.

As far as I could tell, David was the kibbutz's most popular person. He was big, strong, great looking guy. He was jolly and laughed loudly. He always seemed to be smiling. The young women liked him. He was fun, and he was just a sweetheart of a guy. Same as Yaakov, David had completed his military service and was a military reservist who was paid to live on the kibbutz. He was part of their skilled security force. The border was across the road, and if attacked, they would have to defend themselves until the Israeli Defense Forces arrived. All Israel borders with their Arab neighbors were dangerous and needed to be protected. There was one woman who I met living and working here who was serving out her last year of military service.

David caught my attention and pointed to Joseph. "Tonight, I'm David's interpreter," said Joseph. This was David's story as told to me by Joseph: "The 1967 war took place in June last year and lasted six days. Israel captured the Gaza Strip and the Sinai Peninsula from Egypt. They also captured the West Bank—including East Jerusalem—from Jordan, and the Golan Heights from Syria. After the war, David was stationed at the Suez Canal in the Sinai Peninsula. The Egyptian soldiers were close by, on the other side of the canal. The Egyptian soldiers carried their weapons with them as they moved about, as did the Israelis. It was a dangerous place to be."

Joseph warned me that David had no shame and then he continued with David's story. "The Egyptians were fed beans and bread every day. The Israeli soldiers, on the other hand, were eating good food. David being David, at the beginning of each meal, would wave his food high in the air at the Egyptians and yell over to them, 'Hello Egyptians, look what I am eating.' David would show and tell what was on his plate, and then laugh and laugh just as he was doing now." I could picture his story clearly. "One day, an Egyptian soldier got angry at David's antics. He aimed his weapon at David and fired. The bullet missed David. The Egyptian soldier could have caused an outbreak of war. The Egyptian officers took quick action and took away all their soldiers' weapons. The weapons were left at the ready, but they couldn't be touched unless ordered to do so. That way, there were no more incidents. David continued to wave at the Egyptians every mealtime, holding up his food and calling out to the soldiers." When Joseph and David stopped laughing, they continued. "One day, David got sick and he left the front line. Mealtime came, and mealtime went. No David. Each meal that David missed, Egyptian soldiers would yell across the Suez Canal, 'Where's the fat pig today?'" Daniel and Joseph roared at the end of his story. We all laughed. David had no shame.

I asked David, via Joseph, about his part in the 1967 War. But David had nothing to say.

I left the dining hall and went back to my house. My roommates were all there. Because it was Friday night, Benoit visited us briefly and brought a gift: we were in for a big treat. Benoit presented us with a large bottle of vodka. We wouldn't be working tomorrow because it was the Sabbath. He also brought some goodies in a box, but little attention was paid to them. I could see cigarettes, airmail envelopes, and bottles of shampoo at the top.

The four French in the front room joined us five in the back. We gathered close and passed the bottle around. No one passed up their turn. It was an opportunity to have fun. Everyone was laid back and appeared to be happy. Some were quickly getting drunk. Colette decided to do her toenails. She told Robert that I badly needed a haircut and, if he wouldn't mind, would Robert cut my hair? Robert agreed. She hadn't asked me my thoughts on the matter.

"Do I need a haircut?" I asked.

"When was the last time you had one?" Colette replied.

"Not since I can't remember. Robert, have you cut guy's hair?"

Colette translated the question to Robert. Robert smiled and answered, "Only a few times. But I was always drunk."

Without giving it another thought, I agreed to the haircut, since he had experience cutting while drunk. Besides, it was Colette who would have to look at me every day.

Robert pulled out a pair of scissors and went to work on my hair. There was plenty to work with. A big problem was that the lighting in the room was bad. I was sure that it wouldn't be a problem for Robert. Colette did warn, "Do a good job, and don't cut off his ears." That made me feel better. She cared.

When Robert was finished, I looked at Colette, "What do you think?" Colette gave a thumbs up and handed me her tiny cosmetic mirror. I refused to look. I would wait until morning. I felt both ears. They were still there, and neither of my hands were bloody. "Good job Robert," I said. Screw the haircut. It's little things in life that are important, like hearing.

The next morning, I could see that Robert had cut my hair short on the top and front, and left it longer on the sides and back. It looked great, different, European. It was perhaps my best haircut ever. It had been cut and styled by a drunken French art history student. I checked my ears. I was pleased that Robert hadn't given me the Van Gogh look. I wondered how good he was sober?

CHAPTER 17

We volunteers didn't work on Saturdays. No one worked on Saturdays, as far as I could tell, with the exception of the cow guy. The cows probably couldn't wait until the Sabbath ended to be milked. Despite having the day off, Yaakov woke us up at 7:30 a.m. He didn't want the volunteers to miss breakfast. He told us to meet back at the house directly after breakfast. We were all going for a day trip to Lake Kinneret. "Pack a towel and bathing suit," he said. I guessed it would be packed with weekenders since Jewish people didn't have to work.

At 9 a.m., the French, Yaakov, the driver, and I boarded the same truck that had picked us up in Haifa a week earlier. The ride was much more comfortable this time. For one thing, we didn't freeze to death; for another, it was daytime. We could see the beautiful countryside and the towns we passed through. Interestingly, our truck was the only vehicle on the road. It had to do with it being Saturday, the Jewish Sabbath.

When we reached the lake, the truck turned off the paved road that would have taken us into Tiberias, and headed north onto an unpaved that ran parallel to the lake. The truck eventually stopped when the road ended. We were near the northwest corner of the lake. There were tall trees behind the beach. There were no other people or visible buildings. We had the whole beach area to ourselves. I was pleasantly surprised.

The driver stepped out of the truck with Yaakov, and Yaakov announced, "We are at Lake Kinneret. Swim. Rest. Relax. Later, we will eat. We have

113

toilet paper, but no toilets. Men go there." He pointed. "Women go there." He pointed to a different area of woods. "But stay around here. Don't wander off."

I wasn't familiar with the name Lake Kinneret. I was to learn from of the French students that the lake was also called the Sea of Galilee. The modern Hebrew name, Kinneret, comes from the Old Testament. In Hebrew it is spelled כנרות, Kinnerot. Kinneret was found among the "fenced cities" in Joshua. The origin of the name comes from the Bronze and Iron Age city of Kinneret.

It was beautiful. Across the sea were the Golan Mountains that ran parallel to the lake. The same mountain range far up north was the Golan Heights that overlooked Syria. It was very far away for us to see. There was no boat traffic. It was the Sabbath on the lake.

Colette went off with two females to find shrubbery to hide behind so they could change into their bathing suits. I had worn mine there. Carrying my towel and still wearing my glasses, I walked down to the water's edge and got my feet wet. Up the beach, I saw the most amazing thing. A huge, long stone column, not unlike the columns I had seen in the ancient parts of Rome, was lying on the ground, the lower half submerged in the lake. *Where did that come from? What's it doing in the lake? Who put it there?* For sure, that column was ancient and appeared to be Roman. It had to have come from somewhere nearby, unless it had been carted off to here. Since it was impossible for a building to have just one column, the additional columns had to be close to this place. I looked around. Again, I didn't notice any structures nearby, ancient, or modern. I would have to be standing at a higher elevation to fully view the area, or go for a walk away from the group. Yaakov's instructions were to stay close, and I wasn't about to break that rule or any other rule. Maybe more columns were lying on the bottom of the lake?

I was ready to swim, so I laid my glasses and my towel on the column. Since I was the first to go for a swim, I wasn't sure about any creatures and rocks in the lake, So, I did my best to keep my feet off the bottom seconds after I entered. If asked how deep the water was, I had no idea.

I swam parallel to the beach, searching for other submerged columns, but found none. I returned to the column and splashed water on it to cool it down so that I could lie on it. With my head and upper torso out of the water, I turned my head away from the group and laid my head down. I listened carefully, waiting for an ancient voice to speak to me. If it did speak, it probably would have said, "Go to sleep," because that is exactly what I did.

Sometime later, someone shouted that it was time to eat. I woke up, climbed down from the column, and entered the water for one more refreshing dip. If the column had spoken to me in my dreams, I had already forgotten what it said. Whatever this column had witnessed throughout the centuries, would have been wonderful to listen and see. Not that I had the time to sit through each day.

I toweled off and saw Colette lying in the sun. I sat down on my towel beside her and listened to her conversing in French. I loved listening to her speak French. Yaakov handed me a sandwich and a cold lemonade. But soon I realized that Colette wasn't Colette. She was stoned or drunk. How could I tell? Her speech was slurred; her pupils were contracted. She put my arm around her and put her head on my chest until she realized that I was eating my lunch over her head.

As far as I could tell, no one had any alcohol. And I couldn't smell marijuana. If she had gone off into the woods to smoke, her clothes or hair would smell of it. It must have been a pill she took. Or maybe she ate something. Hashish? I never confronted her about it. I didn't care. She looked happy. I was happy. The people. The setting. We didn't have to work. Everything was perfect.

When it was time to get ready to go back, I didn't want to leave the beach. Being there was a vacation from my vacation. Some of the French changed into dry clothes. The French were highly skilled at changing clothes in public. I was not so skilled. I struggled under a towel to get my wet bathing suit off and pull on a pair of kibbutz shorts. I should have gone off to the woods to change.

Dominique changed her bathing suit bottom under a towel where she had been sitting near the water. She put on a tee-shirt and unhooked the back of the bathing suit top, untied the top strings and pulled the swim top out from under her tee-shirt. She was sexy in a tee-shirt without a bra. I had not seen her smile the whole day. Since her New Zealander boyfriend had left her, she appeared to be mourning his loss. She had fallen hard for the guy in just a short time. That sounded familiar…

CHAPTER 18

A week later, the volunteers were no longer needed. Yaakov announced, "The apples are not ready to be picked. Take a week vacation." I was thrilled. To my surprise, Colette decided that she and I would travel alone for the week. We packed up and left immediately after lunch. We rode a westbound bus to the Israeli coast. I loved how Colette looked in her sunglasses, a pair of jeans, and her shirt-bottoms tied together in the front. With her hair pulled back into a ponytail, she was precious. Or as my dad would say, she "looked like a million dollars." I was thrilled to be with her and to share this adventure with her. This was such a welcome change from my travels alone for so many weeks. And traveling with a female would surely be much safer for me than traveling with a male. At least, that was how I felt after my Italy and Greece experiences.

We arrived in Acre in the middle of the afternoon and stuffed ourselves with honey buns and coffee. We walked and walked. Colette had to see everything for sale and not for sale. Darkness arrived too soon. We had no idea where we would spend the night when we were approached by a cheerful, young man about our age, who asked in a distinctly New York accent, "Do you need a place to spend the night?" Colette gave him a quick "yes" before I could even process the question.

"Come with me. I'll explain on the way," the guy said. "My name is Joel."

Joel explained that he was an American student studying nearby. What exactly he was studying he didn't tell us. He claimed that the apartment he was taking us to was owned by the Cuban government and that he didn't pay anything to live there. I found the *free rent* part of the story suspicious. Israel-Cuba relations were bad. Although Cuba had had relations with Israel for many years, that gave way to Arab pressure right after the War of 1967.

We followed him to a beautiful two-bedroom oceanfront apartment, close to the Mediterranean Sea. We had our own room for the night. The shower was hot and wonderful. It would have been nicer if I had had a certain young French girl join me in the large shower, but that didn't happen. The bed was queen size and comfortable. It would have made a great honeymoon bed; it was that nice. But I wasn't on my honeymoon. A sexual relationship with Colette had not made it out of the batter's box. I had never French kissed her. Baffling? I thought so. Unfortunately, tonight would be no different. She wrapped herself in a blanket, turned her back to me, and was instantly asleep.

After a good night's sleep, we ate our host's hard-boiled eggs, pita bread, and coffee. We hitch-hiked, and within minutes had a ride down the coastal road into Haifa. We spent most of the day there. We once again hitchhiked. We were lucky to catch a ride that took us halfway down the coast to Tel Aviv. We took our time from there. One time we walked across the beach to wet our feet. Colette loved the beach and the sea. I also did. But being with Colette and not being alone, was special.

Before dark, we found a small grocery store and bought fruit, yogurt, and juice. We crossed the road and sat on the beach in the dark, enjoying our simple meal and an opportunity to rest. When we finished, Colette bounced up. "Can we walk the beach?" I laughed because the answer was never going to be "no." I didn't share my thought that we should return to the road and find a hotel to spend the night. After a brief walk on the beach, Colette stopped in front of an interesting sand dune. It was horseshoe-shaped, with fine sea grasses covering it. It was tall, and it's only opening faced the ocean. No one could see the front entry from the road. The front entry was maybe six feet wide and was cave-like. Unless local lovers in need of a private place to run off to, this was the place. It was a good place to spend the night—if sleeping on sand was acceptable and if there was no fear of the unknown. Colette had no doubts that this was where she would be spending the night. I didn't object, for I was certain she would have slept there alone if I walked off in pursuit of a comfortable room. But I wouldn't have left her alone for the world.

We laid out our sleeping bags. Colette put her arms around my neck and gave me a quick kiss goodnight. She then slipped into her sleeping bag, took off her shirt, pulled off her pants, turned her back to me, and fell immediately to sleep. Romance was doomed in the dune tonight. There was nothing surprising about that.

The sun was up when we were awoken by bells, lots of bells. We sat up straight. Then we crawled to the opening of the sand dune and peered out. We were surrounded by sheep. Lots of sheep. Bell ringing came from every direction. The sight of all those sheep made us laugh. A Palestinian family, that was my guess, whose oldest child looked about twelve years old, had driven their sheep across the beach to the ocean's edge. The horseshoe-shaped sand dune literally split the herd in two. The male sheepherder dragged the sheep into the water, one at a time, to be washed in the saltwater. What a wonderful mixture of sounds: bells ringing, sheep bleating, children playing, and tiny waves lapping the shoreline.

We eventually dressed—she in her sleeping bag, me standing—and packed up our belongings. We walked back to the store where we bought food the previous night and purchased breakfast items. The reluctant clerk, under sweet persuasion from Colette, allowed us to use their bathroom that was not available to customers. That's what the sign on the door read in English. From there, we rode a bus to Tel Aviv.

We wandered along streets filled with shoppers. Tel Aviv looked like any modern European city. At lunchtime, we ate outside at a bistro on a picnic table close to where the pedestrians passed. Four French women were seated at a table behind us. Colette had a good view of them and was listening to their conversation while pretending to read her menu. She listened when the waitress took their order. When their food arrived, Colette gave it her full attention. One young woman carefully examined each dish as it was placed in front of her tablemates. When she realized that the entrée she preferred was not the one sitting in front of her, she told the waitress, "I didn't order this." She pointed to the dish she wanted. "That's what I ordered." The waitress took her plate back to the kitchen.

Colette whispered to me, "She lied. They served her what she ordered. That's the French for you."

We were at the end of our meal when two soldiers carrying Uzi submachine guns walked out of the restaurant. Only one walked past. The other soldier stopped dead in his tracks when he saw Colette. He was seeing what I saw every time I looked at her: a goddess. He was a good-looking fellow with dark hair and couldn't have been older than me. When he stopped staring, he sat down at our table across from us and spoke at me. "Do you want to trade?" he said in English. He pointed to Colette. I smiled, I thought I would play along with his game, and I pointed to the soldiers' Uzi. The soldier immediately handed over his Uzi to me. I was amazed that the he was so reckless. But before the soldier could claim his prize—and thank God he couldn't—a shout rang out from another soldier walking up from behind him. The young soldier stood. I quickly handed him back his weapon before he even reached for it. He accepted the weapon reluctantly. The deal was off. The Uzi had been in my possession for maybe five seconds. He walked away very disappointed, and possibly in big trouble.

What had happened was surreal. How could that soldier just hand his weapon over to me? I was certain that he was getting an earful for what he did. I wouldn't have traded anything for Colette. Not that I ever had the power to do so.

"That was fun," I said. "I never would have traded that gun for you. It was a game, a joke; you understand that, right?"

She wouldn't look at me. She reached for her bag, pulled out some shekels, and insisted that she pay for her share of our lunch. She put on her backpack, and off we went to find a bus that would take us to Jerusalem. I uttered under my breath, "That might have been an enormous mistake."

We found the busy Tel Aviv bus station and traveled on an "Egged" bus to Jerusalem. From the Jerusalem bus station, we walked to the ancient walled city. Just before we reached there, we came upon some workmen who were using mules to carry building rubble down a hill in baskets hanging on either side of each animal. Up and down they navigated a dirt trail, walking alone. The building where the animals was damaged with dozens of bullet holes. Some were larger than others. Serious fighting had definitely taken place here.

Soon, we could see the walled city of Jerusalem. We walked downhill until we had nearly reached the Jaffa Gate, one of several entry gates. A food truck on the street had a sign that read, "Falafel." I stopped in my tracks. I was unfamiliar with the word, but I was very hungry. I moved closer and watched a sandwich being made for a customer.

In the pocket of a large half of pita bread, the vendor placed two fried balls that had the same appearance as hush puppies. He continued filling it with ripe red tomatoes, green tomatoes, and pickles. After that, he poured a white sauce over them. He topped the sandwich with french fries. It looked delicious. When it was my turn, I ordered one for each of us. As we waited, I watched the sandwich maker while Colette stood to the side, taking in the view of the great walled city. We were both half-starved. I paid the man in shekels, about half an American dollar for the two sandwiches. The hush puppies were actually fried balls of chickpea. The sandwich tasted heavenly. I consumed mine quickly.

Colette was ready to move on, but not me. I had already ordered a second. I devoured the second falafel before reaching the gate, truly believing that I was entering a holy site and not wanting to show disrespect. Besides, Colette was eager to continue.

We entered the city with Colette leading the way. With help from a piece of paper she pulled from her backpack, she quickly navigated the stone streets. We were in the Christian section. A short walk later, she walked into a shop that sold religious figures carved from olive wood, and many fabric products: everything from clothing to blankets.

"Can I help you?" the clerk asked her. I lagged behind her, pretending that I was seriously interested in the merchandise. She spoke with the clerk in a soft voice. I couldn't make out what she was saying. The two of them moved farther away from me and continued speaking in hushed voices. I had no idea what was going on. Colette opened her bag, reached in, and handed him something. It could have been money. If it was, it must have been a prepared amount, as she didn't take a moment to count it.

The clerk walked away and made a call from a wall phone just inside the doorway of the back area. He spoke for only a few seconds. When he hung up, he hollered in the direction of the back of the store. He said to Colette, "Let's go." A woman came out from the back to watch over the store.

Colette followed the man, and I followed Colette down ancient streets. They stopped to talked. Colette turned to me and said, "Stay back. Wait for me here." I nodded yes. Slim chance. I didn't like what was happening at all. I continued to follow them.

The storekeeper finally stopped at a wooden cellar door in a busy area of shops. He kicked the door twice and the door swung open. The storekeeper threw down what must have been the money. Then somebody down below threw up a small packet to the clerk. The clerk pocketed the package. The door slammed closed, and the clerk walked off with Colette. Moments later, he handed it to Colette. When I reached her, her "drug dealer" was gone.

"What is it?" I asked.

"Nothing important."

"They told us at the kibbutz that possessing illegal drugs was strongly discouraged in this country, and if convicted, prison terms run up to twenty years."

She ignored me, put on a smile, and locked her arm around mine. It was her way of saying, "I did what I wanted to do, now let's go explore." Later, I would learn that she had purchased a finger of hashish for the equivalent of five American dollars. Her cheerfulness afterwards made me believe that she was full of herself for making the purchase without anyone's help. I did wonder as to who told her about that shop.

We walked along the magnificent streets of old Jerusalem. Almost every building had wiring running up the outside walls: some for electricity, others connected to TV antennas located on the rooftops. We located stairs that took us to the top of the wall. Looking in the direction of the Dead Sea, with the exception of the TV antennas, a few motor vehicles, and some people wearing modern day clothing, I would have bet the this part of the world hadn't changed in two thousand years.

We walked back down and found our way to the Wailing Wall. The men in charge directed Colette to a different area of the wall just for women because women were not allowed to pray with the men. That's because women distract men and therefore men can't properly pray. Back home, the women sat in the upstairs balcony of the synagogue. Downstairs, I had always sat with my father, grandfather, uncles, and male cousins.

A man asked me if I was Jewish. I said yes. First, he gave me a kippah to cover my head. It was similar in form to what the Pope wears. Then, he wrapped my left arm and strapped the tefillin head part to my forehead, and handed me a prayer book. I walked up to the wall and instinctively touched it, brought my fingers to my lips, and read the prayers in Hebrew. I could read Hebrew, but I couldn't translate it to English— except for a few common prayers.

If being at the Wailing Wall wasn't enough of a distraction to my praying, I was distracted by the thousands of small pieces of paper that worshipers had inserted into the cracks between the huge stone blocks that were all that remained of the Second Temple. I guessed the papers contained prayer requests written to God. Sooner or later, they would fall to the ground and be swept up and stored away. Others were intentionally removed to make room for new notes. Since most had God's name written upon them, none were ever trashed or burned. Instead, they were buried on the Mount of Olives.

I was brief as I could reasonably be. I didn't know if Colette had gone up to the wall herself or if she had been denied access because of how she dressed. She was Catholic, and the wall might not have been important to her. We had never discussed religion. I finished a few prayers and blessings, and once I was uncovered and unbound, I returned to Colette. She looked at me like a proud parent. We kissed. Using Colette's pen and paper, I wrote a note to God asking him to keep all Americans away from Vietnam. Asking only for myself would have been selfish. I went back to the Wall and squeezed the note into a crack.

I didn't want to go up to the Temple Mount to see the Dome of the Rock mosque. Colette wasn't going anywhere without me, so there was no question about her going up there alone. Instead, she bought some Dome of the Rock postcards.

We quickly found a youth hostel to spend the night. It cost one dollar for each of us. We were separated for the night by sex: males in one section, females in another. My room was packed with double bunkbeds. I had the upper bunk. In the morning, after a great night's sleep, we all woke up at the same time. Colette was waiting for me outside.

We decided the evening before to go to Bethlehem in the morning. When we asked where to find transportation to Bethlehem, we were told that it could be dangerous to go there. Tourist buses and Israeli buses could be targets from troublemakers. Despite the warning, we didn't change our minds. We decided that it would be less risky to take a Palestinian bus from Jerusalem into Bethlehem and travel with Arabs.

For the first few minutes, we were uncertain if this had been a good idea. We were the only foreigners on the bus. Men entered the bus with sandals and feet caked with mud. One man came on the bus carrying live chickens that he stored on the overhead rack near the back of the bus. One older man entered carrying a watermelon that he also stored on the overhead shelf. It was minimally secured behind the ropes running the length of the shelf. The watermelon reminded me of the Mediterranean voyage where I met Colette. But it wouldn't be my only memory of watermelons this summer. That's because the bus bounced one time too many, and the watermelon fell off the overhead and splattered in the center aisle, just one row ahead of me and Colette. Everyone onboard laughed, even the old man.

Watching out the window, I thoroughly enjoyed the large olive trees we passed along the route. It turned out to be a nice, safe ride to Bethlehem.

When we arrived, we carefully exited the bus trying not to step on the smashed watermelon that no one had bothered to clean-up during the ride. Uncertain where to walk to next, without even having to ask, a woman pointed us in the right direction. Soon, we entered Manger Square. We could see a large parking lot and the Church of the Nativity, a basilica built over the manger where Jesus Christ had been placed after he was born.

At the basilica doorway, we had to stoop to enter. The doorway was deliberately cropped low to prevent Ottoman raiders from entering on horseback. We could see that the actual entrance was much taller and wider. Now that the Ottoman raiders were long dead and the Ottoman Empire had retreated from the Middle East, I was surprised that the doorway hadn't been re-worked to its original size. With head bowed to avoid running into the low doorway, I followed Colette in.

Bowing down to pass through the entrance, I noticed that the floor was made of wood. Farther in, a small area of the wood flooring had been removed to show the original mosaic floor, a floor that dated back to the fourth century, when the church was first built. I memorized some of the geometric patterns, as they had potential as wallpaper designs. I would start sketching the patterns first chance I had. The walls had mosaics depicting Christ ascending to heaven, and Christ entering Jerusalem riding on a donkey. Toward the front of the church, the lecture pulpit was on the left.

Management of the basilica was shared between the Roman Catholic Church, the Greek Orthodox Church, and the Armenian Orthodox

Church. Just to the left of the altar, a priest was selling candles. He was either from the Roman Catholic Church or the Armenian Apostolic. A Greek Orthodox priest was also selling candles beyond the right side of the alter. Colette made a donation and lit a candle. She bowed her head and appeared to say a prayer.

The Grotto of the Nativity was an underground space that formed the crypt and was the place where Jesus was born. Situated underneath the main altar, it was accessed by two staircases on either side of the chancel. The grotto was part of a network of caves, that could be accessed from the adjacent St. Catherine's Church.

The cave had an eastern niche that contained the Altar of Nativity. The exact spot where Jesus was born was marked beneath this altar by a 14-pointed silver star with the Latin inscription *Hic De Virgine Maria Jesus Christus Natus Est-"717* ("Here, Jesus Christ was born to the Virgin Mary"–1717). It was installed by the Catholics in 1717, removed allegedly by the Greeks in 1847, and replaced by the Turkish government in 1853. The star was set into the marble floor and surrounded by fifteen silver lamps representing the three Christian communities: six belonged to the Greek Orthodox, four to the Catholics, and five to the Armenian Apostolic. The significance of the fourteen points on the star was to represent the three sets of fourteen generations in the genealogy of Jesus Christ: first, fourteen from Abraham to David, then fourteen from David to the Babylonian captivity, then fourteen more until Jesus Christ.

We exited the room and found ourselves in a small hallway. It was just the two of us. A bible was sitting on a small table. Colette picked it up and opened it.

"Hello," said a priest who appeared from nowhere. Imagine that. We were in the most famous church in the world, and a fairly young, handsome priest stopped to say hello and chat in English. "Are you Catholic?"

"Yes," she said. There was no time for me to answer because the priest had moved closer to Colette. He asked her if she had any questions about what she had just experienced. The two spoke for five minutes. Colette left smiling.

We returned to Jerusalem and continued with our sightseeing. We visited the Room of the Last Supper, the Church of the Holy Sepulcher, and took a walk on the Mount of Olives. There we met a Palestinian boy who might have been twelve-years-old. He insisted on showing us the Chapel of the Ascension. It was a small round church or mosque that was both a Christian and Muslim holy site. He insisted that we take off our right sandals and place our bare feet on a dirty footprint that was made in the stone from where Jesus had ascended to heaven.

After that, he took us to a store. He wanted coins to buy a cigarettes. Colette gave him some coins and he was grateful. He went into the store and came out with two cigarettes and gave Colette back her change. We found a place to sit, watched him smoke, and then we listened to his story.

His father was an Israeli Arab who worked as a bus driver in Jerusalem. According to the boy, his father made a good living. He said that he hated the Jordanians. I asked him why. "Because they removed the headstones from Jewish graves and used them to build their houses. It was wrong for them to do that." We eventually said our goodbyes and offered him money for being a terrific guide. But he refused.

It was after dark by the time we finished eating and returned to the youth hostel, only to learn that it was too late to get beds. All were spoken for. While standing there not knowing where to go next, the hostel woman offered us outside accommodations. "You can sleep on the grass." She pointed to a lush grassy area close to the hostel entrance. We thanked her and turned to go when she added, "Forty cents each." I was amazed, but quickly agreed to the price because we had no choice. I treated Colette. It was a rare occasion when she let me pay her share of anything.

We rolled out our sleeping bags side by side; they didn't separate by sex for lawn accommodations. We went inside to use the facilities. When we finally settled in, Colette gave me a kiss and thanked me for traveling with her. Once again, she quickly turned away from me and, within seconds, was fast asleep. Not thirty feet away from us, a guard leaned against a wall facing us with Uzi in hand, clip in, guarding us and the others. The guard watched over us all night. For sure, "*That was the best eighty cents I ever spent for a night's lodging.*"

Early the next day, we left the youth hostel and traveled to Jericho in an Arab bus. There, we observed one of the first Israeli archeological digs in the area following the 1967 War. The dig overall was only a few feet wide and long. Workers told us that the structure they were excavating was from an ancient city that dated back to when Abraham had lived. Colette and I could see that the building was small, and that the archway entrance was similar to an Eskimo igloo entrance. It was neat to see. Although Colette hoped that the diggers had properly dated the site and that they weren't telling us a made-up story, I said to Colette, "they are full of shit."

We wandered through the nearly deserted city. Before the 1967 Israeli War, Jericho's population was 100,000. Now, the population was somewhere around 2,000. The Palestinian inhabitants and hundreds of thousands from other Palestinian areas, fled the West Bank to Jordan, located on the other side of the River Jordan. Jericho is connected to Jordan by the Allenby Bridge. Although the bridge was destroyed on June 7, 1967, the third day of the War of 1967, what remained of the bridge allowed for continued foot traffic across the extremely narrow Jordan River.

As we walked past one deserted house after another, the place was silent. We didn't see people or animals. We turned back, walked past the dig once more, and headed towards the ruined Allenby Bridge. Nearly in sight of the bridge, an Israeli soldier intercepted us. He walked toward us shouting, "Turn back. There are snipers. Turn back." We reversed direction and quickly walked back into the city. We hadn't gotten close enough to see the crossing, or get shot at.

From Jericho, we hitch-hiked to Ein Gedi on the Dead Sea.

CHAPTER 19

The Dead Sea is an extremely salty lake loaded with a very high percentage of minerals that makes your skin feel oily and in need of a freshwater shower. Located some 1,300 feet below sea level, you could smell the bromide in the air. You would also be surprised how quickly the sun set in the west. The sea's surface was the lowest point on earth. And in the summer, the area could be unbearably hot.

The bromide smell was known as a female sex stimulator. It works that way for most women. But not all. Unfortunately, Colette was a not all. I don't know if we have bromide smelling bodies of water in America. It was well known in America that sex stimulation for women could be bought in expensive jewelry stores. I decided to keep an eye out for one.

It was entertaining for us to watch first-time Dead Sea swimmers slowly, reluctantly made their way into the mineral-rich water. When the water reached mid-chest level, bathers no longer stand upright. Each bather would flip forward or backward. To flip forward was a bad experience. The bather needed to exit as fast as possible in search of fresh water to rinse out his eyes. On this beach, there were freshwater showers very close to the shoreline. If the bather flipped backward, and most bathers did, the sea positioned your body into a "rowboat" position, as legs rose up and knees were forced to bend. To move around, you had to row yourself using your arms to propel yourself backwards. Legs were of no help to move about. Once the bather realized that he couldn't sink after flipping into the boat configuration, his or her face was all smiles.

After watching a number of bathers enter, we finally changed into swimsuits and went into the water for a swim, despite the strong smell of the bromide. We kept walking until we were waist deep. With blind faith, we lay back. With our legs flexed up and in rowboat position, we used our arms as paddles to move about. I thought it was great fun until I accidently splashed some water into my eyes. I hustled out of the water and ran to the freshwater shower. Despite that, it was a fun time for both of us.

The Dead Sea was known for its healing properties. It was no lie that it could cure conditions such as psoriasis. Germans flocked to the Dead Sea courtesy of the German government's healthcare system. Patients spent a small part of their day at the water's edge covered in Dead Sea mud, soaking in the sea, and breathing the bromide air. But most of their day was spent behind large privacy curtains that separated the men from the women. There they walked, talked, read, and rested in the sunshine naked.

It was of interest to note that when the Dead Sea mud and water were removed to distant locations, significant healing did not take place.

After bathing and showering at the water's edge, we decided to explore a spring that appeared to be an oasis. It was between the sea and the entrance road. Small, unusual animals inhabited the springs called "rock badgers." Officially, they were called "rock hyrax" and they lived around mountainous places that had fresh water. Hyraxes were believed to be the *shafan* mentioned in the Old Testament. They were also known as "rock coney" or "rock rabbit." They appeared to be rodents, but were in fact ungulate mammals, more closely related to elephants. That was hard to believe. Apparently, their feet resemble those of an elephant, just not big. They didn't appear to have tails and didn't have trunks. The hyraxes in the Middle East were the only non-African members of the hyrax family. They were among Israel's cutest animals and fascinating to watch. Active in the mornings and evenings, they were also highly sociable, living in family groups with one adult always standing guard while the rest of the group fed. They ate the vegetation that grew at the springs.

From there we went back to Jerusalem by bus, and once again had a good night's sleep on the lush lawn of the Jerusalem youth hostel.

The following morning, our last morning in Jerusalem, we decided to hitch-hike north through the West Bank. Before the day ended, we hoped to reach Tiberias. We walked north. Colette stuck out her thumb at a passing military truck, a large one. Slim chance of that truck stopping. But it did stop. A soldier climbed down from the cab and gave Colette a big smile.

"Where are you going?"

"We are going to Nablus."

He smiled again. "We will take you there, but we have to make one stop along the way. Climb in the back."

Hell, I thought, *if I weren't here and she told him she needed a ride to Tiberias, he would have driven her there in this truck or a stolen one. I have no doubt.*

We went to the back and climbed in. Colette didn't need any help. It was an open top vehicle. The truck sped along the road for several miles and then turned off the paved road and traveled east. The land appeared to be desert, not only from the blazing hot sun, but also because of the herd of camels racing on a parallel course to the road off in the distance. The camels couldn't keep up with the speeding truck and soon dropped back. We couldn't see the Arabs or Bedouins to whom these camels must belong. Soon, the truck slowed and entered a very small fenced military camp. The truck drove through the security gate. The guards at the gate saw us, but didn't react to our presence. The soldiers got out and told us to stay on the truck. All around us were military tanks.

The soldiers were gone for less than five minutes. They returned, turned the truck around, and raced back to the highway. Once again, we traveled north. When we arrived in Nablus, the same soldier got out and met us at the back of the truck. He gave us a stiff warning. "Get out before nighttime. There are bad people here. We will drive through here later today. If we see you are still here, we will take you with us. It is very dangerous here at night." We thanked him.

I didn't give any thought as to daytime danger. It was never discussed. We explored Nablus. We walked the dirty, smelly streets, with open trenches on either side. Flies and bees dined on partially covered honey cakes displayed on the sidewalks in front of shops. We wandered about, but stayed out of the shops. Eventually, we walked back to the main road. An Arab bus stopped for us. The driver opened the door, as if surprised to see us, and said, "Yes?" He drove us to Jenin. From there, we rode a bus to Nazareth, where we bought food and drink. By then, it had gotten dark. We waited another two hours before we caught a ride.

CHAPTER 20

The driver of the small truck dropped us off just below Tiberias late that night. He pointed out the direction we should walk to reach the Sea of Galilee. We didn't know how far the sea was, but I needed a bed and a bathroom. We walked for a while and came to a park. It was a noisy one. Constant screams that sounded female and joyous, loud male shouts, and running sounds were all coming from the far side of the park. I guessed that the males were chasing the females in some kind of mating game, and a military installation or a college was located nearby. We entered the quiet sector of the park and quickly found park benches long enough to stretch out on. Without a word said, and at the speed of light, Colette rolled out her sleeping bag on the closest bench, zipped herself in, turned and faced away from me. I stood next to her with my bag in hand. I spoke to her, but she did not respond. I sat down on a bench across from her. I was angry as hell. But there was not a thing I could do.

We were close to the street and close to an apartment building. It was a terrible place to sleep; it was noisy, I didn't feel safe, no toilet, no water, and no food. I couldn't leave her to search for what I needed. I sat there all night watching over her as if I were her Guardian Angel. Why? The hell if I knew. When did I become her body guard? And how did she know she could trust me so?

At dawn, just before I could wake her, she popped up wide awake. A minute later, with sleeping bag and hand bag in hand, she said, "Let's go," and off she walked at a fast pace with me trailing behind. Not a word did she say to me. She could have said, "How are you doing? Get any sleep? No? Thank you for watching over me." I was miserable. The sooner I found a toilet, a cup of coffee, and a place for a short nap—preferably in that order—the better. I wasn't desperate for breakfast, a shower, and sex with Colette. I certainly wouldn't hold my breath about the sex. The apartment on the Mediterranean and the sand dune on the beach would have been perfect places for it. I plodded behind her without a word. We walked north. We should reach the sea going that direction.

It was very early morning. No one was outside but us. No motor vehicles were on the road. We were in a neighborhood of new houses on both sides of the street. It was exactly like an American neighborhood. The houses were perfect, probably brand new. The lawns were very lush and manicured.

Colette had a bounce in her step. She knew that we were in Tiberias. She appeared to be having a great vacation. Our nightlife was nothing special, but the daytimes were grand. Until… the bombshell event that exploded just down the road. It had to do with the devil. I'm certain of it.

The devil himself appeared in disguise minutes after we started to walk. With Colette feeling great and me feeling awful, an adorable puppy appeared from between two houses. He was the cutest little puppy this planet had ever seen, with a wagging tail and a walk only a young puppy can have. Colette stopped. The puppy walked directly up to her. She sat down on the sidewalk and wrapped the dog and held him against her chest. She petted him, kissed him, and spoke softly to him in French. That was precisely what was absent in our relationship. The puppy, in return, kissed her repeatedly. They kissed each other more in twenty seconds than Colette and I had ever kissed. Her sitting on the sidewalk while I suffered, was killing me.

Finally, I said, "Colette, we need to go." Surprisingly, she agreed. She put the puppy down, picked up her belongings, and walked away. But the puppy followed. No problem. Colette stopped, set her belongings down, sat down on the sidewalk, and once again played and made out with her new friend.

"Colette, we need to go. I'm desperate for a bathroom." Once again, Colette put down the puppy and we continued to walk.

But the puppy followed us, staying about twenty feet behind us.

I told her, "This puppy is not going to stop following you. He has no collar. He is getting farther and farther away from his home. He is going to get lost." Colette kept walking. If this were a test of patience, I failed. This dog needed to go home and we needed to hit the road. My eyes were starting to turn yellow from all the pee that had collected since last night. I asked her nicely to start walking. I stepped between the puppy and Colette, picked up the dog, and carried it several feet back the way he came, and shouted at him, "Go home. Go home." The dog sat down on the sidewalk. I walked away from the puppy, but it stood and followed me.

Drowning in pee, cranky as hell, and now suffering a splitting headache, I wasn't myself. I was no longer in full mental control. I picked up a small stone and threw it at a spot about ten feet to the left of the puppy. It didn't hit him; it missed. It was supposed to miss. But it scared the puppy. He backed up a few feet, stopped, sat, and looked at me. I walked toward him. He walked in the direction he had come. I followed him. When I stopped, he stopped. Again, I walked behind the puppy until he finally turned off the sidewalk and trotted off between the two houses where he first set his eyes on his lover, my Colette. He was back home and safe. I ran as fast as I could back down the hill toward Colette, hoping the dog wouldn't follow. He didn't.

I should be that lucky. A storm of the worst kind struck without warning. A tornado? No. Worse. I didn't see it coming when it figuratively hit me right between the eyes. Colette was shouting at me in French, nonstop. I assumed that she thought I was trying to hurt the puppy. Or she was angry because I scared the puppy. I thought that I had done my best under the circumstances. After all, the puppy was safely home and we could continue on our way. Whatever I said fell on deaf ears. She turned her bag upside down and dumped all its contents in the middle of the street. She quickly re-packed her personal items, and left mine on the roadway. And then she ran away from me. She ran faster than any woman I had ever seen run. I never saw her run before now.

"Colette. Wait up, wait for me." I shouted in her direction. I stopped to gather up my things. Some I stashed in my pants pockets. Those that didn't fit, I squeezed into my sleeping bag. But by the time I ran after her, she was out of sight. There was no sign of her.

I had no idea that she could run that fast. Although it should have been a who-could-run-faster situation, instead, it was a game of hide-and-seek, pure and simple. We had to talk about this and straighten things out. I ran down the road, peeking between houses as I ran. "Where the hell was she? This can't be happening," I said out loud to no one. I needed to explain to her that I had no intention of harming that puppy. I didn't have a harmful bone in my body for that puppy. I ran from block to block searching for her. I was freaking out. A bullet to my left shoulder right now would have been less painful compared to this nightmare. Have I just lost my girlfriend? Wasn't I suppose to be watching after her? I assumed Benoit gave her permission to travel separate from the French because she would be traveling with me, a trustful young man.

I did my best to stay calm, but I was anything but calm. I refused to risk running through backyards this early in the morning, because there were probably Uzis in every house. Colette could get away with trespassing: I didn't think I could. All I wanted to do was speak with her and pee. I had to tell her that I made a mistake and I wanted to apologize for it. I wouldn't tell her that she contributed to the situation because I had stayed up all night watching over her. I should have minded my own business about the puppy. Why did I feel so responsible for the puppy to return home? Why didn't I pick up the puppy and run the puppy back up the street? I had to make things right with her.

I ran farther until I reached the sea. I knew she couldn't have gotten this far traveling through backyards. But it was a good place to wait for her to show herself. I hid behind a bench by the sea wall. Time passed. Eventually, I grew impatient. I gathered my things, abandoned the bench, and walked until I found a shop that let me use their facilities. I immediately became their best customer. I bought two hot coffees, two pastries, and two bottles of water. My purchases filled a bag; I showed my gratitude. I walked back to the street where I last saw her, and retraced my steps for several blocks. There was no sign of her. I walked back and waited on a bench that overlooked the sea. Maybe being alone, she might become frightened and change her mind about ditching me. "God," I prayed, "make this nightmare go away. Make a storm with huge lightning bolts that will scare her into my arms." I checked the sky. No storm. No clouds. A perfect summer day for everyone but me.

CHAPTER 21

The nightmare didn't go away. I gave up the search after a few hours and walked west along the shoreline towards the bus station. I checked the station. She wasn't there. Hours later, a bus left Tiberias headed towards the kibbutz with one upset fruit picker onboard. She had ditched me. I was hurt. She was alone. This was a terrible day for me, the worst day of this magnificent summer.

I changed buses at Safed and arrived at the kibbutz that night only to find that Colette was not there. I thought she might have hitch-hiked back and beaten me. No such luck. No one on the kibbutz knew of her whereabouts. I explained to Benoit and Yaakov where we had been and what had happened in Tiberias. "We had an argument in Tiberias this morning and she ran away. She was a fast runner and I couldn't keep up with her. She hid, and I left her behind. I had no choice. I feel terrible. I'm worried and I feel terrible for her not returning with me." I nearly cried. It was no act. I was worried. I was in love and felt responsible for her safety.

The French were very upset with me and about the whole situation. What if the French or Israelis accused me of harming her? There was nothing I could do about that. And, at the moment, I didn't care. Her safety was everything. The French ignored me as best they could. I got the silent treatment from them all, that night and the next day. None of the French tried to communicate with me.

When she didn't return the following day, I decided I would return to Tiberias the following day to find her. Curiously, no one else from the kibbutz offered to go with me or without me. The next morning, I stood at the end of the driveway and waited for the 10:14 a.m. eastbound bus. At exactly 10 a.m., the westbound "Egg" bus stopped across the street. Colette stepped off the bus. She stopped at the edge of the road as soon as she saw me. I stepped toward her; she stepped backward. Nothing needed to be said at that moment. I turned around and walked up the driveway. She followed, staying far behind me.

I entered the limestone house and sat down on my bed, removed my street clothes, and put on my kibbutz work clothes. Colette came into the room. Without saying a word, she opened her big bag and started packing up all her stuff. She was moving out of the house.

I asked her, "Can we talk? Can I explain?"

She kept packing without saying a word.

"Where have you been? Everyone, especially me, was worried sick about you." She still didn't answer.

I finally said, "Stop packing. I'll go. I'll find a different place to sleep. Stay with your friends." She said nothing. She stopped packing, picked up a small bag and a towel, and walked off to the shower house. I packed up my belongings and went in search for a vacant bed. I found a vacant tent nearby. It was a good-sized with two cots. I dropped-off my belongings there, and walked to the orchards searching for the French. I found them in an apple orchard and announced, "Colette has returned." Smiles and conversation broke out among the French. Now they knew that I wasn't a murderer—at least not a people murderer. Eventually, Colette will tell them about the American stone thrower.

Colette, who stayed away from orchard, did attend lunch. She sat at the farthest seat she could find from me at the French table. She spoke the entire meal to those French sitting very close to her. She had a lot to say. That was the last meal I ate at the French table. I found friendly faces to sit with at Israeli tables.

CHAPTER 22

It was hard not to be with her. After lunch, I couldn't sleep. Instead of lying around in the hot tent, I dressed and went to the rock field to remove rocks. I was alone in my work. For me, it was the darkness of the bright summer days. I was in pain. How foolish I felt to feel so heartbroken over a girl I had met barely three weeks earlier. All the anger and sadness that I first brought with me from America returned. I was an emotional mess, but I was determined not to let the others, especially Colette, discover just how screwed up I felt in my head and heart.

Another day passed. Colette still would not speak to me. I needed to make arrangements to leave Israel. I had two other major cities to visit: Paris and London. I told Yaakov why I had to leave. "I'll be back in three days. Don't give my bed away." The next morning, I packed some of my clothes and caught a westbound bus to the Mediterranean Sea. Eventually, I arrived in Tel Aviv by train.

Once in Tel Aviv, I quickly found a large storefront travel agency. The windows were covered with giant posters of travel destinations: Italy, the Greek Islands, Turkey, Spain, and so forth. I sat down with a travel agent and explained to him I needed to fly to Rome, from where I could once again use the European trains with my pre-paid ticket.

He searched through a big book. "I can get you a direct flight from Tel Aviv to Istanbul, and that same day you can take a direct flight from there to Rome."

"How much?" It sounded expensive.

"You are a student, so airfare is half price. It will cost you eighty American dollars."

Eighty dollars was cheap enough and seemed well worth it.

I spent that day and night in Tel Aviv. Early the next morning, I rented a moped on the outskirts of Tel Aviv and left for Beer Sheba to visit the famous Bedouin camel market. I had not driven more than a few miles when I came to a stop sign at a busy traffic intersection. The road was very sandy and as I left the stop sign, I accelerated very fast. The moped slid out from under me. I fell, scraped my leg, and banged my head and shoulder on the road. A soldier came to my aid immediately. He righted the moped and pushed it to the side of the road. I slowly followed.

"Are you hurt?" the soldier asked.

"No," I lied. I was embarrassed and didn't want to make a big deal out of it.

"Do you want to continue on, or do you wish to go back from where you came? The direction you are traveling has many sandy roads that are difficult to drive. If you don't wish to continue, I can drive you back to where you rented this scooter. I think it's drivable."

The camels would have to wait. I was glad not to be seriously hurt. It could have been a worse accident, and then imagine what would happen to me? This was a bad idea; I should have taken a bus. "Drive me back to the rental place. I would appreciate that."

The soldier was happy with my decision and drove me back. I dreaded having to pay a lot of money for the repairs. Indeed, the rental people were displeased to see the moped in its "new condition." He was kind enough to stand right behind me and listen in on the conversation that lasted seconds.

"Ten dollars," the older man said. I was happy to pay up, but tried not to show it. He could have demanded more and gotten it. I paid him and left; the soldier had already slipped away.

I left Tel Aviv and traveled north the rest of the day until I reached Haifa. That night, I had a good meal. My skinned knee still burned, but my head and shoulder were feeling better. The pain was no greater than my Colette pain. I wasn't looking forward to my return to the kibbutz. But I had to go.

Early next morning, I traveled from Haifa to Yir'on. When the bus stopped at the kibbutz driveway and opened the door, I wasn't mentally prepared to get off. I changed my mind. "Go," I told the driver and pulled out my money to pay the additional fare to continue to Safed.

In Safed, I found hot food and a clean room for the night. I stayed in my room and created one wallpaper design after another. In the morning, I rode a bus to Tiberias.

CHAPTER 23

I stepped off the bus in Tiberias heartbroken, depressed, and without a plan. I followed my feet for a while, but they did not lead me to anything special. So, I decided to follow my nose and soon came upon a bakery. I opened the door and listened to a bell ring. A young child appeared.

"Good morning," I said.

The child looked at me and yelled, "Mama, a foreigner!" The bakery was not new and shiny. I didn't care. It was poorly lit, but at least it appeared to be clean. A woman a few years older than me came out from behind a curtained area. She greeted me with, "Shalom," and followed with a few more words in Hebrew. She waited for my answer. I pretended to perfectly understand what she said, and pointed to the cookies with nuts on top. I showed her three fingers and said, "Three." Obviously, an American. She bagged my three cookies and showed me the price on my cookie bag. I paid her.

From behind a curtained area came the aroma of coffee.

"Coffee?" I asked.

"*Lo café*," she answered, shaking her head no. Coffee wasn't served here. But I was desperate for a cup.

"Please. I will pay for coffee." She shook her head no. But I was determined. I held out a hand full of Israeli lira and put on my sad face, a face I had shown a lot lately. I pointed to the outside bench that was shaded by an awning. Was she afraid that I would steal her cup? She nodded her head yes, but her face said, "I hate you," and she passed behind the curtained area. She returned with a well-used ceramic coffee cup filled to the top with strong-smelling coffee. She was shaking her head from side to side as she walked toward me. I think she wasn't happy about giving up her morning coffee for a stranger. She handed me the cup.

"Thank you." I held out my free hand, full of Israeli lira.

"*Lo*," she said shaking her head. She would not take my money. I was grateful for the coffee and said so.

There were no tables inside for eating. I went outside and sat on a long bench that faced the street. I took my first sip. To say my black coffee was strong would have been an understatement. A teaspoon might have stood up on its own in my cup. But the taste was good, and I was a beggar, and beggars couldn't be choosey. The cookie was delicious. I was careful not to bite down hard, for I was concerned that the coffee might have softened my teeth. Turkish coffee? I would find out in Istanbul. I ate a second cookie, pocketed the third, and went back inside to return the cup.

Across the street was a liquor shop. I crossed over and entered the shop. "*Shalom*," I said to an older man who sat at a small table reading a newspaper. The old man peered over his glasses and said, "*Shalom aleichem*."

"Vodka," I said. The man got up and walked over to the vodka bottles. I asked, "Do you speak English?"

"Do you speak Hebrew?" he replied in English.

"No." He got me. Reciting blessings, singing hymns, and praying from the Torah are not the same as speaking Hebrew.

The liquor store man picked up a small bottle of vodka and said, "This is good vodka." I picked up a different bottle with an attractive label, and held it up. The shopkeeper nodded his head no. "No good. Drink that and your head will hurt in the morning." He spoke with a British accent. I returned the bottle to the shelf.

"I'll buy that one, but I want a bigger bottle." The man exchanged the small bottle for a larger one. I paid him and carefully packed the vodka into my sleeping bag and rolled it up so that the bottle was zipped in and near the center.

I paid the man and walked for a few minutes until I reached the lake. In front of me were dozens of boats tied to moorings and the dock. As best I could see, none of the boats were out motoring. I wondered where Colette had hid during her time away. Benoit had told me that she had stayed with an old fisherman and his wife. Maybe that was true. And maybe not.

I saw men on their boats and on the dock. There was a young good-looking fisherman, maybe older than me, mending a fishing net. His boat was docked closest to the street. Maybe she lied about the older fisherman and his wife. Maybe she stayed with a younger fisherman for two nights and shared her hashish with him. Had he slept with her? I clenched my teeth when I thought about her and this fisherman together. I took a deep breath and managed to relax. The young fisherman looked up at me, smiled, and waved. I didn't wave back. I already hated him.

I walked away miffed. I followed the lake around to the east. I hadn't pulled out the map, so I wasn't certain where exactly I was headed. I didn't care. I stopped and sat on a bench, while I fed the last cookie to the birds. I closed my eyes and napped for more than an hour. I woke and continued my walk.

I came upon banana plants and a large restaurant on the lake. There were many outside tables scattered along a large pier. No boats were docked there. I sat at a table with a nice view. A gorgeous waitress brought me a menu and a glass of water. "My name is Helena. What would you like to drink?" I asked her for lemonade.

I couldn't keep my eyes off her as she walked back to the kitchen. She was gorgeous. When she returned with her order pad, I looked at her beautiful green eyes and beautifully tanned face. I kept my eyes off her lovely figure so as not to embarrass her or me. I guessed she was my age. She had no idea how much I could use a big hug from her. *That would sure make me happy.*

"Do you know what you want?"

"Yes," I answered truthfully. But I was shy and wouldn't ask her for a hug. Or would I? Maybe she was married. I didn't see a ring. Besides, I would surely be asked to leave the restaurant. "Ah, no," I lied about the hug. "What do you recommend?"

"The St. Peter's fish dinner. The fish are freshly caught from the lake. The sides are boiled potatoes or fries, and coleslaw."

"I'll have fish. With it I want coleslaw, a double order of french fries, and lots of ketchup. I haven't had french fries in a very long time." She wrote it down on her pad. "And coffee later."

"Great. My name is Helena. Oh, I told you that already. Enjoy the view." I watched the "view" disappear inside. I enjoyed looking at her, and listening to her accent. Her accent was different from all accents I ever heard.

Waves lapped the shoreline below the pier. The St. Peter's fish swam in the Sea of Galilee when Jesus Christ called to Peter and his brother to follow him, to leave their nets, and become fishers of men.

She brought me my dinner and refilled my lemonade. "If you need anything, just wave to me. We aren't busy. I'll keep an eye out for you." She had several other tables to cover.

When I was nearly finished, Helena checked to see if I needed a lemonade refill. "Refill?" She held up my lemonade glass."

"Yes, please. The food was very good." It was said that street food in Israel is the best in the world, and that restaurant food was not very good. But not here. The food was delicious. The fish and the fries were hot and tasty, and Helena delivered sunshine with the meal. My darkness had brightened. Life at the moment was good.

I was stuffed when I finished my meal. Helena appeared in a timely fashion to clear my dishes from the table. My dad always said that if a server could remember to bring a teaspoon with the coffee, get the order right, bring the food out hot, and clear away the dirty dishes in a timely manner, he would tip that server until it hurt. He would leave a twenty percent. Helena put her hand on my shoulder and asked if I was ready for coffee. "Yes, please, along with a check and a bottle of water to go." She had the coffee with her. She set the cup down, poured the coffee, and placed a teaspoon next to the saucer. From her apron she removed small packs of sugar. I sipped the coffee.

"Do you take cream?"

"No. It's perfect." The coffee was good. It didn't need milk or sugar. And it was hot.

"By the way, I told you my name. What's yours?"

I told her.

"That's nice. Are you a guest at the resort?"

"No. I'm a volunteer on a kibbutz."

"Which one?"

"Yir'on."

"I know it. It's a shame you aren't working on this kibbutz. It's a lot more fun than Yir'on. They are very serious up there." She turned and walked away. I watched her take an order at another table.

I looked at my Israel map while I enjoyed my coffee. I really did need to get back to Yir'on. I could see that from here, the shortest and most interesting route would be to follow the sea north, then cross the Jordan River just above it, and from there walk and hitch-hike North-Northwest to Zafed. From Zafed, I would take a bus back to the kibbutz. That way, I didn't need to backtrack around the south end.

Helena brought me a coffee refill, a bottle of water, and a glass of water. She put her hand on my shoulder a second time as she served me my coffee from behind. I certainly didn't know her, but I liked her. A hug would have been nicer. If there was any man in need of a hug today, it was me.

"I'll be back with your check."

When she returned with the check, she asked, "More coffee?"

"No, but thank you. I don't want to swim out of here."

"Why not? There's plenty of water," she said with a smile.

"That was funny." I handed her back the check and money to cover my bill, service charge, and tip.

"Thank you very much. You're most generous. Adam, stand up. Please." She signaled with her arms for me to stand. I stood.

"I have to tell you this. It's very important to me. I am going to give you a hug. I promise it won't hurt." Before I could answer, she hugged me. It was a full-body hug. She stood on her toes and pushed her cheek against mine. She seemed to melt into my arms. It was a long hug. And it was as if she had read my mind.

Helena finally backed away. "Thank you," she said.

"Thank *you*," I said. I was astonished. My heart pounded. She gave me a big smile and went back inside the restaurant. *Is she a mind reader?*

I emptied my pockets of coins and placed them on the table. That hug was priceless. Hugs may not be on the menu, but if they were, the price on the menu would have been in the expensive range.

I shoved the water bottle inside my sleeping bag and walked down the pier. When I reached the road, I stopped to look one last time. She was busy at another table. She couldn't have noticed that I turned left instead of right. Only guests at the resort turned left.

CHAPTER 24

I passed a fenced seaside resort lined with rustic brown cabins that extended down to almost the lake. I walked farther up the road until I reached a huge gate. The gate was like the entrance to the Ponderosa Ranch on *Bonanza*. It read in large letters in English: "MILITARY ZONE." There were no "KEEP OUT" signs or "DANGER" signs, though. On each side of the gate were tall chain-linked fences that extended out of sight in either direction.

The gate itself was partially open, just wide enough for a person to slip through. The padlock was hanging on the fence, unlocked. I put down my sleeping bag and held up the map. Travel through here was the best way to go. I didn't consider turning around. Besides, in a few hours, I would be away and no one would know I had been there. I slipped through the open gate, careful not to touch it or the fence. No one noticed me. If they had, I would have been emphatically turned back.

After a short walk from the gate, I came across evidence of the war. On the edge of the road were seven hand grenades with their pins removed. Near them were thirty-six small rockets, two large rockets, and a hand-held rocket launcher. Behind the ammunitions, an army tank was parked. I took pictures, careful not to touch anything, and thought it strange that the military hadn't removed the ordinance.

A war had been fought here one year ago: The Six-Day War. Major fighting didn't occur here, but there was fighting and soldiers died. Elements of the Israel Defense Forces army and airborne soldiers had "mopped up" the area. The United States government referred to the war as the 1967 Arab-Israeli War. While that wasn't inaccurate, it would have been more accurate to call it the Egypt-Arab-Israel War. Even that name should carry a footnote that the Soviet Union had its hand in this affair, militarily supporting Israel's enemies. The Soviet Union had been supporting the Egyptian military since the mid-1950s.

The Historian, Bureau of Public Affairs, from US State Department published their account of the war:

"The 1967 Arab-Israeli War marked the failure of the Eisenhower, Kennedy, and Johnson administrations' efforts to prevent renewed Arab-Israeli Conflict following the 1956 Suez War. Unwilling to return to what National Security Advisor Walter Rostow called the 'tenuous chewing gum and string arrangements' established after Suez, the Johnson administration sought Israel's withdrawal from the territories it had occupied in exchange for peace settlements with its Arab neighbors. This formula has remained the basis of all U.S. Middle East peacemaking efforts into the present.

"The Johnson Administration and the Arab-Israeli Conflict, 1963–1967: Lyndon Johnson's presidency witnessed the transformation of the American role in the Arab-Israeli Conflict. Until the early 1960s, the United States had adhered to the terms of the Tripartite Declaration of 1950, wherein the United States, United Kingdom, and France had pledged to prevent aggression by Middle Eastern states and oppose a regional arms race. The

United States had pressed Israel to withdraw from the Sinai Peninsula and Gaza Strip after Suez, and rejected Israeli requests for all but limited quantities of defensive weapons. By the time Johnson took office, however, U.S. policymakers concluded that this policy was no longer sustainable. Soviet arms sales to left-leaning Arab states, especially Egypt, threatened to erode Israel's military superiority. Johnson's advisors worried that if the United States did not offset this shift in the balance of power, Israel's leaders might launch a preventive war or develop nuclear weapons.

"Initially, the Johnson administration sought to convince Egyptian President Gamal Abdul Nasser and the Soviet leadership to work toward a regional arms control regime, but neither party proved receptive. Thus, in 1965, Johnson agreed to sell Israel M48A3 tanks, followed by A–4 Skyhawk aircraft in 1966. The rationale behind these sales, as National Security Council staffer Robert Komer put it, was that, 'Arab knowledge that they could not win an arms race against Israel should contribute long-term to the damping down of the Arab-Israeli dispute.

"However, U.S. efforts to preserve the regional balance of power were soon undermined by Fatah and other Palestinian guerilla organizations, which began attacking targets inside Israel. The Johnson administration tried to intercede with Fatah's Syrian patrons and to prevent Israeli retaliation against Jordan, from which most Palestinian raids were launched. U.S. officials worried that Israeli reprisals could undermine Jordan's King Hussein, who had secretly agreed to keep Jordan's strategically crucial West Bank a buffer zone. In November 1966, when the Israelis attacked the West Bank town of Samu', the Johnson administration voted for a United

163

Nations Resolution condemning Israel, admonished Israeli officials, and authorized an emergency airlift of military equipment to Jordan."

On November 13, 1966, Israel retaliated for the death of three soldiers killed by a road mine planted by Fatah terrorists, for attacking the Jordanian village of Samu' in the West Bank, and for Jordan for giving aid and comfort to Fatah guerilla forces. In the pre-dawn raid, the soldiers ordered the civilians out of their homes and systematically began to destroy them. They wanted to send a loud message to the king of Jordan to stop the guerilla raids from recurring. Unfortunately, one hundred regular Jordanian troops were unexpectedly in the area and engaged the Israeli troops. There was a lengthy battle. In the end, ten Israeli soldiers died, the Israeli commander died, fifteen Jordanian soldiers died, three villagers died, and ninety-six were wounded. Upwards of 125 homes were destroyed.

"While the administration's response to Samu' helped prevent further Israeli reprisals against Jordan, it failed to address the underlying problem of Palestinian cross-border attacks. By the spring of 1967, the Israelis were retaliating forcefully against Syria, whose leaders demanded that Egypt intervene on their behalf.

"The Prewar Crisis: On May 13, 1967, Soviet officials informed the Syrian and Egyptian Governments that Israel had massed troops on Syria's border. Though the report was false, Nasser sent large numbers of Egyptian soldiers into the Sinai anyway. On May 16, Egypt demanded that the United Nations Emergency Force (UNEF), which had been deployed in the Sinai Peninsula and the Gaza Strip since 1957, withdraw from Israel's border.

Secretary-General U Thant replied that he would have to withdraw UNEF from all its positions, including "Sharm al-Shaykh, which would put political pressure on Nasser to close the Straits of Tiran to Israeli shipping. Nasser remained adamant, and on May 22, after UNEF withdrew, he announced that he would close the Straits. In 1957, President Dwight D. Eisenhower had promised that the United States would treat the closure of the Straits as an act of war. Johnson now had three unwelcome options: to renege on Eisenhower's promise, acquiesce in an Israeli attack on Egypt, or order U.S. forces to reopen the waterway.

"Instead, the President played for time. He sought international and Congressional support for Operation Red Sea Regatta, which called for a coalition of maritime nations to send a 'probing force' through the Straits if Egypt refused to grant all nations free passage through them. Simultaneously, Johnson implored the Soviets to intercede with Nasser and urged Israeli restraint. 'Israel,' Johnson told Israeli Foreign Minister Abba Eban on May 26, 'will not be alone unless it decides to go it alone.' Yet over the following week, the administration failed to gain domestic or foreign backing for 'Regatta.' Meanwhile, Jordan joined the Arab coalition, heightening the pressure for an Israeli strike. Though Johnson continued to caution Israel against preemption, a number of the President's advisors had concluded that U.S. interests would be best served by Israel 'going it alone' by the time the Israelis actually did so.

"The War and its Aftermath: Between June 5 and June 10, Israel defeated Egypt, Jordan, and Syria and occupied the Sinai Peninsula, the Gaza Strip, the West Bank, East Jerusalem, and the Golan Heights. From the beginning, the United States sought a ceasefire in order to prevent an Arab defeat bad

enough to force the Soviet Union to intervene. U.S. officials were also concerned about alienating pro-Western Arab regimes, especially after Egypt and several other Arab states accused the United States of helping Israel and broke diplomatic relations. Yet after June 5, the administration did not also demand an immediate Israeli pullback from the territories it had occupied. U.S. officials believed that in light of the tenuous nature of the prewar armistice regime, they should not force Israel to withdraw unless peace settlements were put into place.

"The administration's concept of 'land-for-peace' solidified following the war. "Certainly," Johnson proclaimed, "troops must be withdrawn; but there must also be recognized rights of national life, progress in solving the refugee problem, freedom of innocent maritime passage, limitation of the arms race, and respect for political independence and territorial integrity." Yet after the Arab states rejected a Latin American UN resolution calling for full withdrawal in exchange for recognition of "the right of all states in the area to live in peace and security" and a similar U.S.-Soviet draft, the Johnson administration scaled back its efforts to promote a settlement. Though alarmed by Israeli decisions to absorb East Jerusalem and establish Jewish settlements in the occupied territories, U.S. officials believed that the Arabs remained too inflexible to justify pressing Israel to withdraw.

"The Johnson administration did not re-enter the diplomatic fray until October, when the Soviets began to circulate a new version of the resolution that they had promoted that summer. Knowing that Israel would reject the Soviet draft, the administration encouraged the United Kingdom to introduce an alternative resolution devised by UN Ambassador Arthur Goldberg. Security Council Resolution 242, adopted on November 22, *called for Israel's withdrawal from 'territories occupied in the recent conflict' in exchange for "termination of all claims or states of belligerency and respect for and acknowledgment of the sovereignty, territorial integrity and political independence of every State in the area and their right to live in peace within secure and recognized boundaries free from threats or acts of force." Interpreted differently by Israelis and Arabs, this resolution would nonetheless remain the bedrock of all subsequent U.S. efforts to resolve the Arab-Israeli dispute."*

I continued to walk. Several times, I came across large bullets that had been pressed into what had once been mud. The mud was as hard as concrete, and no matter how hard I tried, I could not pry loose any of the bullets. For all that I saw and now touched, I didn't hear the voice of reason say, *Turn around. Go back. This is a big mistake.*

Farther up the road, I came across a blackened area, and then a second, where the ground had been burned. A flame-thrower, I do watch war movies, had scorched the earth in both locations. Those flames could have scorched more than just earth. It was easy to picture.

I walked farther up the road and came across empty baked bean cans and flattened tin mess kits. A few large boulders, much taller than me, rested there at the foot of the mountain and seemed strangely out of place.

I passed the first of several two-foot tall brown signs located in the narrow space between the road and the base of the mountain. A word was painted in Hebrew letters. I read the word in Hebrew, but I couldn't translate it. I had no idea why these signs were there. I guessed they were directional markers. I stopped near one and decided to climb. I had to see what was on the other side. The slope was steep, but maybe not too steep to climb. I had to try. Without having a second thought about the matter, I decided to take a chance and climb.

I put my sleeping bag down on the dusty road, careful not to break my bottle of vodka. I zipped open the bag and pulled out my shoes and a pair of socks. Loose-fitting sandals would have led to a fall for sure. I walked past the brown sign. "Here goes nothing," I said out loud. I hugged the mountain and began to climb. I didn't like being dirty, but it could not be avoided. Pulling myself up the mountain with my arms didn't work — there was not much to hold onto. Only by digging into the mountain with my shoes could I gain a foothold and exert downward pressure. This allowed me to flex and extend my legs pushing me upward. I climbed and climbed with my chest rubbing against the mountain. I knew that I was scuffing up my Florsheim shoes, but I had no choice. I had to see what lay beyond the mountain. I was certain that if Florsheim shoes could talk, they would scream at me. *This is intentionally abusive. I won't forgive you. Expect blisters in the morning!* Although I hated abusing my shoes, I pushed aside the hate for the excitement of the moment.

I moved higher and higher, stopping from time to time to assess whether to continue climbing straight up or to move to one side or the other for the easiest tract. Straight up turned out to be the best route. Once I made the mistake to look down. Once was enough. It was a quick reminder not to fall down the mountain. I focused and continued my climb.

When I reached the top, I hung my arms and chin over the sharp but soft crest. My chest and abdomen pressed hard against the surface. The hot afternoon sun beat down on my neck and back. I looked all around. I could see two more mountain ranges that ran parallel to this one. All the groundcover was brown. Nothing green was to be seen. I saw no animals, people, vehicles, roads, or manmade structures of any type. There was no evidence that people had ever been there. This place, the view, were great. I pulled myself up and straddled the mountain. Sea, beaches, grasses, mountains, and valley views flowed through my eyes into my head.

When it was time to climb down, I soon discovered that it was more difficult than the climb up. It was hard to safely support myself on one leg as I dug into the mountain with my other foot. When I could locate one, I used footholds that I dug earlier. I had a fright mid-way down when I dislodged a rock that rolled down and made a knocking sound when it hit the wooden brown marker below.

I reached the bottom, excited by my successful climb, careful not to step down on the wooden marker. Now safe on the road, I pulled my water bottle out from my sleeping bag and drank the last of its contents. But I was still thirsty. I hadn't planned well, and now I was without water.

I changed footwear, gathered up my sleeping bag, and continued my walk north, until the road turned sharply to the east through a mountain pass. There was no road straight ahead, just tall grasses. *How could that be possible?* I thought. *There has to be a road between the Sea and the mountain. The road should continue straight ahead.* But it didn't. *Maybe I have been in the sun too long.* Confused and concerned about time, I walked through the tall grasses down to a narrow beach, unaware of the danger all around me.

I followed the shoreline north until I came to a manmade barrier. A barbed wired fence crossed the beach and ended somewhere in the sea. If this was supposed to be a warning to turn back, I didn't receive the message. I should have, but to turn back never occurred to me. I removed my clothes and sandals, and threw them, along with my sleeping bag, over the fence. I walked into the sea and swam around the barbed wire, careful not to get caught on it. The water was so refreshing that I took my time. It was a nice respite from the heat. After drip-drying, I continued on my way.

Thirty minutes later, seduced by the glistening sea, I stripped down and jumped into the water for another swim. Afterwards, I sat at the water's edge in waist-deep invigorating waters. There was no boat traffic at all. If there had been, a boat might have come closer to investigate.

Once dried and dressed, I noticed the time. It was much later than I thought. Quickly, I gathered up my personal items and packed them in the sleeping bag. With a rolled-up, wet towel in one hand and sleeping bag in the other, I ran along the beach, hopeful that I would reach the Jordan River before it got dark.

I was bone-dry. As apprehensive as I could be, and in full knowledge of the consequences I experienced drinking from a Roman fountain, I waded into the sea and drank. The water wasn't salty, and didn't taste bad, though neither had Rome's fountain. It didn't taste good either. Diarrheal illnesses were caused by germs such as cryptosporidium, giardia, shigella, norovirus and E. coli that could easily be found in the water. I didn't want to become sick, but I had to take a chance. I ran down the beach, hopeful I would be there in time.

I ran past the ruins of Kursi. The ruins were buried and yet to be discovered. It was the land of the Gadarenes, where Jesus cast the demons out of a man who was possessed, into a herd of swine that plunged into the sea and drowned. There was a Byzantine church complex, built to commemorate that event, complete with an enormous monastery dating from the fifth to the seventh century. The monastery was complete with sleeping and eating facilities to accommodate thousands of pilgrims who came to the Galilee sea during Byzantine times. There was a cave chapel where Jesus had encountered the possessed man.

I kept running. There was no time to rest. I didn't slow down my pace. The sea was seven hundred feet below sea level. Kibbutz Yir'on, to the northwest, was more than two thousand feet above sea level. Because the sun set in the west behind that mountain, the sunlight would be blocked sooner than later.

I abruptly stopped running. I didn't believe what I saw. In front of me and on each side, was a dense thicket of marsh. What I didn't see was the beach. It ended. I was at the tip of a peninsula that jutted out into the marsh where the Jordan River flowed into the sea. It was not at all what I had expected. I couldn't see the river because the marsh grasses were much taller than me. I simply stood there, out of breath, sweaty, still thirsty, and dumfounded. If that wasn't bad enough, just on cue, to add insult to injury, the sun, without a hint of betrayal, dropped quickly behind the mountain, and wrapped me tight with heartless darkness. *Damn!*

CHAPTER 25

I dropped my sleeping bag and stood there, frozen in place. Time, that hadn't been a big deal for most of the day, was now a big deal. All that starlight without moonlight added up to no light at all. I was stuck on the beach, for there was no way I could slip into the dark waters and swim some unknown distance to the far shore, a shore I couldn't see even in the daylight. I had reached a place where turning back was not an option. What if I walked into a barbwire fence? What if I didn't, but had to swim around it. I had no choice but to stay here until sunrise.

I unrolled my bag and sat down on it to think. My biggest concern was my thirst. I had no choice but to continue drinking from the sea. I couldn't imagine what it would be like being sick from drinking it.

I lay out on top of my bag, removed my shoes and socks, and stripped down to my shorts. I placed my clothes on top of my Florsheim shoes, a few feet away. It was too hot to get inside the bag. There was no breeze, and the night temperature didn't seem any cooler than the afternoon temperature. It would be nice to go for a swim, but I wouldn't go in, not the dark. What is there was an Egyptian crocodile in there? Egypt wasn't far away.

After a few minutes of rest and star gazing, I sat up. What I saw was disturbing. At first, I thought I was seeing rockets in the night sky, moving from east to west. Moments later, I realized that it was a meteor shower. Now relaxed, it was special to see. Maybe here was a good place to spend the night. I lay down again, thinking about Colette and my lunchtime hug, when I fell asleep.

Nearby, neurotransmitters alerted hungry invertebrates walking the sea floor to scuttle to the feeding grounds on the other side of the peninsula. Food was scarce today, for the Barbus longiceps and Blennius fluviatilis fish had fed heavily on snails. The hungry Potamon potamios—freshwater crabs—made their move under the cover of darkness. They walked along the sea bottom and emerged onto my beach. The feeding ground behind this narrow stretch of beach was grassy wetlands, where their favorite food, dark-patterned snails, flourished. Unfortunately, I was in the direct pathway of a crab. I was soundly asleep and wholly unaware of the coming assault. My right foot was the first human foot this particular crab had ever seen. *Maybe this thing is food,* thought the crab. The crab eyeballed the bottom of my soft right foot. He opened his big claw and gave a pinch.

Yipes! I kicked out at the unseen crustacean. I sat up, grabbed my glasses, and scrambled to my feet. Wide-eyed and half frightened to death, by starlight I could make out a small army of crabs retreating to the safety of the sea. It was an unwelcome surprise attack,

To protect from another crab attack, I sat on my sleeping bag with my knees bent and my feet flat on the bag. I kept my eyeglasses on, not that it helped. I held a sandal up high ready to squash an attacker. I was reluctant to squash any critter with my Florsheim shoes or my vodka bottle. The sandal would have to do. I didn't care if these crabs were a protected species.

Of all the sea life in the waters, Jews could eat sea life that had fins and scales (Lev. 11:9; Deut. 14:9). Shellfish, such as lobsters, oysters, shrimp, clams, and crabs were all forbidden.

With a chance that the crabs might return, I refused to lie back and sleep. I didn't want to be pinched again. But it was still too hot to climb in, so I sat there on guard.

Time passed. I waited for the next crab attack in front of me, but it never came. Instead, all hell broke out when an attack came from the tall grasses behind me. They weren't crabs. They were mice. I could barely see them in the dark as they scampered across the sand and attacked my clothes pile, that was beyond my reach with sandal in hand. I immediately climbed into my sleeping bag. I didn't want mice in it. That would be a nightmare. With one hand holding up the bag, I threw pebbles at them with the other hand. They immediately scattered. I refused to stand up and attack or defend what I could barely see.

It was an endless attack. I threw pebbles; they momentarily retreated. They attacked my clothes once again: I threw pebbles. They retreated. They attacked. Over and over we played out the battles. Finally, I had enough. I climbed out of the sleeping bag. The mice retreated. I quickly dressed. To my surprise, the mice didn't return.

What followed was another problem; I was nauseous. I ran down the beach and threw-up. A minute later I felt better. I scooped up water from the sea and rinsed out my mouth. *I'll bet it was the sea water that made me sick. What else can I expect? Diarrhea?* I prayed. *God, heal me. Make all this go away. Thank you. Adam. Amen.* I should have mentioned to him that I needed a roll of toilet paper just in case.

Instantly, an idea came to me. I walked back to my belongings and removed the vodka bottle. I broke the seal and rinsed my mouth out in an attempt to kill the germs. I didn't swallow. I guessed that the Vodka would make my stomach produce more acid than usual, causing stomach upset, possibly diarrhea, and more vomiting. It was possible that my vomiting wasn't germ-related, but instead an episode of anxiety and stress. If that was the case, alcohol would have been a bad choice. I was dead tired, my throat bone dry. But I was not hungry. I paced back and forth, searching the ground for mice. Never had time passed this slow. I was miserable, and saw no way for my predicament to end before sunrise.

But I was wrong. To the north appeared a bright beam of light moving back and forth against the sky. I had seen light similar to it back home when there was a grand opening of a large retail store. I was thrilled. I wasn't alone out here. The Israelis were here! At least, I hoped it was the Israelis. If I could meet up with them, my nightmare would be over. I stood at the end of the beach, cupped my hands and shouted, "*Shalom!*" Over and over again I shouted, "*Shalom, Shalom, Shalom.*" The lights moved slowly move south, toward Ein Gev.

I continued to shout. Surely the searchlight would have changed its movements if someone had heard me. But nothing changed. The silent night was only interrupted by my shouts. That changed when I lost my voice. I realized too late that the searchlight operator was too far away to hear my *shalom*. I stood there on the beach with my hopes crushed, my stomach churned, and my brain overheated and confused. My situation was hopeless. I needed a miracle. How else could this nightmare end?

But it did end! My miracle in the sky! My prayer came true. What miracle? This miracle: a shinning partial sphere rose from the east and lit up the night. It was a waning gibbous moon, three days after the full moon. It rose quickly from behind the Golan Mountain. I could see my surroundings. I was no longer a prisoner. I packed up, determined to meet up with the people with the searchlight.

Because I was on a peninsula, I raced down the beach the same way I had come, the opposite direction from the searchlight. After running half of a mile, I decided it was time to leave the beach and try crossing inland through the tall grasses that stood between me and the mountain. There had to be a roadway on this side of the mountain. If I was blocked by swamp, I would return to the beach and try crossing farther down.

I stepped into the tall grass and quickly stepped back. Critters scattered. Mice? Lizards? There might be poisonous snakes in there hunting their next meal. Ten species of venomous snakes belonging to three different families could be found in Israel. Three of the species posed a serious threat to humans. Antivenom is available locally for only two of the species.

I quickly changed into long pants, shoes, and socks. I gathered all my courage and stepped into the tall grass. Unseen critters scattered. I took several critter scattering steps, and stopped abruptly. Unreal. In front of me was a wide trench that ran parallel to the beach. Jordanian soldiers had dug it in preparation to defend the area from the Israelis. I couldn't tell how deep it was because I couldn't see the bottom. Moonlight could not reach the bottom: the moon wasn't high enough in the sky. I didn't have time to find a way to walk around it—the trench could be miles long. The searchlight was getting closer. This was where I had to cross, and I had to do it now.

The distance across the trench, even with a running jump, was too long for me to clear. But my adrenaline was flowing and I was a fast runner. I had to try. I had no idea what was on the bottom of the trench. I assumed it couldn't be more than four or five feet deep. I got the creeps. With my head busy with cowardly thoughts, my arms forced the issue: they threw the sleeping bag over the trench. I was amazed. It was decided. Now I *had* to jump.

I backed up several steps through scattering critters. I dashed towards the trench and jumped as far as I could. I landed short. My arms grabbed hold onto the far side, and my chest crashed against the dirt back wall. It was a frightening moment when my shoes hit bottom. I sprung up and out, pulling up hard with my arms, and literally *flew* out of the ditch. I rolled over onto my back. Now the critters had a fair chance, but the cowards chose not to fight.

I stood quickly. With my heart racing and perspiration flowing, I grabbed my sleeping bag. I had to hurry; the searchlight was getting closer. I walked quickly through the tall grasses until I stood on a dirt road at the foot of the mountain.

The searchlight had not yet reached here. I wasn't too late to meet up with them. I was excited. I felt safe, for help was on its way.

CHAPTER 26

The searchlight was becoming brighter and brighter against the night sky. The sound of a truck engine was growing louder. The Israeli soldiers—I hoped they were Israeli soldiers—were getting closer. And then it dawned on me. There would be risk in being rescued. *What if they shoot me? Maybe I should hide and let them pass by. But I can't hide. My footprints are all over the dusty road. If they find my footprints (and how could they not), they'll know someone is near. Where would I hide? In the tall grasses? Surely not. Up on the mountain? No way. I need out of here tonight, not tomorrow. I would greet the soldiers.*

I waited for them until I couldn't wait any longer. With sweat dripping from my face, I picked up my sleeping bag and began walking up the road. I cleared my head and tried to focus. How was I going to handle this? I needed to be seen in a non-threatening way. But just how would I do that? I had never been in a predicament like this before. Who had? I needed to identify myself quickly: *Jewish, American, student, volunteer on Kibbutz Yir'on. I got stuck out here.* What if they didn't understand English? Sadly, that wouldn't matter if my voice was still gone. I decided to test my voice. "Shalom," I said out loud. My voice was back. I decided not to speak again until I had to. I might have only one *shalom* left. I would speak out instinctively if given a chance to speak. I realized that what was about to happen was much more dangerous than anything that had already happened. *Damn it. Why was that gate unlocked? And why was I so stupid to hike out here in the first place?*

The soldiers were very close now. I stopped walking. Only a hill separated us. My adrenaline was pumping. It was fight or flight time. I looked down and realized that I was dressed in green Levis and a green cord shirt with epaulets on the shoulders. Shit! They will think I'm a soldier. And not one of their kind. The truck was nearly on top of the hill. It was too late to do anything about it.

When the truck tipped downward about thirty yards away from me, the searchlight was pointing toward the tall grasses. I screamed, "*Shalom.*" No human being on this planet had ever shouted "*Shalom*" as loud as I did. No one. Ever. "*Shalom*" smashed into the mountain, echoed across the tall grasses, and frightened the fish feeding in shallow beach waters.

Despite the loud noise of the truck's engine, the soldiers heard. The driver slammed on the brakes and turned off the truck's engine. I immediately dropped my sleeping bag, quickly raised my arms, and placed my hands-on top of my head, just before the searchlight found me. I couldn't see what was behind the bright light, but the truck's occupants probably had weapons drawn and pointed at me. To the silent light I shouted out again, "*Shalom,*" and without pause I quickly added, "My name is Shea Ben Noah Haisenberger. I'm an American Jew working on Kibbutz Yir'on, near the Lebanese border."

From behind the bright light came a burst of Hebrew from one soldier.

Of course, I didn't understand a word. "I don't speak Hebrew," I quickly shouted back.

"Who are you?" came a commanding voice, speaking perfect British English.

I answered, "I am Shea Ben Noah Haisenberger. I'm an American Jewish kid. I pick fruit on Kibbutz Yir'on near the Lebanese border, near Kibbutz Baram." A second passed. Another second passed. I shouted out the song, "*Adom Olam,*" but I was cut off before I could sing "*a-share.*"

"Come here!" ordered the soldier.

I stepped forward and got screamed at. "Put your hands back on your head!" My hands shot back on my head. I focused on my external chest, hoping a bullet wasn't about to burst through it. I nearly reached the truck, but stopped when the blinding light aimed at my face stopped me cold. It made me tear up as if I was crying. I wanted to tell them that I wasn't crying, but didn't dare.

"Who are you?" the soldier said, incredulously. I repeated my words. My life depended on convincing them that I was Jewish and not their enemy. The soldier spoke in Hebrew to the other soldiers. He probably said, "He's one of ours. Unbelievable. I almost shot the fool!" I know because they turned off the searchlight. The truck headlights were no bother to my eyes. I could see that there were three soldiers in uniform in the heavy-duty vehicle. It was about four times larger than a jeep. He then said, "Go get your things."

I put my arms down. Before I turned to go, I said, "I'm not crying. The searchlight made the tears." I walked towards my sleeping bag. Halfway there, I glanced back at them when it occurred to me that they might have changed their minds. But not one bullet came whistling in my direction. I thought about the writing on the wall in the Vatican, "God is Great," for they would let me live.

I took my time walking back toward them. I walked to the passenger side of the large, roofless military vehicle, where the front-seat passenger stood outside, waiting for me. In English, he said, "Where did you come from?"

The tone was friendly. I could now see from the uniforms that they were Israeli Defense Forces. It was over. I was safe.

"Ein Gev."

"Didn't you read the sign?"

"I read the sign. It didn't say keep out, and the gate was open. If I may ask, do you have anything I could drink? I have been drinking from the lake all day." I didn't mean to deflect the subject, but I was desperately thirsty.

"We have lemonade, but the lake water is good to drink."

I smiled. The soldier poured me a cup of cold lemonade. I thanked him and drank quickly. Without hesitation, I held the cup up and asked for more. Lucky for me, they had plenty.

I was not frisked for a weapon, nor did they search through my sleeping bag. I thought for sure that they would want to see my passport, or write my name down. But they didn't. Apparently, they felt I wasn't a threat. I wasn't sure how they could. I would not have been so trusting. No way. I would have cuffed me, searched me and my belongings, examined my passport, and questioned me before uncuffing me. Maybe a short apology at the end and an offer of a ride out of here. I watch movies.

The same soldier said, "You are lucky. We almost shot you. It was 50/50 we would shoot. We are afraid out here. Arabs come here, and if they found you before we did, they would have killed you. Where were you going?"

"North. Up that way," I pointed. "I was going to cross the Jordan River just above the lake, walk west until I found the main road, and I catch a ride to Safed. From there, an Egged bus would take me to my kibbutz."

The soldier shook his head. "If you continued up this road, you would have reached a military base where we train new soldiers. They are very young and very afraid. There are very few officers. They would have shot you. I am one hundred percent certain." If those words should have frightened me, they didn't. I was safe, and that's what mattered.

"What are we supposed to do with you?"

That was a concerning statement. Was he kidding? "I don't know," I said. "But I think it would be a very bad idea to leave me out here."

"We are not going to leave you here," said the driver. My chest relaxed. "But we can't take you back to Ein Gev right away. We are on patrol working our way back to Ein Gev. Climb in the back seat."

It was time to patrol. I climbed in and sat next to the third soldier, who hadn't spoken yet. He was holding a shotgun that looked like a cannon. He sat up high on the back part of the truck with his boots planted on the back seat. He was older than me, but younger than the other two soldiers. His face appeared stern, unlike the others. I wondered whether the guy was angry because he hadn't been given the order to shoot me.

Within five minutes, the truck stopped in the middle of the road. The soldier next to me stood his weapon upright with the stock on the truck's floor, barrel pointing upward, and told me, in English, to hold it for him. I grabbed hold of it to keep it from falling over. It seemed very trusting of him. I was surprised. He jumped out, walked around to the front of the vehicle, lifted up the hood, and poked around, acting very concerned. I asked the soldier in the front seat what was happening.

"Engine trouble," he said. The soldier under the hood said something, then lowered the hood and climbed back in. He reclaimed his shotgun, and off we went. After a minute, I leaned forward and asked the soldier in front of me what was wrong with the engine. He answered, "No problem."

I didn't realize, but I had just passed their test. The soldiers had to know who was traveling with them. The soldier in the back seat pretended to be checking the engine. The front seat passenger had unholstered his handgun and held it where I couldn't see it. It would be a deciding moment. If I had made a threatening move with that shotgun, I would be shot. They had to know who was riding with them. It was a good thing for me that I didn't screw that up.

The truck continued rumbling down the road, the searchlight sweeping back and forth across the road, searching for Arabs. Up ahead was an ambush site, located between two very large roadside boulders. Just before we reached it, the driver sped up, turned toward the ambush site, slammed on the breaks, and cut off the engine. The searchlight pointed straight ahead. Weapons were drawn. The soldiers in the front seat aimed their Uzis, and the back seat soldier aimed his shotgun. Silence prevailed. I only felt the pounding of my heart in my chest. It was a scary feeling. I should have been issued a gun. This was serious shit. Seconds passed. Finally, a soldier called out in Hebrew, "Move on." With the engine once again roaring, we backed up and continued on patrol. I noticed that the truck tires never left the roadway.

Patrolling paused when the driver stopped the truck and pointed down the road. He asked me, "Are those your shoe prints?" I stood up and saw my shoeprints on the dusty road along with the imprint of my sleeping bag next to them.

"Yes, they are. I stopped there to climb up the mountain."

"Why did you climb up the mountain?" he asked in disbelief.

"I wanted to see what was on the other side."

"And what did you see?"

I told him what I saw.

"And did you see that brown sign over there, maybe three meters away from where you climbed, and more signs identical to it along the roadway?" He pointed to a small brown sign on a stake not far from the imprint.

"Yes. I saw it. And the others. The signs were written in Hebrew. I can read Hebrew, but I can't translate."

"What is written is, 'Minefield.' You walked through a minefield going up there and coming back down. Most of this military zone was mined, especially in the grasses and beaches between here and the lake. There are some 200,000 land mines throughout the Golan. They are everywhere. Some are hard to detect. Others are difficult to dispose of. It will take many years to rid the area of them. This road is safe, but nowhere else."

"Amazing," I thought. I wasn't shaken by it. I hadn't gotten hurt. I wasn't under arrest. There was no longer risk for stepping on one.

Patrolling continued. At one point, I was taken by surprise when the driver slammed on the brakes. In the middle of the road, I could see two wolves caught frozen in the truck headlights. In an instant, one wolf ran off the road into the tall grasses to the right. The other dashed to the left and climbed the mountain. Soon, the searchlight found the wolf, frozen in the searchlight about two-thirds of the way up. I knew how he felt. I had been in a similar predicament only two hours earlier. The soldier next to me stood was aiming his shotgun at the wolf. He was prepared to shoot, but the driver ordered him not to. Unhappily, he put the shotgun's safety back on and lowered his weapon. The driver fired up the engine and off we went, leaving the wolf unharmed.

I leaned forward and asked the front seat soldier over the roar of the engine: "Wolves?"

"Apparently. We have never seen wolves here."

"Why didn't he shoot?" I asked.

"The wolf was in a minefield. We couldn't go up there and bring him down."

Wolves in minefields were protected from hunters. That was a good conservation program. Not the best, but it had worked for today.

We patrolled until we arrived at the gate. I was relieved to be back. One soldier jumped out and swung open the gate. We quickly drove through. The soldier locked the gate with the same padlock that I had seen dangling open from the fence earlier that day. It was hard to believe that all this had happened in just one day.

We drove a very short distance and parked between two cars a stone's throw from the resort's entrance. The truck would stay the night waiting for a different team of soldiers to patrol the following day. The soldiers jumped out of the truck, grabbed their gear and weapons, and stowed them away in their car trunks. The front seat soldier and the shotgun soldier drove off in one car so quickly that there was no time for a goodbye, something I didn't understand.

At that point, I wondered where I would be spending the night. The driver walked quickly to the front gate. I followed him. I was unsure what would happen next. Behind the gate stood a guard with an Uzi cradled in his arms.

The driver told the guard to open the gate, and for him to find me a place to sleep. The guard told him that his orders were to admit guests and employees, no one else. He was not going to open the gate. This angered the driver. The driver raised his voice and repeated his orders to the guard, but the guard ignored him. Now, the driver was livid. He began shouting at the guard. But still, the guard would not open the gate. Many guests heard the commotion. They left their cabins and gathered close to the gate. The driver continued to shout and berate the guard, but the guard simply would not let me enter. There was no way that he was going to open that gate for me, and the stand-off continued.

More vacationers joined the others. Some quietly questioned the guard's judgment. The guard finally hollered at the vacationers, "My orders are not to admit anyone who doesn't belong here. That person," he pointed to me, "He does not belong here."

At that very moment, the unexpected happened. A dark-haired, well-groomed, middle-aged man had made his way through the crowd. Actually, the crowd parted to let him pass. He walked right up to the gate, stood in front of the driver, and he asked what the problem was.

"*Shalom*," said the driver. He told him the story about tonight's patrol and the need for me to sleep here tonight because there was nowhere else for me to go at this late hour.

The vacationer, ignoring the guard, immediately opened the gate and, speaking English, told me to follow him. The guard did not try to stop him or say a single word. The guard must have known this man, a man of importance, and didn't obstruct him. I turned around to thank the driver, but the driver had already run off to his car.

I followed the man past brown rustic cabins, until we reached a plush, grassy area. "Sleep here. Where the lights are, is the shower house."

"Thank you," I said.

The man said nothing else and walked off to the closest cabin. I rolled out my sleeping bag. The vodka bottle had not broken. And once I got back from the shower house, I undressed and partially covered up with the sleeping bag. To my surprise, the man returned, this time with a woman. She gave me a sandwich and a bottle of juice. She turned back without saying a word. He said "Goodnight" and followed her. I guessed that she came to get a closer look at the nut case. It may have been her idea to feed me.

"Good night, Ma'am. Goodnight, General. Thank you," I called after them. He acted like a high ranking military officer. The woman continued walking. He called back without turning around, "It's Colonel."

I woke in the middle of the night and sat up. I listened intently. I thought a wolf. I lay back down, not knowing what I heard was real, or if it had been a dream. I quickly fell asleep.

I was wide awake by sunrise. No one else was moving about. I dressed quickly, used the shower house, packed up my sleeping bag, and walked as quietly as I could past the colonel's cabin and up to the front gate.

Last night's guard was still leaning back against the wall, Uzi held in two hands across his abdomen, at the exact spot where he stood last night. He gazed stoically at me. I paused. The guard made no effort to open the gate for me, so I gently opened the gate, and closed it behind me. No words were spoken between the two of us.

Once I passed the fish restaurant, I relaxed and played back yesterday's events in my mind. Deep in my heart, I believed that my survival was a miracle. I wasn't religious, but a miracle was a miracle. I had new interest in God. I set the miracle idea aside for another time to ponder, though, as now I needed to return to Kibbutz Yir'on as soon as possible. Apples needed to be picked, but above all, I wanted to see Colette. Maybe she had a change of heart. Maybe we could talk and be friends again. "Miracles happen," I said out loud and chuckled.

CHAPTER 27

It was Saturday, the Jewish Sabbath. I walked along the lake and didn't stop walking until I reached the bus station. Of course, the station was closed for the Sabbath and no buses were operating. So, I kept walking. On the outskirts of town, I tried to hitchhike, but had no luck. With the sun blazing down on me, I walked on, still hopeful that a car or truck would come by. It didn't take long before I was desperately in need of water. Eventually, I came around a bend in the road. There I found a roadside café with a huge, modern tour bus parked out front. After several teenagers boarded, the driver closed the bus door and started to drive forward. I waved to him, hoping the driver would stop. He did stop, and opened the door. "Hello," he said to me in American dialect English. "Where you headed?" I smiled from ear to ear.

"I'm headed to Zafed and then farther northwest to my kibbutz."

"Come in, I'll take you to Zafed," the driver said, "but first, we have to meet up with the rest of our group. They are down at the lake not far from here. From there, I'll take you to Zafed."

I was thrilled as I climbed in. The driver had ten American teenagers onboard, aged roughly fourteen to sixteen. I said hello to them and soon there was the buzz of conversation. One of the teenagers, a boy, was from my hometown. It was hard to believe. I knew his older brother.

We arrived at the sparkling sea. I stepped into the waters to cool down my very hot feet and then left the water to sit under a shady tree. The bus driver came by and tossed me a bottle of water. My exhaustion quickly dissipated and I felt grateful.

Less than an hour later, all the adults and teenagers loaded into the bus. As promised, I was dropped off at the Zafed bus station. Because I wasn't sure if buses were operating, I tried hitchhiking again and got lucky. Just after dark, a small truck stopped for me. The driver dropped me off at the foot of the kibbutz driveway.

I walked directly to my tent. I didn't see anyone. I stripped down and wrapped in a towel. When I returned from the shower house, I fell deeply asleep. The next thing I heard was a kibbutz guard hollering for me to wake up. How did they know I had returned?

Fifteen minutes later, while sipping a cup of hot coffee, I was among a large group of British students. They arrived yesterday. That was a surprise. A bigger surprise? I asked about the French. "They left yesterday morning. They were gone before we arrived." I forced myself to smile. I couldn't speak again if I wanted to. I needed a moment. Then I introduced myself to the others. The French were on their way home. Only the French nurse, Dominique, remained. Disappointed, heartbroken, and stunned, I developed a nasty headache.

Yaakov assigned the groups to the wagons. I didn't hear much after that. The tractor pulled our wagon down a different road. I could tell from a distance that this new orchard was very different from the others. Dark fruit hung from these 15-foot tall trees. They were plums. The plums

194

were smaller and easier to pick than the other fruit. The fruit came apart from the tree with the slightest twist of the wrist. And the plums didn't make my lower arms itchy. I could only imagine how these trees smelled in spring when they were in full blossom. Unlike cherry trees, plum tree blossoms had a very sweet smell.

The first plum I picked, I ate. The plums were delicious, sweet, and juicy. I ate two at a time, trying hard not to ruin my appetite for breakfast. In all, I ate sixteen delicious plums, and later, a big breakfast.

Shortly after returning from breakfast, I felt the first pangs of an upset stomach. Minutes later, it became clear that I was in serious trouble. My bowels were calling out to me, "Emergency. Prepare for sudden diarrhea attack." I unhooked from my fruit-collecting basket and sprinted to the shower house that seemed to be miles away. I ran past the dining hall and the tents. When I reached the shower house, I took the steps three at a time and shoved the door open. I was in luck. No one was here. Better yet, there was plenty of toilet paper.

Reading material was limited to one magazine: *Time*, May 31, 1968, with Charles De Gaulle on the cover with a banner above his head that read, "France: Beyond the Deluge." I went outside for fresh air and did some more reading. I was stuck here until my intestinal situation returned to normal. I sat on the shaded front stoop of the shower building while my stomach rumbled.

There were major articles about France and France's President Charles De Gaulle. France had a lot of problems with unrest from workers and students who disliked how powerful De Gaulle had become and disliked how he ran the country.

How timely. There was an advertisement for Braggi cologne by Revlon. A bucket of cologne splashed throughout the shower house would be of great value right now.

A sign of the times? Dr. John Kenneth Galbraith wrote of "a worldwide revolutionary movement" in America, Africa, Great Britain, western Europe, and parts of eastern Europe.

Military experts were predicting that 50,000 to 60,000 American military soldiers, airmen, marines, and sailors could die by the end of the Vietnam War. I was not going to be one of them.

I dropped the magazine and ran inside to the toilet. Directly after, I jumped in the shower and dried off with paper towels. I came out of the shower house feeling poorly.

I read how the Pentagon spent over $21,000 for an Israeli institute to investigate how kibbutz life affects young men's leadership abilities. I would have been interested to see the results of that ongoing investigation.

Pediatrician Dr. Benjamin Spock was currently being tried in court for conspiring to aid draft dodgers. He was a major protester of the Vietnam War.

El Al airline owned seven Boeing 707 jets and leased two additional planes. More than half of their pilots participated in the Six Day War in 1967.

Thirty minutes had now passed since my last run into the shower house. It wasn't lunch time. I made a risky decision to go back to work. I walked cautiously back to the plum orchard, and grabbed a picker's basket. All the ladders were in use. I was grateful for that. I received a few smiles and waves from the Brits. Yaakov welcomed my return. I did a shoulder shrug and said, "You didn't warn me." Until today, my experiences with plums were that they came from grocery stores, and were not free. With my big appetite, what a disaster.

I was grateful to have finished my morning work alongside the Brits. At lunch, a British male passed by and patted me on my back. "Good show, governor." A second passed by and told me, "You run jolly fast." I could only chuckle.

The Israelis just looked at me and some laughed—but not Dovid. He brought forth an eruption of laughter so loud that his laugh ended in a coughing spell. The French woman, Dominique, who had ignored me since the Colette break-up, smiled. I smiled back. I managed to eat lunch, a small one, devoid of fruit.

CHAPTER 28

Three days passed. I would leave tomorrow morning for good. I had mixed feelings about leaving. I enjoyed it here. My head was full of good memories. Except for the loss of Colette, my stay here was grand.

I wrote to my sister and Uncle Rick. I told them about my travel plans to fly to Turkey, fly back to Rome, and from Rome take a train ride to Paris. I was excited about Paris. I knew something about Paris and France from studying history, watching movies, and from *Time*, the magazine.

I left my tent before dinner and walked to the future "vineyard." I never mentioned my idea to Yaakov. Why risk being laughed at. I sat for a long time. It was quiet and peaceful. My remaining time on the kibbutz could be measured in hours. Tomorrow, after breakfast, I would catch the westbound morning bus to the Mediterranean Sea and then travel south to Tel Aviv. From there, my thoughts returned to when I first saw Colette on the auto-ferry ride between Athens and Haifa. So much had happened since meeting her. Although I missed her, my pain was nearly gone. Was it for the best that she was gone when I returned from Ein Gev? I would never know.

I was quiet during my last dinner. I sat at the long table with the Brits and the French woman. After dinner, I went to the library. The door was unlocked. I turned on the lights and got comfortable in an armchair.

I relaxed for a few minutes. "What the hell." I found pencil and paper and wrote about my idea of creating a vineyard instead of another fruit orchard in the rock orchard. On the back of the paper, I sketched rows of grape vines next to a peach orchard laden with fruit. When I finished, I laid the drawing on the big desk and let myself out.

I stripped down and wrapped myself in a towel. With soap and toiletries in hand, I made the short walk to the shower house. I stood under the shower with tepid water flowing down my neck and upper back as I slowly soaped up my body. My mind wandered. I couldn't remember taking shower without my mind wandering. Tonight, the torrents of water made my mind spin like a turbine generating a steady flow of thoughts: Israel, the kibbutz, and Colette. Tomorrow, I would leave the kibbutz and begin a lengthy trip that would have me arrive in London before Labor Day.

I showered. When I got back to my tent, I left the tent door flap open to catch the evening breezes that would minimally cool down the room. Rain would have helped, but it hadn't rained a drop since I arrived here, nor was any rain expected for several months. I slipped on a pair of kibbutz shorts and sat on the edge of the bed deep in thought. I was mentally prepared for tomorrow's departure, but I wouldn't have minded staying here for a few weeks longer. It would have been a real opportunity to get to know the Israelis once the volunteer fruit pickers had moved on. But there was no place for me here once the fruit harvest was finished. I was ill-prepared to stay. I didn't speak Hebrew, had no mechanical or electrical skills, and no training with weapons, although there was probably some rule that prohibited foreigners from handling one. More importantly, I found kibbutz-style socialism unsettling.

I wasn't sleepy. I grabbed a drawing pad and colored pencils, and drew a picture of the house where I had lived with Colette and the French. Then I switched to wallpaper designs. When I focused, new designs flashed into my head. I paused after my third drawing, and reached down and pulled out my vodka bottle from under the bed. It had sat untouched since I returned from my great adventure. Propped up on my bed, I had a clear view through the open doorway. I unscrewed the cap, said *L'Chaim* ("to life"), let out a breath, took a big swig of my "no headache tomorrow" vodka, and exhaled the high octane vapor.

Dominique passed, dressed in a mid-thigh robe, with a towel draped over her shoulder. She was carrying a wash bag on her way to the shower house. She glanced into my tent as she walked by and saw me on my bed with a large vodka bottle at my lips. She didn't stop. Too bad. It would have been nice for Dominique to stop by to have a goodbye drink with me. She knew that I was leaving tomorrow. *Perhaps, I could stand at the tent entrance and invite her in when she passed back by?* Silly idea. I turned off the light, but didn't stop thinking about her.

On her return from the shower house, she stopped in front of my tent. Through the open-door flap, she could see that it was dark inside. She stepped in and asked, "Adam? Are you awake? It's Dominique."

I had only turned off the light a few minutes earlier. Half asleep, half drunk, I quickly sat up and turned on the light. "Dominique?"

"Yes. I need to come in." I didn't know she spoke English.

Amazed and a drunk, I said, "Please come in. What a surprise." She closed the tent flaps behind her. She stepped forward and stood in a short robe with her head wrapped in a towel. She never looked better.

"Hi," she said. She looked around just in case I had a tent mate. "I just wanted to say goodbye to you.

"It is nice of you to come by. Have a seat." I pointed to the foot of my bed. I had no chairs, and the other bed was covered with all my possessions.

She hesitated, then sat down, taking great care to keep herself covered as best she could. "Adam, could I have a drink, please? I just happened to notice you drinking when I passed by earlier. A toast to your safe travels would be nice."

"It would be. I hate drinking alone." I handed her the vodka bottle. A glass wasn't needed. We had drunk together from the same bottle for several Friday nights. "It's good to see you. You came to say goodbye?" I knew she was here for the vodka, but I asked to be polite. Seeing her sitting on my bed stirred me sexually. *Sex.* I hadn't had sex since Rome, and that was weeks ago.

"I did. Where are you going from here?"

She drank two mouthfuls that went down like water, and passed the bottle back to me. "Italy, France, London, and finally back home by early September."

"I also came to apologize for treating you so badly after your breakup with Colette. It wasn't nice of me. And you deserved better from her."

"You didn't treat me badly, Dominique. You just ignored me, as did the rest of the French. And you speak English."

"I know. Sorry." She said in a sincere manner.

I drank half a mouthful and handed the bottle back to her. "I'll accept your apology, but only if you stay here and drink with me and talk for a while. By the way, the vodka is expensive. You won't wake up tomorrow with a headache if you drink too much."

She didn't answer. She drank another mouthful and handed me the bottle. I drank a small amount and handed the bottle back to her. My guess was that she didn't want to get drunk, and that she simply wanted the bottle. But she had no choice. Somewhat inebriated, she drank a large mouthful, stood up, and handed the bottle back. Then she said, "I need to go back to my tent for just a minute and change. I'll be right back." She appeared to be uncomfortable in her short robe. Maybe she wasn't wearing underpants. But her short robe interested me. I didn't want her to change, if that was her reason for leaving.

"Listen," I said. "If you leave now, I know that you are not coming back. You are beautiful and sexy the way you are. Please don't leave. If you do, it's lights out and I am off to bed." She sat back down, angry at me. "Sitting here drinking with you will be a good memory for me to leave with. These last few days, I haven't had many good ones." I lied. Despite the loss of Collette, I enjoyed the work and the people who would speak with me and even those who couldn't because of language differences.

She held the vodka bottle in both hands. The big bottle was now down to three-quarters full. Her eyes locked onto it. She was smiling. "Beautiful and sexy," she said softly. She took a short sip and passed the bottle.

"I'm staying."

It was quiet for a minute. I placed the bottle on the floor next to me after taking a sip. "We could talk about this summer, or we could talk about Camus, De Gaulle, or our sex lives," I suggested.

"Sex life," she said while staring down at the floor. "Did you have sex with Colette? She was just a child."

"What do you mean 'just a child'?"

"She was seventeen."

"What? The truth?" She nodded. "No. Of course I didn't know that she was that young. Why didn't someone tell me on the ship, or since we arrived here? You knew that she pushed our beds together. How is it no one told me?"

"It was discussed among us, but we decided not to hurt her. She was no different from the rest of us. We all wanted this to be a fun time. She chose you. And you chose her. In terms of sex, she could have been sexually active. I think it mostly turned out well for both of you, except for the ending."

204

"You are right. It was painful ending."

"Yes, sorry about that."

"Now that I know, I'm glad we didn't. I was fooled by her age, and I was fooled by our relationship. She needed a male companion, not a boyfriend. I don't regret being with her. She was great company, attractive. But I was hooked on the idea of being her lover someday.

"I could never forget your watermelon," Dominique said. "After you gave her watermelon on the auto-ferry, she was fascinated by you. She told me. You were the first American student she had ever had a conversation with. You made a good impression. She hardly knew you when she asked Benoit for permission to join us. She knew right away what she wanted and she was determined to get it. I watched her when the kibbutz director had to decide whether you could come along with us. He could not say no to her."

"And if he had?"

"Believe me, she would have made a scene, screamed her bloody head off. Maybe threatened to jump into the Sea. She wouldn't give you up. You were a godsend, perfect for her." She drank and passed the bottle back to me.

Dominique was so desirable, sitting with her robe partially open exposing the inside part of her left breast. She was drunk and unaware; I was drunk and very aware. I sat up and scooted down the bed and sat right next to her. She laid her head on my shoulder. I responded by putting my arm around her. She fell asleep, and though I wasn't in any hurry to let go of her, it was getting late.

"Dominique, you need to wake up. It's getting late and morning will be here soon." I gave her a gentle shake. She woke up quickly and straightened up. She did not seem to notice how uncovered she had been. She looked at me and said, "How long have I been asleep?"

"You nodded off for about two minutes ago," though it was for longer. "You laid your head on my shoulder. Then I held you, trying to keep you from falling off the bed."

"You are sweet."

Now fully awake, she stood up, bent over, and gave me a kiss goodbye on my forehead. "Thank you very much for a delightful evening." She had some difficulty finding her flip-flops, but I found them for her. She held onto my back as I bent down and helped her slip them on.

She waved goodbye and walked toward the entryway. She stopped before opening the door flap. Making no effort to open it, she turned around. "I want to take that bottle with me. You leave tomorrow. I have six more nights here. Let me have it, please?"

It was no big deal for me to give it to her, but the thing was that I wanted to make love with her and pictured making love to her right now. Instead of showing her what a good guy I was, I stood up and responded without making eye contact, "I'll give you the bottle if I can make love with you." I couldn't believe I had told her that. If she had walked up to me, stuck her face in mine, shouted at me or slapped my face, I would have said to her, "Sorry. You can have it. Didn't mean to upset you. No hard feelings?"

But she didn't. She looked shocked. She turned to me and said, "I am a beautiful, sexy, drunk French woman. I know I will regret this in the morning. I already do. But I am going to fuck you. When I am done, I am going to leave here with that bottle." She pointed to the vodka sitting on the floor. "Agreed?"

I nodded yes.

"Say it."

"After sex, you leave with the bottle."

"Have you done something stupid like this before?"

"No. Of course not."

"I'll be right back. I need to go to the shower house." And she left.

CHAPTER 29

When she returned, she laced up the door flap so that no one could see in. She walked over to where I was seated and said, "Pull your pants down and lie on your back." I happily did what I was told."

She turned off the overhead light and straddled me, still wearing her short robe whose fabric brushed against my belly and thighs. My hands felt nothing—she had my arms pinned down.

She finished before I did. I had not been in a hurry. She quickly climbed off me, turned on the light, and grabbed the vodka bottle. I sat up, disappointed as hell for not having been given enough time. She pushed me back down.

"Not fair," I said. "You stopped too soon! I didn't finish."

"You had more time than you deserved. It wasn't nice of you to demand sex for this bottle."

"I didn't demand. I asked nicely."

"It doesn't matter. This bottle is mine now. I got what I wanted." Was she referring to vodka or the sex, or both?

"I'm sure you must be disappointed. But if you had taken the time to charm me, I would have given you a much more and more time."

She turned to leave when I said, "Dominique. I'm having the adventure of my life. I was with Colette, a goddess—I know, a very young goddess, but a goddess nonetheless. As I said, she and I never had sex. But when you walked in here looking beautiful, I thought how fantastic it would be to have sex with you. I know your New Zealander boyfriend enjoyed you."

Slowly she said, "What do you know about him and me?"

"I saw you both in the men's shower, but only for a second. Didn't mean to see."

She paused for a few moments, sucking on her lower lip. Her anger was growing. "He was a handsome man."

"Yes."

"Adam, sit up." I sat up. "I have to go. But first, close your eyes. I am going to kiss you goodbye. You can enjoy me kissing you, or you can imagine that you are kissing Colette goodbye. Just close your eyes and wait for the kiss." I closed my eyes. Quickly, she covered the bottle with her towel and swung it hard against the side of my head.

I woke up in the morning with a nasty headache. *How did that happen?* I wondered. *The vodka was expensive.* I tried to remember what had happened. Was it a dream that Dominique was in my tent? I looked for the vodka bottle. It was gone. She had been here. I thought I had sex with her, but I wasn't sure. *Did I dream I had sex with her?*

Despite the headache with minor dizziness and a touch of nausea, I worked from 5 a.m. to 8 a.m. picking apples. At breakfast, I said my goodbyes. Dominique smiled at me and said, "*Au Revoir.*" If she have been curious about what I remembered about last night, she didn't ask. I was curious, but said nothing.

After breakfast, I finished packing. I was in no rush as I walked down the driveway for the last time. I was alone; everyone else was doing their job. I was certain I would never return. I was lucky to have been here at all. I crossed the quiet road and waited for the westbound Egged bus to take me to the Mediterranean Sea. I stood a short stone's throw from Lebanon. I was certain that I was being observed from both the Lebanese and Israeli installations located high up on the mountain tops.

When I thought the bus would never arrive, I heard the bus approach before I actually saw it. I quickly filled my eyes with the last images of a remarkable place. I stepped up onto the bus, paid the fare, and sat in the first empty row. As the bus drove-off, I looked back one more time.

CHAPTER 30

In late August, I arrived in Paris. It had been a long summer of travel and work. I was in tremendous need to stretch my legs after flying from Israel to Istanbul to Rome, and then the long train ride from Rome to Paris.

I called the young French couple I had met waiting in line to buy lemon gelato when in Rome a few weeks ago. No one answered. They told me in Rome, "When you get to Paris, call us. We have a place where you can stay." I looked forward to spend time with them. Instead, I found a room in a small hotel. The rate was double compared to Rome.

That first afternoon I visited Notre Dame Cathedral. I was surprised that a woman walked up to me and made me pay to sit on a bench in front of the cathedral that overlooked the Seine River. If they were to charge me just to sit, it made sense to sit elsewhere for free. I found a bistro and sat for free while I enjoyed a cup of coffee.

After coffee, I walked along the river, crossed one bridge after another as I wove my way along the river. I lost count but was certain I had crossed twenty bridges, maybe more.

I loved how the French dressed. I was dressed like a foreigner. I might as well have "American" written across my Levi pants. There were many booksellers and artists scattered along the river. It was such a different city compared to those I had previously seen. In the evening, I walked past the Louvre and the Eiffel Tower.

The next morning, after a delicious breakfast, I called the French couple again. This time, I got through. "It's Adam. We met in Rome. Lemon gelato? Do you remember me?"

"Of course! The American. Where are you?"

I told her.

"I'm home. I will give you my address and you can come to my apartment now if you want."

"Now is good. I'll see you soon."

True to her word, she had a place for me to stay. We rode the elevator to the eighth floor of an apartment building. It was her personal studio apartment: bedroom and bath. I had a fantastic view of the Arc de Triomphe with the Tower in the distance. "I have removed what I need down to my parents' apartment on the fourth floor. They are away on holiday. Me and my boyfriend are very busy studying for university exams in September. I will spend my days studying in my parents' apartment, so you can use this apartment any time. When we have time to be with you, it will be in the evening. If you want to eat lunch here, buy what you want from a shop. Bring extra for me. I will prepare it for us both."

"Steak. I haven't had a steak all summer. Where do I buy it?"

"Step outside the building, turn right and it's a short walk. The shop is on the same side. Look in the shop windows and you'll know. Ask for steak."

I didn't want to be a bother for her, but steak is definitely what I wanted. I got up early the next morning, extremely excited to be in Paris. I walked down a number of streets looking into every shop window. The Seine River, the bridges, the people, the booksellers — it all fascinated me. The only thing missing was romance, not only a woman to share all of what I saw and felt, but a special person to hold hands with and sit on a public bench kissing unashamedly the way the young French couples were doing. I felt so incomplete here being alone.

Near noon, I found the grocery shop that my host had recommended. I had an unusual experience while buying string beans. I nearly set-off an international crisis when I reached out and touched the beans.

"No!" shouted the grocer.

Touching and self-service were not allowed. The grocer asked me a string of questions in French that I could not possibly answer. I understood nothing. I pointed to the string beans and said, "kilo" and gave a hand signal for half a kilo.

I wanted a thin, long bread. I watched how a customer handled his bread and copied the procedure flawlessly, fearing another near international crisis.

In the back of the shop, I found the fresh meat department. I had no problem asking the butcher for beef steak and showing him the size needed with my hands. "Two persons." I held up two fingers and said "*Elle* and *moi,*" — she and me. I was proud that I remembered that from the French group. They thought I only knew the cussword *merde*.

The butcher understood perfectly. I wished I had an opportunity to say *moi* again, not because I could pronounce it correctly, but because it made me smile to say it. It made me shape my mouth in a funny way. I enjoyed the French language and was disappointed not to have studied it and practiced speaking on the kibbutz. I sure had the time.

I brought the food to my French friend, and in no time, she whipped up a nice lunch of steak, steamed string beans, tomato slices, bread and butter, and red wine. She had one sip of wine for herself. Test preparation was her priority. After lunch, with Frommer's book in hand, I went off to explore the Left Bank.

CHAPTER 31

I was enjoying the beautiful streets of Paris, when loud shouts and banging sounds came from a street up ahead. The streets were crowded. I saw a flag I didn't recognized waived above the heads of a crowd. What I thought to be a celebration turned out to be a demonstration by Czechoslovakian students and their supporters parading through the streets of Paris to protest the invasion of Czechoslovakia. Soviet military forces and their allies, some 500,000 troops in all, had invaded Czechoslovakia yesterday. The noise was coming closer. I had no reason to believe I was in danger, until I saw a policeman yank the camera from a CBS cameraman filming next to me. The policeman opened the film box on the side, pulled out the film canister, and shoved it into his coat pocket. The cop closed the side compartment and handed the camera back to the cameraman and quickly walked away. The whole time the cameraman kept saying, "I have a permit for that. I have a permit for that." But the deed had been done.

Up ahead, I saw policemen dressed in military uniforms. They wore helmets, and carried batons held high in one hand and shields in the other hand. They were the CRS national police placed in Paris for crowd and riot control. Trouble. I ran off the street onto the sidewalk, searching for a hiding place. One shop's door was open. I ran in. The shopkeeper hiding in the back of the store heard me enter. He stuck his head out from the back and signaled me to hurry to the back where he and others were hiding. I ran to him. Behind a back wall, I and a half dozen others remained silent. At first, all I could think about were the batons and protesters. Were the police beating the demonstrators? I hoped the clubs were used only to threaten—a show of force.

The shop was a frame-shop and art gallery. A large tabletop work area was in the center area behind the counter. Framed paintings, posters and photographs hung from the available middle and upper wall surfaces. While waiting for the danger to pass, I looked at the framed photographs on the walls in front of me. My eyes focused on a beautiful photograph of two young women seated on redbrick wall that circled a small tree in the middle of a courtyard surrounded by redbrick buildings. I walked over to the photograph to get a better look. One girl was a redhead and the other was… Colette, *my* Colette. I couldn't believe it! It was her. The redhead had to be her best friend who she often spoke about.

The shopkeeper looked at me. "Something interests you?"

"Something does. I want to buy this photograph, unframed." I pointed to it. "I don't see the price." The price was steep, but I didn't care. "I wish to mail it to my home in America. Can you help me with that?"

"*Oui.*"

"The woman in the picture is my friend. Her name is Colette. It is important that I speak with the photographer. Does the photographer live here in Paris?"

"Oui. But it is difficult to meet with him. It's August. Everyone is away."
Maybe the shopkeeper thought I was trying to save money and buy more
pictures directly from the photographer.

It grew quiet outside. The street was mostly empty. All of those taking
shelter left, except for me. After I paid the shopkeeper for the picture
and for the postage to America, I asked him again, "I need to speak with
the photographer."

The shopkeeper ignored me. I stepped back and leaned against a cabinet.
"I'm not leaving. This is very important to me." I guessed this man was
a reasonable man and the police would be too busy for a minor
complaint of trespassing with all that was going on in the streets.

It worked. The shopkeeper made the call.

"What is your name?"

"Adam Haisenberger."

The shopkeeper repeated my name. "He is an American." Pause.
"*Merci*." He hung up and wrote down the photographer's address and
slid it across the counter. I was smiling. With no protesters or police in
sight, I left contented.

It was a long walk to the photographer, but I was up to it. I located his
building on the busy street that ran along the Seine River. The building
appeared to be his home and not a commercial business. It was four
stories tall, and each side except the front touched or almost touched

apartment buildings that towered above it. It might have been a small apartment building.

I pushed the bell buzzer next to the gate handle.

"Bonjour." A male voice greeted me through the intercom.

"Bonjour. I am sorry to bother you. I hope you speak English."

In English, he said, "Yes?"

"My name is Adam."

He interrupted. "Where are you from?"

"America."

"Where are you coming from?"

"Israel."

"Why are you here?"

"I saw a photo of two young women in a picture frame shop. The shopkeeper told me that you shot that picture. One of the women was Colette who I met in Israel. Do you know her? Or is she a stranger to you?"

The photographer pushed a button that electrically unlocked the front gate. A young man about my age came out onto the porch shirtless, wearing dungarees, and barefoot. "Come through. Close the gate behind you."

I walked up to him. We shook hands. "Adam."

220

"Jean. Come inside." I followed him in. "Close the door tight."

"The girl in the photograph…"

Jean completed my sentence, "is my younger sister, Colette, with her friend Amy."

If it were easy to catch flies by opening one's mouth, I would have collected enough flies for a meal.

"I know who you are. You're welcome, but Colette isn't here. She is in the South of France with my mother. I'm preparing breakfast. You're just in time. My father is busy in the house somewhere. Now that you are here, I don't have to eat alone. I hope you're hungry. Coffee is ready. I have croissants. Come to the kitchen and choose what you want. Cheeses. Butter. Fruit spreads. This kitchen is packed with food that makes it difficult to find what I am looking for." We toasted, sliced, spread, poured, and finally loaded two trays with breakfast goodies, coffee, silverware, and cloth napkins.

Tray in hand, I followed Jean. We went up a staircase to the second floor. The house was beautiful. Paintings and photographs covered the walls. I followed Jean to the third floor, and then to the fourth floor. It was as if I were visiting an art museum. Finally, the staircase took us up to the roof. On the roof were chairs, tables of different sizes, some with umbrellas, some with lounge chairs. In the back area, stood a large barbeque grill. There was plenty of room for a very large gathering of people.

I was distracted by everything, especially the view. Before I could sit, typical of an excited kid, I walked over to the chest-height wall at the front of the building. Down on the street were pedestrians and motor vehicles. On the far side of the street were two booksellers and an artist painting a portrait of a young woman. Behind them, was the Seine River. I couldn't believe Colette lived here. I was glad she wasn't here though. She might have pushed me off the roof. On second thought, a face to face conversation might have made it easier to move on with my life. Not that I felt wounded or in pain. It just could have been nice.

"What a place," I said softly. Jean opened up the table's huge umbrella that shaded the table and two lounge chairs adjacent to it.

"So, you are Adam. Can I tell you about my sister?" He didn't wait for my response. "My sister liked you since her first mouthful of your watermelon. By the way, that was a clever way to introduce yourself to a girl. I'll have to try it sometime. But she is just a young girl. Everyone enjoys her except the boys who fall in love with her. She tosses them away, breaks their hearts. Are you one of those boys, Adam? Did she break your heart?"

"I adored her even though she broke my heart. But I healed quickly once I learned how young she was. She had already left the kibbutz for France when I found out. Jean, I know better than to come here still hurting. That would be foolish of me."

"Adam, you broke your own heart. She didn't do it. You did. You threw a stone at a dog." I didn't correct him. "She adored you. She's only seventeen. You had no chance of having a real romantic relationship with her. I know my sister. We were together for one evening this week without friends or family. She told me everything about her trip. Let's eat and drink coffee while its hot, and rest our heads for a few minutes."

Taking a break from conversation to focus on the meal had never occurred to me. But it worked. The food and coffee were divine.

He spoke first. "Adam, please eat, but allow me to continue. I'll make us more coffee in a moment." I bit into a chocolate croissant. I had no idea such food existed! "You are the first American Colette had spent any time with. She found you funny and interesting. For some reason she felt amazingly safe when she was near you. You made it easy for her to be with you at times, and be with her French friends at other times. And when the two of you traveled in Israel on holiday, she couldn't have enjoyed herself more. She sent us postcards every day. She said when she told the French where she wanted to travel to, no one was willing to go with her. But you were agreeable to everything. You never said no to her."

"Yes, that's me. But that's her too. She is a real charmer," I said.

"She ran away from you and went into hiding after you became *Adam the stone thrower*. She was angry with you! Nobody finds Colette until Colette wants to be found. She would be world champion of hide-and-seek if there were world championship games. Tiberias was the first time she had been on her own. She met an older Jewish couple who had a boat. She trusted them. They fed her and made a place for her to sleep on their boat. When she returned to the kibbutz, she wasn't surprised that you were about to leave to search for her when no one else was, or that you moved out of the house instead of her having to move out. But she was surprised that you didn't leave the kibbutz right away and move on with your holiday. So, I have to ask: Why didn't you leave?"

"I didn't leave because I enjoyed the work and the people. I had fallen in love with Israel and the kibbutz. I didn't have a better place to be. And you're right. I watched out for her. It was easy. She was charming, and I adored her—maybe more than adored. When I was with her, I felt special."

Jean spoke up, "Her English wasn't very good, but she knew how to fool people with her English skills. She could guess correctly what people were speaking about. She says that the two of you didn't know each other because you didn't have a language in common. How good is your French, Adam?"

"I learned a total of ten words. How can a language that sounds so beautiful to my ears be so difficult for me to learn?" I didn't tell him that I was too lazy to try to learn.

"I don't know." Jean stood up. "I am going downstairs to make more coffee. *S'il-vous-plait*, you stay here and enjoy the view and the food. I'll be back shortly."

I was leaning over the front wall looking down on the street below when I someone spoke to be me from behind. *"Bonjour."* It wasn't Jean's voice. I turned around.

"Hello Adam, I am Colette's father. Glad to meet you. Colette spoke highly of you. Jean told me that you and Colette are no longer friends. He also told me how you found us and your mishap today. Paris is rarely that dangerous, I promise you."

It turns out that the father was a winemaker and importer of hard liquor from Great Britain. Wine-making was a minor business compared to his primary business of importing and distributing major brand hard liquor and cheaper brands throughout France.

"I have to run out for a meeting, Adam. You were very good to my daughter. I was worried about her. I called the kibbutz and I spoke with that young man, Benoit. He told me not to worry because Colette had an American friend named Adam who watched over her. He said, 'Charles De Gaulle could do with a bodyguard as committed as this guy.' That's what he said. After that call, both her mother and I worried less about her safety. What can I do for you, Adam? Do you need a place to stay?"

"No sir. I have a place to stay."

"Can I give you money?"

"No sir, I have plenty."

"Have you done any fine French dining, here in Paris?"

"No sir. The idea is intimidating. I haven't brought my fine clothes with me." In reality, I didn't own any. I spent most of my life wearing cutoffs, untucked long-sleeve collared shirts, and loafers without socks. I rented a tuxedo for formal occasions. And I was not about to eat alone in a fancy restaurant.

"Give me a minute, Adam." Jean's dad left and returned a few minutes later with a piece of paper and a business card that he handed to me. "Tonight at 8 p.m., you have a reservation at this three-star restaurant. Casual dress is acceptable, but no blue jeans. Hand my card to the maître d' and he will take care of you. You will be made very comfortable, I can promise you that. Your meal and the people you will meet are tops. I need to be going. It was nice meeting you Adam. If you need anything, call me. *Au revoir.*" He rushed off.

"Good bye," I hollered, and quickly realized I should have said *Au revoir.*

Jean didn't return. It was time for me to leave. I ventured down the staircase that was covered with photographs. The lights were off in all the upper floor rooms, so it was difficult to see what was beyond doorways. Finally, Jean intercepted me at the bottom of the second-floor staircase, and walked me downstairs to the front door. I thanked him and asked him to convey a message to Colette. "It's a shame you never let me explain about the puppy. Thank you for the good times. I won't forget you." We shook hands. Jean saw me out.

At 8 p.m., I walked into the beautiful French restaurant that had been "recommended" to me. I waited my turn to speak with the maître d'. I almost turned around and walked out after the way he looked at me. I made eye contact and handed him her dad's card. The maître d' instantly became a new man. "Monsieur Adam, I have been expecting you! Please follow me, sir." He led me in the opposite direction from where he had led the others. I thought he must be taking me to the employee lunch room. We entered the huge kitchen and walked to the far end where a table large enough for eight dinners stood. He chose my seat and promised me that I was in for a marvelous time. He left a wine menu and a dinner menu and disappeared from the kitchen.

An English-speaking cook came to me with a big welcoming smile. "Welcome Adam! Tonight, you are a guest of our best customer. It is my job to see to it that you have a dining experience that you will never forget. Do you enjoy wine?" I nodded yes. "Can you read the menu? It's in French." I shook my head no. "Forget the menu. I will be your menu. Are you very hungry?" I smiled. "Good. Do you want full portions, or do you want to sample a variety of appetizers, soups, entrées, and desserts? Of course, I will serve the appropriate wines."

"No soup, please." I explained that I wasn't a big drinker and perhaps the wine should be served in small quantities.

"I suggest you start with a variety of hors d'oeuvres and appetizers."

I was nearly finished with liver pâté, my last appetizer, when the maître d' came to my table with a stunningly beautiful older woman. She was at least thirty-five years old.

"Adam, may I introduce you to Madame Bonaparte. Madame Bonaparte, I am pleased to introduce you to Adam Haisenberger." I stood. The woman walked up to me, initiated a handshake, and quietly directed me to kiss her cheeks. I did as I was told. I had seen this same kissing many times in Paris and Rome. I would have preferred a hug, but cheek kisses were enchanting with a woman of her beauty.

"May I sit next to you?"

"Certainly." The maître d' had me stand and stand aside while he seated the lady. But before I could sit back down, a waiter appeared with a full table setting for her. She ordered a glass of wine. I was reseated with the assistance of the maître d'.

She spoke first. "The man paying for your meal tonight? I am his mistress. He asked me to join you tonight." She put her hand on my mid-inside-right thigh. "He didn't want you to dine alone. Now that I see that you are such a good-looking young man, I am very pleased to be seen here with you. I love this table. To be seated at this table is one of the most special places in the whole world to dine. Where are you?"

"Where am I?"

"I speak about your meal."

"Ah, the meal." I had forgotten about the meal. "Entrées are next."

The same cook appeared at our table and poured her wine. She spoke to him in French. "I ordered what you are having." She continued speaking about herself and her family, followed by Colette's family. Without stopping, except for an occasional sip of her wine, she discussed Paris' troubled times and her optimism that France would have a better future once De Gaulle stepped down. When I informed her about the Czechoslovakia demonstration and how it was handled, she expressed anger as she raised her voice in English, then in French, and then back to English punctuated with hand gestures. She was delightful to watch and listen to. But the attention she gave my right inner thigh was stimulating, unexpected and historic.

From each small plate, my dinner partner ate less than half of what was served to her. She discussed each of the different wines that were served. Her words were wasted on me, for I was well on my way to a state of inebriation. I hoped that it didn't show. She didn't seem to be affected by the wine.

When a large serving tray, with beautiful presentation of decorated meat, carrots, mashed potatoes, and a green vegetable rolled past our table on the way to the dining room, I asked her what it was. "Châteaubriand for two. Have you ever tasted it?"

"No."

She waved to the cook, who immediately came to our table. The cook spoke first. "Apologies, I know what you will ask. It is not possible to have extra Châteaubriand. I am so sorry."

"I don't want it for me. I want it for my date. Who did you serve it to?"

"I'll check." The cook stepped into the dining room and returned quickly. "The ambassador from Norway and his wife."

She looked at me. "I know them. I will go speak to them." She removed her hand from my thigh. "Let me pass." She went directly into the dining room. Minutes after she returned to the kitchen, a waiter wheeled the Châteaubriand just inside the kitchen. A portion of Châteaubriand was served to me. I found the dish to be heavenly.

When I was done eating, the cook cleared the last of the dishes and announced that he would return shortly with dessert suggestions.

The beauty sitting next to me asked, "Adam, are you happy? Are you depressed? Tell me the truth."

"It has been an amazing summer. I am having the best meal of my life with an extraordinary woman. I am very happy."

With a big smile on her face, she pulled her thigh hand away and placed it against my cheek and said, "You are a lovely young man. I am pleased that you are happy, and you are drunk, yes?" I nodded yes. "I have enjoyed our time together. But I am tired and I must go home. I must rest for a busy day tomorrow. Since you are so special to my lover's family, and because I find you to be so attractive," I was certain she was exaggerating, "I must tell you that if you were unhappy or depressed, I would be obligated to take you home with me so that we could enjoy ourselves in privacy. But you are in good spirits and I must go. Please let me pass."

Before I let her out, I asked her with my most successful face, my sad one, "Is it too late for me to change my answer?"

"Yes." She kissed me on the lips, told me that she had a wonderful time, hoped I enjoyed her company as much as she enjoyed mine, and again asked me to let her pass. I reluctantly obliged. Before leaving, I hoped she would tell me, "Next time in Paris, look me up." I would have responded with, "Only if I was depressed." Cheek kisses were followed with, "Ciao." Moments later, she was gone.

Alone, but still feeling special, the cook returned to discuss dessert. I asked for coffee and gelato. I was too full for a serious dessert. I asked him, "She is a beautiful woman, yes?"

"Monsieur Adam, every woman-loving man in this kitchen tonight was highly jealous of you. And they will be jealous of you long after you leave tonight. Be careful. They work with sharp knives." He paused. "I am kidding of course, but I am not kidding about jealousy."

I learned my lesson. The next time a beautiful woman asked me if I was happy or depressed, I knew what to say.

I woke the next morning feeling the effect of having eaten and drank too much the night before. But I couldn't delay. It was time to leave Paris. I needed to get to London, my last stop of the summer.

I swore I would return to Paris someday. My generous friend, who looked exhausted from her endless hours of study, was willing to call me a taxi after I told her the details of my memorable meal. She was envious of the meal. I failed to mention Madame Bonaparte's lovely left hand.

CHAPTER 32

I arrived in London in good spirits. Paris had been a blast. I found a room, showered, and went off to sightsee. I noticed large posters in a storefront window advertising, "Hong Kong Tailors - Custom Tailored Suits." I went in and bought one woolen suit off the rack for forty-eight dollars, and paid fifty-six dollars for a custom tailored wool suit. The latter had slanted front pockets that were identical to Johnny Carson's suit pockets. The custom-made suit would not be ready for two weeks, but it would be mailed to me. The other suit I would carry home with me. With all this travel and work over the past three months, I had lost twenty pounds. I was determined for my new suits to still fit a year from now.

I called Susan. I had met her at Tivoli Gardens in Copenhagen. She was a university student living in London who often spent her weekends as a private tour guide. That same night, we got together for dinner. After dinner, she drove me to her house in a London suburb.

"Susan, I see a lot of chrome and glass furniture." My family's house was upholstery, oak, cherry, and mirrors.

"Our family business manufactures most of this furniture."

"Your home is also a business showroom?"

She laughed. "No way. In England, a person's home is a very personal place. 'A man's house is his castle.' Only family and close friends are invited here. I'm a surprised that I brought you here. This is a rare chance for you to visit a private English home." I told her I felt honored.

Soon after, her parents returned from visiting a farm. Their faces showed surprise when they first saw me. For their sake I was glad Susan was standing next to me. Only seconds past surprise and a short introduction, her father asked me if I was hungry, and before I could answer, he insisted that I try some fresh cream they had brought home from a farm they had just visited. The cream turned out to be similar to sour cream, only it wasn't the white dairy product I had experienced back home. This sour cream was yellow, tasted much better, and the texture was also distinctly different. With the addition of a small banana, he insisted I add a banana, the dish was a real treat.

Later, Susan drove me back to my hotel. We made a date for her to take me sightseeing on my last full day in England before returning home to America.

Three days later, we went sightseeing together. She was a lot of fun. We did not visit museums or clocks. We did drive past one castle. It reminded me of my uncle's "miniature" castle back home. We visited Harrods department store. We walked past private neighborhood parks where we could look into but couldn't enter. We ate delicious, freshly made ice cream that was from another planet.

After sightseeing, neither of us wanted to say goodbye. Susan suggested we see an American movie that had just opened in London theaters. She was a big John Wayne fan.

The movie turned out to be *The Green Berets*. I watched for as long as I could, then I whispered to her, "You stay. I'll be conversing with the popcorn man. Can I bring you popcorn? This movie is making me ill."

She decided to join me. Many others had quit the movie before us. John Wayne fan or not, we didn't enjoy watching John play a soldier in the Vietnam War. Susan also opposed the war.

From the movie, we went to dinner. I asked Susan to help me choose a meal. From my experience, the food in London was bad. I had tried minced pie and had no doubt that the recipe originated during a period of time when England had nothing to eat. A venison dish I tried was no good either. From then on, I mostly ate fish and chips and drank beer with meals.

After she ordered a chicken dish for me, I asked her, "Tell me about your parents. Were they sore about me visiting your home?"

"Not at all. They were happy to see me bring you home. It was a surprise, but they were happy for me. You're my friend, you're a nice person, and you're the first American in our house since forever, or longer. If Dad had a problem, he would never have shared his favorite cream with you."

She talked about her brief travel to Denmark. When I had met her in Copenhagen, she had been traveling with her Austrian first cousin who she described as a snob and a bore. He was incapable of adventure. That kept them out of trouble, but also kept them out of reach of the unusual or ridiculous.

My stories had her in stitches, especially the time I got locked in the toilet in Brindisi, and when I was escorted to the police station in Athens with all the children taunting us along the "parade route."

She told me, "Your stories are good, but your story-telling is what makes them terrific."

Not being use to receiving compliments, I didn't respond. I asked her, "Susan, have you been to Israel?"

"Not yet. Tell me about Israel."

"Do you want the three-hour story or the five-minute story?"

"I'm flexible."

I decided on a fifteen-minute story—I didn't want to bore her. So I began my story in Cyprus. I lied to Susan about what caused Colette to end our relationship. Yet, the longer I spoke about Israel, the more I realized I might never visit Israel again or any of the other countries I traveled to. That meant I wouldn't ever again meet up with the people I had met along the way.

"Susan, I have to ask you something. How many years have you been offering tours of London to Americans?"

"Three years."

"Do they ever tell you that they are coming back to visit London?"

"Most do."

"Do they return?"

"Not usually."

"I'm not implying that your American customers had a problem with your service and they chose to tour with someone else on their next visit. I just wondered."

"I know what you mean. They do refer their family and friends to me. But no, I usually don't see them again. My tour guide friends rarely see their American customers again either. We have discussed this among ourselves. Your point is that people say they will return, but they don't?"

"That's exactly my point. Something in their life changes, or they simply want to go where they have never been before. But they don't return. There is a good chance I may never come back, or go back to Israel. Not a very uplifting thought."

She changed the conversation. "How many years of university do you have left?"

"I'll graduate next summer, and a month after that I'll be reporting for my military physical. No way will I flunk that physical. I'm very healthy. The Vietnam War will still be raging. The next American president isn't going to end that war any time soon. I don't care what he promises the American people. Nothing is going to change, at least not soon enough to change things for me. I don't want any part of that war. And honestly,

Susan, I'm not crazy about returning to America. That war makes me crazy."

We silently ate our dinner for a whole minute.

"Could you live in Israel?"

"I hadn't given it any serious thought. It's an amazing country. I loved being there."

"If you do, are you concerned about future wars in Israel? Israel isn't the safest place to be living. The 1967 War was not the war to end all wars. If you go to Israel, you will have to serve in the Israeli military."

"Susan, I'm not a reluctant soldier. If I move to Israel, and Israel has another war, I will fight. It makes complete sense to defend your country. The Vietnam War has nothing to do with defending America. I will not serve in the American military until that war ends. At times, I imagine the pain our soldiers are going through right now, today. It doesn't matter whether they volunteered or were drafted into service. Our politicians are responsible for the killing and maiming of those men. For what? We couldn't win Korea. Why expect a better outcome in Vietnam? Not one person in all the countries I visited ever told me, 'Our country is blessed to have the Americans fighting in Vietnam for our freedom.' Not a single one. They know America's military doesn't belong there."

"I know," said Susan. "We get daily Vietnam War news. But Adam, have you considered moving to Israel? That way you can avoid fighting in the Vietnam War! Though if Israel fights another war, you'd have to fight for Israel."

"I haven't thought about living in Israel or any other country. I'm not committed to any of them. Regarding my kibbutz, I was only a summer volunteer. No one ever sat me down and said, 'Adam, consider joining the kibbutz. You are a hardworking, educated fellow. Find a girl. Settle down. Raise your children here. It's a great life.' It never happened."

"They missed out on a good man."

"Thank you."

"Do you have to decide now? You said that you have one more year of university. Doesn't that mean you have one more year to decide whether to stay in America or not?"

"Yes. But no, I don't."

"Why?" asked Susan, looking very confused.

"Think about your customers that don't return to London. Susan, once that plane takes off for New York with me on it, the door to Israel or any other country will be closed to me. I have no doubt. In a few months, Israel will have slipped out of my mind and heart. The only options left will be serving in Vietnam, or become a military draft dodger, an illegal avoider of the armed forces. To do that I would need to move to Canada. The Canadians are welcoming American draft dodgers. Canada is a big country, second only to Russia, with plenty of cold places to live. Running away, living in Canada? Vietnam is wrong.

But Canada isn't the answer. Besides, its empty for me. I have no love for Canada: no hate either. They are a good neighbor to America.

"If you don't go home, what will you do for money?"

"I have a job with a wallpaper company in New York City. I work from anywhere as long as it has good postal service. I send away original wallpaper designs, and they pay me for the good ones. I have a savings account. Someday, I'll receive an inheritance from my parent's estate. I don't know how large it will be. I don't have access to it until I'm twenty-five. I have an uncle who my sister and I live with. He is wealthy. I can count on him to help me out if I have need."

"Maybe you should stay in England and marry me. Seriously, Adam the wallpaper designer, the 10,000 Pound Sterling questions are: What will you do and when will you do?"

"Miss game show personality, I'll have to decide that before I set foot on my flight home. That's my final answer."

"No prize. And the rules of the show forbid me to express an opinion. Thank goodness. Good luck to you. Audience? The audience half heartly applauded. There were several boos. Lean forward. I want to tell you something. Closer. Closer." She kissed my forehead. "This is making you crazy—good crazy, not the bad kind of crazy. Listen to Susan. If the military thought that you were crazy, and you could prove it to them, maybe they would find you unfit for military service and that would put an end to this mess! Do you understand what I'm saying? If they don't like crazy, then give them your best crazy. But mind you, if they like crazy, and you show them crazy, you're screwed!"

"You're very wise Susan. Why are you wasting your time in this backward, old-world country? The New World awaits you. By-the-way, aren't you Brits at war with someone? All your old enemies are so near. Germany. Portugal. Spain. Hell, France is only a few golf shots away when the wind is blowing from the west."

"You're funny. Too much British beer in you? I know that we are involved in the Vietnam War indirectly. I also know that hundreds of our soldiers are in Vietnam, having quit the British army, and joined the Australian and New Zealand armies. Did you know that?"

"No, I didn't."

"And some of the old world has become the New World. I guess you didn't notice."

"We are still friends, right?

"Of course."

It was getting late. I picked up the check and refused to split it with her. I walked her to her car and thanked her profusely for her good company and her advice. We hugged and smiled at each other just before she drove off.

I returned to my hotel room. It was a short walk from the restaurant. I laid out my clothing and packed the rest. I washed, brushed my teeth, set my alarm clock, and turned off the light. Usually, I fall right to sleep, but not tonight. My brain wouldn't call it quits. I turned the light back on, turned on the television, and drew pictures while watching a soccer game. I drew scenes from the Sea of Galilee, including one where I was lying on a Roman pillar still half-submerged in the sea. I sketched the Wailing Wall, again. I sketched the open cellar door with Colette and her drug pusher the moment the hashish was tossed up in the air. I sketched and sketched until I fell asleep. Four hours later, and now fully awake, I washed and dressed and waited in my room for breakfast to be served.

Susan was a sweetheart and interesting woman. London didn't interest me. The English language, as foreign as it sounded to my ear, wasn't foreign enough. Even with all the other similarities: America's British roots, democracy, freedom of speech, law and order, a sense of decency, a degree of common gene pool, and many national enemies in common, I felt no attachment and no tourism excitement. Maybe if England's Renaissance had been similar to Italy's, it would have been different. England's Renaissance was music and literature. The Italian Renaissance was paintings, sculptures, fountains, and architecture.

I would never forget my sightseeing in Norway, Sweden, Italy, Greece, Israel, and France. Maybe I would return to those places someday. I already missed Israel, especially Kibbutz Yir'on and the Sea of Galilee region. I did have relatives on my mother's side living in Jerusalem. If I wanted to live in Israel, I could prove my mother was Jewish. I had developed an attachment to Israel and felt it important to visit again.

I only had coffee for breakfast. It was the first time in three months I passed up an opportunity to eat the morning fare. The food was fine, but I wasn't. I felt unwell, and I was very tired and very cranky. I finished packing and paid my hotel bill. The front desk called me a taxi just like in the movies that dropped me off at Heathrow. I arrived early, much too early, but I thought it was a better plan than hanging around the hotel and missing my flight due to some unforeseen event.

At the BOAC ticket counter, the line was moving slowly, I grew impatient. When I couldn't wait any longer, I stepped out of line and found a seat where I could watch the people walk by. They were mostly well-dressed adults. Two men were wearing turbans. Male Hasidic Jews passed by. Everyone was so different.

The lines were shorter now at the BOAC counter, but I wasn't motivated to get in line. I picked up my bags and went for a stroll. I stopped when I saw the El Al Airline ticket counter and sat where I could watch the passengers standing in line.

Perhaps it was Lady Fate who selected my seat. Between me and the ticket counter was a framed display advertising the Green Beret movie, with a life-size portrait of John Wayne himself wearing his Special Forces camouflage uniform. Missing was the movie theme song: "The Ballad of the Green Berets." I remembered two lines from the movie theater: "Silver wings upon their chest. These are men, America's best."

That song brought forth mixed emotions: I was patriotic, and I was a grateful American. But it also brought forth all my anger towards the federal government because of the war. The war continued to be a dagger in my heart. I had no doubt that the Green Berets were the best soldiers on the planet. I strongly believed it was horrible that they were being killed and injured, but on the other hand, they were killing, injuring, and breaking things. They made widows and orphans. And for what? Nothing! I said out loud, "John Wayne, I am not convinced." Now I was hardly calm and collected. I was sweating. I teared up, not because of John Wayne, but because I wasn't ready to go. Solutions to my problems are not awaiting for me back home.

What I needed was a miracle. I laughed out loud. I had just come from the land of miracles: Israel. The Holy Land. It had saved my life. I probably wouldn't find another in America. I would be kidding myself if I thought I could.

After twiddling my thumbs for ten minutes, I pulled out my American Express Travelers Checks. I had $600 in $20 denominations. I spent seven hundred and twenty-five dollars since I left home. Before the trip began, I spent four hundred and twenty dollars on airfare to Europe and for my Eurail train pass. It was enough money for now. *I'm going back*, I whispered.

I walked over to John Wayne and saluted, then walked back to my bag. It was time to get in line at the ticket counter. The line moved slowly. When it was my turn, I stepped up to the counter and said, "One please, the cheapest seat you have to Lod Airport, Israel." The words brought forth a touch of dizziness. I held tight to the counter top. I wasn't certain if this was a smart decision.

"Passport, please. When do you wish to fly?"

"First available seat. I'm not leaving this airport except on an airplane flying east. I'm prepared to eat fish and chips and drink beer for as long as it takes for me to get out of here." I smiled at her. She smiled back.

"In that case," she said, "I'll see what we have. If I can't accommodate you here," she paused long enough for me to outguess her next words: "*I will take you home and accommodate you there.*" But she didn't. And I was glad. I couldn't handle outside interference that might sabotage my newly made plan. Instead, she said, "I'll check with the other airlines. I know there are no available direct flights with us until much later today. And that flight on short notice is super expensive. I'll see if we have a one-stop flight. You would have to change planes in Greece. Would that meet your approval?" She said this in such a sweet British accent that I almost fell in love with her then and there.

"Excuse me. Where are you and your accent from?"

"Liverpool."

I thought, *there is a female English accent to fall in love with! Who would have thought it would hail from Liverpool?*

"Yes, that would be fine." She found me a flight with a three-hour layover in Athens. Problem was that mine was a middle seat in the smoking section at the very back of the plane. But it would do.

With ticket in hand, I sent a Western Union telegram to Uncle Rick. "Not arriving today. Flying to Israel. Unfinished business. More later.

Love Adam." I paid the man. I wrote a note to BOAC/ I told them I was going to miss my flight intentionally: "There is no reason to delay the flight for me to board. I'm will not fly back." I would have told them in person, but I refused to stand in that long check-in line, again. I skipped the line by stepping up to the ticket counter and leaving both the note and my ticket on it. I left, ignored an "excuse me" that came from behind the ticket counter.

I was stressed about my decision. I walked into a bar and sat at a small table in the back area. I ordered a drink and asked for something— anything, to snack on. One hour and two drinks later, I knew what I needed to do in Israel. I would return to the mountains above Ein Gev. That's where God was, and that's where my miracle was to take place. He will free me from fighting in Vietnam and make me feel terrific. If He had a plan for my future, that would be a good time to reveal it. I was committed. The ticket in my pocket proved it. I finished my gin and tonic, and ordered a third.

Gin mixed with tonic has similar results as 3-in-1 oil: it loosens you up and keeps your joints from squeaking. Now pleasantly loose with silent joint movement, I picked up the green paper napkin next to my drink and pushed it into my left shirt pocket. It looked exactly like a real decorative handkerchief with the top half stuck out. It was my "green badge of courage." I was certain that once I arrived in Israel, all the final details I needed for my plan to work would be realized. It had to be that way: there were no solutions to my problems in America.

My name was announced on the airport public address system, something about me contacting a BOAC agent. That wasn't going to happen. I carried on as if I had never heard the name Adam Haisenberger. I was not about to chicken out and change my mind. I pulled out my new plane ticket. My flight was to Greece. I would change planes for Tel Aviv.

For lack of something better to do, I took out my colored pencils and my sketch pad. I wasn't in the mood to design wallpaper. Instead, I designed toilet paper. It had nothing to do with my Rome dinner date. The only idea that came to mind were alligators with their mouths wide open. "Ouch!" I mumbled. "Can you imagine that headed for your ass?"

I boarded the aircraft and stowed my carry-on luggage on the overhead shelf. I asked a stewardess for a cup of coffee. I couldn't tell if I had on my funny face, begging face, sad face, or smiley face when I asked her.

She replied, "I'm sorry. We don't begin beverage service until after we level out and the seat-belt sign is turned off." Five minutes later, she returned with a steaming hot coffee in a paper cup with a closed lid. The advertisement on the cup was for a fish and chips eatery. "Sir, we found this on the boarding bridge and we believe it belongs to you. Is that correct?" She squinted at me and nodded her head yes.

"Yes ma'am," I nodded back. "That's mine for sure. Thank you for bringing it to me."

"No trouble, sir. Glad to be of service." If not for those perfect lies, my coffee would certainly have caused a stir onboard... or worse! The coffee was hot and delicious. I felt special.

CHAPTER 33

It was early morning when the plane landed at Lod Airport, a few miles Southeast of Tel Aviv. Without a moment's delay, I rode a bus to Jerusalem and rented a room at the YMCA, located directly across the street from the King David Hotel. I had coffee and a sweet roll. Afterwards, I walked directly to the Wailing Wall. I prayed that what I was about to do would succeed, thanks to God's help. I also prayed that my headache would go away. From there, I left the old walled city and went back to modern Jerusalem to shop. In a large hardware store that sold camping and gardening tools, I found a yellow watertight bag. I bought the bag, along with a three-inch pocket knife, fifty feet of rope, two canvas camping ground sheets, and a garden trowel. I also bought a roll of duct tape and several long garden stakes.

"Anything else?" asked the shopkeeper.

"No. That will do it." I paid the man, filled the bag, and left the store.

In a nearby pharmacy, there was a small area of party supplies. There, I purchased a bag of balloons and then returned to my room to take a long nap. I woke up without a headache.

That evening, I ate pizza for dinner. Afterwards, I found an eatery near the YMCA with outdoor table service. I sat at the only available table, a table for four with one chair—not a problem since I wasn't expecting company. I ordered a draft beer. The waitress brought me draft Goldstar beer. It was delicious. It had a sweet taste that was as satisfying as good food. I watched people walk by, always on the lookout for someone I knew. It was possible. The women soldiers looked cute in their uniforms. But I wasn't interested in meeting one. I told the waitress how much I enjoyed the beer and asked for a second. She told me that it tasted sweet because it was an incomplete beer. "Don't drink too much of it. In the morning, your head will hurt. Maybe you should switch to a different beer." I changed my mind about a second beer and returned to my room and went directly to bed.

The next day, I traveled to Tiberias. That evening, I checked into a small hotel that overlooked the Sea. I hand-washed my clothing. They hadn't been machine washed all summer. I hung them out to dry, showered, and went out to eat.

When I returned to the hotel, I found a comfortable chair behind the hotel with a view. With ample light to write letters, I wrote two: one to my uncle, and the other to my sister. I wrote my sister about London. I told her not to worry, but that I didn't know when I would return home.

To Uncle Rick, I wrote about Uncle's team, the New York Mets. I had caught up on the latest Major League Baseball news from a British newspapers. The Mets were in the midst of a poor season. My uncle had tried many times to convert me to be a New York Yankees fan. "That way," he would say, "You'll have fewer disappointments." But the Yankees season was not going well. They had a low team batting average, were many games out of first place, and far behind the Detroit Tigers. Detroit had a strong team and could win the World Series. I told my uncle more than once that, "I would eat dead rats before I would root for the Yankees." Why? I had no idea why I hated them. I just did.

After a good night sleep, I finished packing and went to the front desk to pay for two more nights. I needed the room to leave behind my travel bag and my new suit. With the waterproof bag half-full of clothes, toothbrush and paste, and all the purchases I made in Tel Aviv, I left on foot.

I stopped at a bench by the sea and sketched. I sketched the boats tied up along the docks and those moored beyond them in the deep blue waters; they no longer caused me hurtful memories of Colette, though I still had memories of her. Most were good. What was important was that I no longer was taken by her. My head was filled with more important matters that would soon play out. Time was passing, but I needed a few minutes to calm down. Sketching worked wonders for me. I enjoyed sitting by the sea. People passed by behind me. Some walked dogs, couples held hands, and others pushed baby carriages. I closed my eyes and visualized the task ahead, and prayed to God that it would succeed.

When I was calm and collected, I put away my pad and pencil, grabbed my bag, and crossed the street. It was too far to walk to Ein Gev, so I decided to hitchhike. A small white truck with pull-down seats in the back stopped for me. The driver went out of his way to take me directly to the fish restaurant. I walked out on the dining pier and sat at the table closest to the rail on the north side of the pier. I was glad that the restaurant was closed and that there was no one around to interfere with my plan.

I looked over the railing to judge how far I would have to swim with the bag. The distance was farther than I had calculated, but it was doable. The bag wasn't heavy. Inside, the top half of the bag was taken up by inflated balloons. I hoped that would make the bag buoyant. I didn't have a bathtub in my room to test it.

CHAPTER 34

"It's plowed earth that drinks the rain." – Haitian Proverb

Meaning: "You must be prepared for opportunity."

"Hello," came from behind me. It was Helena, the waitress from the last time I had been here. I thought I was alone.

"You're back! The food must have been good. And the service, outstanding. You did have a very good waitress. Coffee?"

"Yes, and yes. I'm surprised. I didn't think that you were open."

"We are not open. No milk or sugar, right?"

"You remembered."

She smiled. "I didn't remember because you drank your coffee black or because of your double order of french fries. And it wasn't because of the ridiculously large tip you left me—by the way, why did you do that?"

"It was the most enjoyable meal I had all summer."

"Really? Did I hug you?"

"Yes."

"That was nice of me. Could you use one now? You didn't marry since the last time you were here?"

I shook my head no.

She stepped up to me and hugged me tightly. A quick kiss on the lips followed. "I'll get your coffee." I watched her until she disappeared into the kitchen.

This wasn't part of my plan, but after a welcome like that, she was worth a short delay. I had forgotten how stunning she was. The hug, the kiss? Why me? The hell if I knew.

She returned with two cups of coffee, two teaspoons, a small creamer and two sugar packs on a tray. "May I join you?" She sat down in the chair next to me before I could answer.

"Why did you kiss me?" I asked. She decorated her coffee with cream and sugar, and gave it a quick stir.

"I'm attracted to you. Did you enjoy the kiss? I can do better when I make the effort."

"The kiss was nice."

"Tell me more about the tip you left me."

"You were nice to me. If you remember, you put your hand on my shoulder. It felt warm and comforting at a time when I needed it. And you hugged me. Not a mom hug, but a lover's hug." I was intrigued, and it wasn't just because she was beautiful.

"So, I earned the tip?"

"Yes, you did."

"Thank you."

"You're welcome. Are you early for work?"

"It's my turn to set up. I volunteered for this job, filling in at lunch time. This is not my regular job. My job is in the kibbutz business office. I am a secretary and a soldier. The kibbutz owns this restaurant, and I'm here because our sweet waitress, who is much too young, is about to give birth to a baby. I'm covering for her until other arrangements can be made. Those other arrangements are taking forever because our workers are very busy this time of year."

"That's nice of you."

"It's expected of me. How else could we make things work around here?" Without pausing, she said, "The first time I saw you, I pointed you out to the dishwasher. She saw a good-looking college guy, maybe an American. I saw a very handsome young man. Funny, there are plenty of handsome men who come through here, both tourists and Israelis, who have never interested me. Men look good in uniform. You look good without a uniform. Tell me," she giggled, "Tell me, are you the guy I've been waiting for?" I could only smile. I didn't know what to say.

She said, "I'm not kidding. It's not difficult for me to date. I could have a boyfriend waiting list if I wanted one. I'm not desperate for a serious relationship, but if the right man comes into my life, why not let him know that he could be that man. If I think it's you, then we should get to know each other. But not if you are not just passing through."

"Are you saying I might be the right man?"

"It could be you, but probably not. You are a tourist, You are one coffee refill away from me never seeing you again."

"Maybe I'm not passing through. I have business to take care of today. When my business is finished, I'll come find you. There is a chance that I'll be living in Israel."

"Really? You might not go back to America?"

"I might not. It will take some time to figure out where is best for me. Right now, home is America. But in the past several weeks, I have grown to love Israel."

I sipped my coffee. I had a plan, and Helena's arrival was unexpected and, at the moment, an obstacle. Or was she now part of the plan? I glanced at her not wanting to be caught staring. She was lovely.

"Will you ask me out on a date?"

"Yes."

"That's nice. I can't wait. I'll make myself look nice for you. We'll eat in a nice restaurant. Someone else will be the waitress. I can picture it. Can you?"

"You would intimidate me if you looked any nicer. Hell, I'm already intimidated and suffering from eye strain."

"You'll get over it."

"I don't think so."

256

"If you are seriously considering living in Israel, then ask me."

"For?"

"A date. We don't have to eat. We can watch the sunset. We can walk and hold hands. You can buy me a flower, and I'll buy you a cold beer. They pay me big money to work here," she joked.

I smiled. "You'll buy me a beer? You're funny, Helena. Will you go out on a date with me when I get back?"

"Yes, I will. How long will your business take?"

"Maybe two days."

"I can wait two days. But not much longer. More coffee?"

"Please." She walked off, and caught me looking at her backside. I quickly showed her my best "I couldn't help it" shoulder shrug with elbows down, palms facing up, and eyebrows raised.

CHAPTER 35

After Helena disappeared into the kitchen, I removed twenty dollars of Israeli money from my wallet, and shoved it into my shirt pocket.

Helena returned with my hot coffee, put her hand on my shoulder, and told me she had to get back to work in the kitchen. When the restaurant opened, she said she would return with my lunch. "Can I choose lunch for you?" She kissed me on my lips, and walked off without waiting for my answer.

I wrote her a note: "I look forward to our first date. Will be back soon. The traveler's check is for you. Buy something nice." I left the note and money under the coffee cup where she would find it.

I pulled out an eyeglass strap and secured my eyeglasses tightly to my head. I put my passport, wallet, sandals, tee-shirt, and dungarees into my waterproof bag. Dressed only in my bathing suit, I walked to the north edge of the pier and threw my bag into the water. As I expected, the bag floated.

I leaped into the sea and swam as fast as I could, parallel to the shoreline, shoving the bag ahead of me in the direction of the resort's beach. It was located on the far side of the restaurant. When I reached the beach, I grabbed the bag and jogged along the beach. I smiled when I passed the guests. I didn't want to alert the guests and have them interfere with my plan. To the guests, I was simply a young guy out for a run carrying a big yellow bag.

At the end of the beach, I reached the military zone fence. An extremity of barbed wire jutted into the sea. I ran in, swam around the barbed wire, and entered the all-too-familiar military zone.

As soon as I swam past the security fence, the guests who'd witnessed this stood up in amazement. One ran to the beach emergency phone located on the wall of the restroom building. He called and alerted management as to what had happened. They called the police.

I reached the deserted white-sand beach where I stopped, pulled out my sandals, and slipped them over my wet feet. With my feet covered, I ran as fast as I could through tall grasses, staying as close as I could to the chain-link fence. I was certain there were no mines here. The area had to been rendered safe for the fence's construction workers.

When I reached the road, I stopped in front of the huge gate I had entered previously. It was locked. If it hadn't been, I would have tried to lock it. I was concerned about being intercepted by a military patrol. If I heard the loud truck motor, I would climb the mountain as fast as I could.

I switched my footwear from sandals to shoes. There was no time for socks or wiping-off the last drops of seawater from my feet. There were shouts from the other side of the fence. People were running toward me. I didn't know if they had a key for the gate lock. Regardless, I sprinted up the road the best I could schlepping my bag.

Male voices shouted in Hebrew, and a woman's voice called out my name. It was Helena, but I couldn't stop and explain. I just raised my free arm over my head and waved it back and forth.

I followed the road north until I found a good place to climb. Unfortunately, a brown marker stood at the bottom. I continued until I found a better place to climb, a place with no brown markers. Only a narrow strip of land remained between the mountain and the truck tracks, so there was less chance of a mine planted there. About halfway up the mountain, the climb became steep. To avoid this, I would have to climb up and then sideways until the mountain became less steep, and continue up from there. Farther to my left was a brown "mine field" marker. Hopefully, I wouldn't step on a mine or fall on the sign. I peeled off my wet swimsuit and dried off as best I could. I unzipped the bag and changed into underpants. With the bag secure on my back, I approached the mountain and began to climb. The bag made climbing difficult. When I reached a height of 40 feet, I worked my way to the left until the mountain slope became less steep. I continued to the top.

CHAPTER 36

A customer on the pier witnessed my jump into the lake. He ran to the kitchen entrance and shouted in what he had just witnessed. Helena came out of the kitchen and noticed my absence. She ran to the edge of the pier and spotted me exiting the water. She called to me. I couldn't stop. I responded by waving my free arm back and forth over my head. I didn't dare turn around. I was not turning back.

Helena turned to leave, but stopped when she saw my note protruding from under my coffee cup saucer. She found the paper money with it. She quickly read it. "Helena. I am looking forward to our date. There is something I need to take care of first. Will explain later. I will return to you as soon as I finish my business. Don't worry. Adam."

She shoved the note and money into her pocket. She watched me reach the end of the beach and run into the water. "Oh God," she said, standing at the railing among a crowd of customers. She ran off the pier and followed the road past the cabins. She stopped at the padlocked gate. Others arrived at the gate next to Helena. They could see me off in the distance. Helena yelled, "Adam!" Again I waved my arm high above my head without looking back.

The man next to her asked, "Do you know him?"

Unwilling to give up on me, she thought of a way to stay connected to me. She turned to the man and said loudly for all to hear, "Yes! He's my fiancée," and walked away on the verge of tears.

CHAPTER 37

I reached the mountain top exhausted. I hung my arms over the rim. As soon as I caught my breath, I pulled the bag off my back and dragged it to the crest, careful not to let it fall off the other side. I pulled myself up and straddled the crest, facing my bag. I rested again. I carefully unzipped the first foot of zipper and pulled out a hand trowel I bought at the hardware store with the string I had attached to it. I put the string around my neck. I used the trowel to pop all the balloons. I pulled out work gloves and put them on. It was very risky to climb or step over the bag, so I turned around to access the mountaintop. From my location, I noticed an area close by that was wider and made for a good place to set up camp. I cautiously moved along the ridgetop on all fours and began my site-improvement project. I scraped down the mountain to make a flat surface for sitting and lying down. I calculated I would need a five-foot-wide by ten-foot-long platform. It was a lot of work to accomplish the task. I was exhausted when I finished.

When it came time to leave the mountain, I would push back the dirt and restore the mountain top to how it had been. I carefully walked on all fours back for my bag and dragged it along the top until it was secured on my camp site. To say it was important for me not to fall off, was an understatement. At ground level directly below me, were two large boulders. Between them was a brown sign that marked a minefield.

When my strength returned, I flattened a length of the peak to form a narrow walkway so I could exercise. At the far end of it, I cleared an area just below the peak on the backside for a privy where I could not be seen from the road.

I had nearly finished when I heard a military truck approach. I returned to the platform and unzipped the bag. I slipped on kibbutz shorts and a yellow tee-shirt. I pulled out a small radio and a headphone set. I had found a music station and turned up the volume. They stood on the road. One soldier looked up at me and cupped his hands around his mouth. I hadn't a clue as to what he might be saying, nor did I care. I had nothing to say to him. I was determined not to leave here until I was ready to leave. When would that be? I didn't know. In the meantime, I was comfortable in one of the most beautiful places on the planet.

CHAPTER 38

When I awoke from my nap, it was already dark. I sat up to enjoy the view. I listened to Israeli music. I planned to stay up all night just in case wolves made an unexpected visit. I put on gloves to keep my hands clean, and crawled across the crest until I was above the latrine area where I had dug into the backside of the mountain. I stepped down to the lower level and peed down the backside of the mountain, unaware I had been observed by the night patrol. I carefully climbed up to the crest and inched my way back to the level platform area. At this point, the truck driver flashed his high beams on and off several times. So much for privacy.

Knowing I was watched from both sides, I did not need to worry about Arabs and wolves. I could safely sleep. I opened up a small bottle of water, drank half, and returned the bottle to the bag. I felt around and found a small bag of nuts. I finished those, then finished the water.

At first light, I awoke hungry and thirsty. I ate a cracker and walked along the mountain crest to the privy. Last night's military patrol behind the mountain was nowhere to be seen. I returned, pulled out my sketchbook, and drew Helena. I finished one drawing and began another. The more I sketched, the more I realized I didn't know her face as well as I thought. She was a stranger who I wanted to know better.

I put the pad down. I thought about the Vietnam War again. I truly believed if I were sent there to fight, I would be killed there and return home in a coffin. These past three months of summer travel had been a major distraction from the pain I had left behind in America. But it was a reminder: if I returned to America, all the stress I left behind would be waiting for me.

A full day had passed. My plan was to pray for a miracle that would make my military draft problem disappear, and in turn, save my life. Once I received the miracle, I would pack up, repair the part of the mountain I had flattened, surrender to the soldiers, and meet up with Helena for our first date. I firmly believed I wouldn't be locked up by the Israelis, I wouldn't be deported to America, and Helena wouldn't lose interest in me. How would I know if I received my miracle? I don't know. It was a mystery. But I was certain I would soon find out.

The daytime heat was oppressive. The soldiers' truck appeared below me and shouted up, "Do you need anything?" And after a few moments of silence, "Are you ready to come down? If so, we can help you." They didn't say how. But it didn't matter, because I ignored them.

I urgently needed water. The presence of soldiers blocked my access to the lake. They were always there. When a second truck pulled up next to the first, the first truck turned around and drove off to Ein Gev.

I gazed out over the sea for a long time. I relaxed and let my mind wander. Time passed.

"Shalom!" Again, the soldiers were below. One hollered up to me. "Do you need anything?"

I forgot my plan had been to ignore them and shouted down to them, "No."

"Are you sure? Water? Food?"

"No. Go away. Leave me alone. You interrupted me." I closed my eyes again. I was back on Kibbutz Yir'on telling a story to British volunteers.

After a nap, my thoughts turned to all the good times I had over the summer. Colette was no longer a source of pain. My thoughts now about Helena. Our restaurant conversation had been brief. I learned very little about her. She was extremely attractive. I wished she was with me now so I could wrap my arms around her and hold her tight. I had never seen in person a woman as beautiful as she was. I remembered her face, her hands, those slender fingers and nails manicured to perfection. And I couldn't wait for our first date.

As the day wore on, it was more and more difficult for me to remain awake. I sketched angels playing on the beach. The naked angels were Greek; the Roman angels were dressed in fine linen. Rome and Athens were an education in addition to all the fun and adventure I experienced this summer.

I was holding on as best I could. Instead of asking God for a miracle, I repeated the Shema blessing— the first line only, for I didn't know the rest. My Rabbi had told me once I said this prayer, God automatically would forgive any sins I committed against him, though not any sins I committed against individuals. Immediately, I thought of Dominique. My asking her to trade sex for vodka may have been a sin. If she were here, I would ask her for forgiveness. Strange, but I felt like I had already been punished. Since that hazy night, my headaches had gotten worse.

I can't be sure, but I think the Shema blessing was the last words a Jewish person said before he died. My preferred final words would be, "I love you." I certainly didn't pray the Shema because I thought I would die up here. I had no intention of dying. Besides, I doubt anyone ever died up here. It's just not a good place for it. But I had to wait, waiting for a miracle.

CHAPTER 39

By late night, something was different from all other nights. I was teary-eyed and sad. I felt utterly terrible. My mouth was dry. I felt weak and couldn't easily sit upright, so mostly I reclined; but I never got comfortable. I felt dizzy. I had a throbbing headache. I couldn't sweat anymore. My legs were cramping and I was lightheaded. I became agitated and fearful once I became aware that l didn't remember why I was on this mountain in the first place. I couldn't remember how long I had been up here. I wasn't aware that my time for a miracle was running out. Little did I know, I was slowly dying from heatstroke and dehydration.

Earlier, I hallucinated about the military truck below. It was parked in a grove of red maple trees. Beneath the trees, I saw tiny "helicopters" rain onto the truck. The "helicopters" were seed-pairs. They dropped off trees when seeds had dried and cracked open. The two seeds broke apart and twirled down like helicopters. The hallucination ended when the truck engine turned on and roared off to Ein Gev. Finally, I was alone.

Now was the time to make a run for the lake: drink all the water I could, fill my small water bottle, and return here without getting caught. But it didn't matter that they were gone. I couldn't stand, climb, or run. I was a prisoner here of my own making. I couldn't leave if I wanted to, unless I got stupid and rolled down. No rolling today, thank you!

I was at peace, observing blurry stars overhead, when from nowhere a row of angels appeared to me. They sat along the mountain crest on both sides of me. Were all these angels sent to protect me, or to cart me off to heaven? I didn't know. The angels sat there. I didn't speak to them: I didn't want to scare them away. Maybe my guardian angel sent them because she was very busy elsewhere. It all made perfect sense to me as I sat there, slowly losing my mind. I sat patiently waiting for God or my guardian angel to speak to me or perform a miracle of some kind.

From the direction of Ein Gev, I could hear a truck. and see its headlights shine back this direction. It hadn't been gone long. What terrible timing. *Why now?* It will scare away the angels.

CHAPTER 40

Helena was in the kibbutz social hall when an army officer walked into the hall.

"Shalom. Helena?"

"Shalom. Yes sir?"

"We need your help. We have a situation. The resort security told us that you have an American fiancée who."

She cut him off. "Is he alright?"

"He is conscious. He has camped out on a mountaintop not very far from here. He has refused help from our soldiers. But we think he may respond to you. We need him down from there at first light. I want you to go to him now. A helicopter will come to pick him up at sunrise. You need to get him to cooperate with us. He is not to climb down. It's too damn dangerous. Below him are mines."

"I'll help."

"Get into your uniform. And hurry. I'll arrange your transportation."

Minutes later, Helena was dropped off at the Military Zone gate, where a patrol truck was waiting for her. An Uzi rested on the front seat. She climbed into the driver's seat.

A different officer approached her. "A patrol will follow you and will stop two kilometers away from him. I don't want him to see them. If you need help, honk the horn. Help will reach you in two minutes." He showed her my location on a map with penciled-in landmarks. "Don't drive or walk off the roadway. The area is mined."

Helena and the second truck set off. The second truck parked half way there, well out of sight. Once Helena reached the first of the two large boulders, she parked the truck. She shone the headlights onto the boulders and turned off the noisy truck engine. She stepped down from the truck, and stood between the boulders, with the headlights shining on her. She didn't dare step beyond the roadway. She saw the minefield sign off to her left as she faced the mountain. It scared her. She couldn't see me, so she shouted up to the top, "Adam. It's Helena. Are you up there? Can you see me? I can't see you."

Facing the roadway with my legs hanging over the mountainside, I looked down when a female voice rose up from down below. Truck headlights lit up the roadway and I could make out what looked like a soldier with a woman's voice. I wasn't feeling, hearing, or seeing well. A fine dust that covered my eye-glass lenses, make my vision somewhat hazy. Why was she here?

"Soldier. I'm waiting for my guardian angel. Go away."

"You're waiting for your guardian angel?"

"Go away."

"Oh, no," mumbled Helena. "He is out of his mind. He doesn't know it's me. And he doesn't want a soldier around. He wants his guardian angel? If he wants one, I'll give him one." She walked past the truck headlights into the darkness. She removed the elastic from her ponytail and fluffed up her hair. She removed her army shirt, walked back into the truck headlights, and called up to me, "I am your guardian angel. I am here to help you, Adam."

I strained my eyes trying to see better. "Are you my guardian angel?"

"Yes, it's me."

I glanced at the angels seated nearest to me, then looked back to her. "What kind of guardian angel are you?" I knew only two kinds: the clothed angels from Italy and the naked angels from Greece.

"What kind?"

"Roman or Greek?" I said.

She hesitated. "Greek," she shouted back to me.

"No way. Greek angels are naked. You are not my guardian angel. Go away."

She ran back to the truck, hidden in the dark. She quickly unlaced and removed her boots, then her pants, and the rest of her clothing, and threw them on the back seat. She raced back naked, again centered herself between the boulders. She was lit up, mostly from behind by the truck headlights. She cupped her mouth and shouted up, "Adam. I am your guardian angel. I am here to help you. I will be here to watch over you so no harm will come to you. At sunrise, help will arrive and get you safely down from there. You need to come down. But it is too dangerous for you to come down by yourself. Wait until sunrise. I promise to get you down safely then. I'll stay here and keep you company."

I could hear her but I couldn't see her clearly. I closed my eyes: my headache was terrible. I opened them quickly when I heard, "Tek a luk dung there, man…" Was it the voice of a Jamaican male? I turned my head toward the angel sitting next to me. The angel was looking down the mountain. I looked but couldn't see clearly. I removed my glasses and wiped them with my shirt. Now clean, I looked down again. I couldn't believe my eyes. My guardian angel was down there facing me. Lights were shining on her back. I couldn't see her face and the front of her body. I strained my eyes and leaned forward, trying to get a better look, when I was pushed from behind. Down I went. I grabbed at loose dirt. "Woah!" I screamed. I managed to twist my body around and was now facing the mountain. I tried to stop my slide, but found nothing to grab hold of. Friction from my hands, chest, knees, and bare feet scraped along the dirt and somewhat slowed me down. I screamed. The scream alerted Helena, and she reacted quickly. She ran to the truck and dove headfirst over the back door and onto the back seat.

About half way down, my foot dislodged a large rock that slowed me down. The rock tumbled down and landed on a land mine. There was a flash of light followed by an explosion. Shrapnel hit the boulders and

Helena's truck. I screamed when a piece of shrapnel struck me in my left buttock.

I hit the ground and rolled over onto my right side. Unfortunately, I rolled on a hot piece of metal. I screamed and rolled off onto my back. I felt as if I was on fire. I screamed again from lying on my slashed buttock and continued rolling, this time on my stomach facing the road. Loud ringing noises filled my ears.

Helena pulled on her pants, put on her shirt, jumped out of the truck still barefoot, and ran to the edge of the road. She looked at me, expecting to see me blown to pieces. I lay quietly moaning without body part separations. I was beyond her reach from the roadway, and four feet away from the minefield sign. I narrowly missed being impaled on it. She couldn't get to me without risk of being blown up by a second mine, so she hollered, "Adam, Adam. Can you hear me? Don't move, don't move. Stay there. There could be another mine. Help is coming." The explosion had certainly raised the alarm.

I lifted my head and opened my eyes. Though barely visible through my dirt-covered face, I could see my guardian angel. I smiled even though I was in terrible pain. I reach her by pulling myself along the ground with my forearms. Just before I reached the road, I reached out one arm. She grabbed it, and dragged me onto the dirt roadway.

She got on her knees and put her hand between the dusty road and my face and frantically told me, "Please don't die." She turned me onto my side. With my head now on her lap, I lifted my head toward her voice and saw a lovely, tearful face between two large breasts. I smiled. "My guardian angel. You saved me." My head dropped down into her hands as I slipped into unconsciousness.

CHAPTER 41

From what I learned days later, soldiers arrived shortly after the explosion. They laid me on the back seat with my head on Helena's lap. A second soldier climbed in the back seat and applied pressure to my buttocks in an attempt to stop the bleeding. Then they sped off to the kibbutz infirmary.

Helena comforted me as best she could. She talked to me; she held me close. She told me over and over again, "Don't die." I might have died right there in her arms.

The doctor and nurses were waiting for me. The doctor arrived yesterday from Tel Aviv and was given a cabin across the road for as long as he was needed in Tiberias. His specialty was trauma surgery and trauma care. He was not told why he was sent to be my doctor. It was a mystery.

The medical team at the infirmary heard the explosion and prepared to receive an injured patient, me. If others were injured, only I was to be treated here unless my injuries were life threatening. All others if injured, would be rushed to the hospital. The doctor called the hospital and ordered a portable x-ray machine to be rushed here by ambulance. The ambulance would remain here on stand-by. Hopefully it wouldn't be needed.

When the military truck arrived at the infirmary, the soldiers quickly lifted me off of Helena and the back seat and rushed me inside. By the time Helena reached the entrance, she and the other soldiers were being shooed out of the clinic. Helena never made it inside, but she wasn't about to leave. She sat down on a lawn chair near the entrance and waited.

They stripped me naked and immediately addressed bleeding and dehydration. A piece of shrapnel had torn into my gluteal muscles but didn't lodge in there. The doctor cleaned the wound, stitched it closed, and heavily bandaged it. I was given a hydrating enema composed of sugar and salt. He treated my burn wound around my lateral rib cage, and examined me for internal injuries. There were signs of concussion. Further concussion evaluation would be made later. I had mild to moderate abrasion injuries about my chin, chest, fingers, knees, and toes. X-rays were taken from my head to my pelvis using the portable x-ray. Cassettes were rushed back to the hospital and quickly processed.

The radiologist reported back: no broken bones. I had several cracked ribs all on the right side, the same side as my burn injury. He noted a left side skull fracture that was partially healed. None of my ribs had punctured my lung or were in danger of doing so. Pumping saline into me was more important than all the other procedures once bleeding was contained. Deemed in stable condition and now out of danger of dying, the doctor decided to keep me at the infirmary.

When Helena realized she wasn't going to learn anything about my condition, she went back to her room.

I slept through the night. My doctor spent the night in an empty patient room next to mine. "Help!" I shouted.

The doctor reached me before the nurse. "Adam, I'm your doctor. Are you in pain?"

"What?" I shouted.

The doctor raised his voice. "Are you in pain?"

"Yes!" I shouted back.

The doctor entered my room and called out for a nurse. "I need pain medicine, right now, " I demanded.

"The nurse will bring morphine. I'm your doctor. You are in the kibbutz infirmary in Ein Gev, across the road from the fish restaurant where you went for a swim several days ago. You experienced a bad accident when you apparently slid off a mountain. A land mine exploded before you hit the ground. The explosive materials and the fall injured you."

"An explosion?"

"Yes, from a land mine. You are lucky to be alive. But don't worry. You are in stable condition. You are responding to treatment." The doctor continued, "About me. I was sent here from Tel Aviv to attend to you. I am a surgeon and trauma specialist at a Tel Aviv hospital. You are my only patient. You are being cared for like a very important person. I don't know why. Do you?"

"No."

"That's strange. Okay then, I want you to drink water, lots of it. I'll have a meal sent over, including fruit and fruit juices, and I will make certain they are always within your reach. I'll answer any questions you have. And when you feel up to it, I want you to tell me what happened to you out there." He pointed toward the military zone. A nurse entered the room and injected medicine into the I.V. apparatus.

I asked him about my injuries. He told me all he knew. He was surprised about my nearly healed skull fracture. I told him I wasn't aware of such an injury. Then he said, "Is this a good time for you to tell me what happened to you out there?"

"I'll try." It took a few seconds for me to gather my thoughts. "I remember I was up high, sitting on top of a mountain with a group of angels. I saw my guardian angel at the bottom of the mountain. I was trying to get a better view of her when a hand pushed me from behind. Next thing I knew, I was sliding down the mountain in the dark. There was a bright light and a tremendous explosion. I remember lying on the ground, and looking up at my Greek guardian angel. She grabbed me and pulled me along the ground. What I remember next was her holding me as we bounced along in a loud vehicle, probably a military truck, with me moaning in pain. I woke up here. The whole event sounds like a bad dream, doesn't it?"

"Yes, it does. Except you did fall off the mountain. There was an explosion. Helena, rushed you here, where I performed surgery and treated your other injuries and conditions."

"Helena, the waitress, was the one who brought me to you?"

"I was told she is from the local kibbutz. Since you two are engaged, they thought she could be of help. She went with a group of soldiers to get you off the mountain safely."

"Engaged? You said engaged."

"When she comes to visit you, check her out. I'm sure your memory will return. Temporary memory loss is common from what you experienced."

"Thank you for patching me up."

"You are welcome. I assure you it was a team effort. You're a tough guy. Not everyone could have survived what happened out there. You were dying. Remaining up there any longer would have killed you. If you weren't a healthy guy, you would have been dead long before you fell off the mountain. You mentioned seeing angels and a guardian angel. I assume you were hallucinating."

"I don't know. It's difficult for me to believe they weren't real. It's even more difficult to believe my guardian angel wasn't real. She was there: I could see, hear and feel her. She was a life-size Greek guardian angel, and she was beautiful. She was supposed to protect me. She didn't do a great job. I fell. Wasn't she supposed to catch me?"

"You're talking about a female Greek guardian angel?"

"Yes. A naked tall size Greek angel. She called up to me from the bottom of the mountain."

"What did she say?"

"My name. But I couldn't make out what else she said. Then from nowhere, a hand, it felt like a hand, pushed me forward and I fell down the mountain."

"A hand. Alright. What you just described suggests a head injury. I have diagnosed concussion. I will have a neurologist from the hospital come here and examine you. In the meantime, get some rest. Can I trust you not to sneak out of here and go mountain climbing again? Do I have to tie you to this bed?" I smiled, closed my eyes, and went silent. The doctor let me be. Additional questions would have to wait.

CHAPTER 42

When the lunch crowd had slowed at the restaurant, Helena walked briskly to the infirmary. Outside the infirmary, she saw a doctor. She walked up to him and said, "Hi. I'm Helena, Adam's fiancée. Are you his doctor?" He nodded yes. Cat got his tongue for a moment. She was stunning!

"How is he? Can I see him?"

"Excuse me for asking, but about your engagement. Is it a recent one?"

"Yes. No one on the kibbutz knows Adam and I are engaged. We met at the kibbutz restaurant across the road where I waitress. We had a date and we fell in love." She wasn't an experienced story fabricator, but she was a fast learner. "I told Adam I worked here at the kibbutz and I couldn't leave Israel and go back to America with him. I told him to come back here if he thought I was the woman of his dreams. He returned, and we talked about our future. We were so sure about it, we got engaged. He left me a few days ago to take care of business, and said when he returns, we would live here together until I finished my military obligation."

Her story sounded credible. "You know he was up on a mountain?"

"I saw him running away toward the mountain."

"Do you know why he went there?"

"No. He said he had to take care of some business and would return in a couple of days. How is he?"

"Adam is doing well considering what he had been through. But he's still in rough shape."

"Can I see him now?"

The doctor showed her to my room. With a big smile on her face, she walked over to me and put her hand on mine. "Hello Adam, remember your favorite waitress?"

"Yes."

The doctor pulled up a chair for Helena. "Adam, this is your fiancée, Helena. She has been waiting a long time to visit you. I'll leave you two alone."

"Hi. Of course, I remember you."

"How do you feel?"

"I've felt better. Actually, I feel very little pain. They give me morphine and they've been extremely nice about everything. My doctor tells me I will be as good as new. Now, my doctor told me that you're my fiancée?"

She leaned over and gave me a long kiss on the lips. "I didn't bring you anything. So, a kiss is all I had to give you."

"It was a nice gift."

"I enjoyed giving it to you."

"And you're my fiancée?"

"Oh, that. It's like this. You established yourself as a man of interest to me."

"Because of what just happened?"

"Despite what just happened. I just got crazy about you. I connected with you. When you ran off into the military zone, I invented the story about me being your fiancée. I didn't want to be kept away from you. Remember, we agreed to a date after you returned from taking care of business? As your fiancée, I was able to join a group of soldiers who were on their way to help you that night. But before we reached you, we heard an explosion. We found you wounded, laying on the road. My team quickly loaded you on a truck and rushed you here."

"Thank you, and apologies to you, my favorite waitress, and to the soldiers. I guess I put you all in danger."

Helena smiled. "I'm no longer your favorite waitress, or anyone else's. Today was my last day waitressing. Tomorrow I'll return to the kibbutz business office doing my regular work."

"Congratulations!"

"Thank you." She smiled at me, and took a moment to focus on what she was about to say. "Adam, there is more I need to tell you about me being your fiancée. I have fallen head-over-heels for you."

"You are in love with me?" I asked.

"Yes, and I got it bad."

"You're sure?"

"Yes, I'm sure. And I know you're interested in me. You couldn't keep your eyes off me at the restaurant. You told me I was the most beautiful woman you had ever met, my hugs were the best, and you wouldn't mind receiving two of my hugs every day, one when you woke up in the morning and one before going to bed. It's what you said. Do you remember?"

"I think so." I didn't.

"Do you know if you're going back to America, or staying here in Israel?"

"I don't know yet. I might not have a choice. Israel may deport me for trespassing, illegal camping, mountaintop flattening, and littering. On the other hand, it might be difficult to throw me out when my belongings are still on top of the mountain, including my passport and shoes."

"I don't think they'll bother you. You belong here, with me. You're a brave guy, maybe a little crazy, but one of the bravest I've ever met. Promise me you're not going back there, ever."

"I promise."

"You may have hurt your head from the fall. They don't know how it can affect you later. But I love you. I need you to be here in Israel, not somewhere else. Israel is my home. I have no intention of relocating. If you give me and Israel a chance, you will discover how happy you would be here with me. We would make a nice couple. Look, I don't want to be separated from you. I'm asking you, although I wouldn't rule out begging, may I be your fiancée for real? As your fiancée, I can visit you and help you any way I can. In time, we'll see how things work out for us. If it does work out, then we can really be engaged. If it doesn't work out, I not going to think about that."

"Because you love me."

"Because I love you." She bent over and kissed me.

"Helena, I am forever grateful for your help. You are gorgeous. Your hugs knock my socks off. And I am enchanted by your accent. What I find so incredible is that you want to be with me so badly."

"I do, and I can't offer you an explanation as to why. Moving forward, let me cheer you up and help you with your recovery. Here, I'll show you how." She leaned forward, cupped my face, and kissed me passionately on my lips.

"Your kisses are nice. If I agree to be your fiancée, do I have to get down on one knee and ask you to marry me?"

"No, please don't ask me to marry you. You don't love me yet. Give it time. It will happen. Go ahead and ask."

"Helena, will you be my fiancée?"

"Yes, I will Adam," she answered sweetly. "Adam, I don't know your last name."

"Haisenberger."

"Adam Haisenberger, I am Helena Mansour Greenfield. Yes, Adam, I will. You just made me a very happy woman." We kissed, and lightly pressed our foreheads together without speaking.

After a long pause in conversation, Helena said, "I want to tell you about me and my family before our life in Israel."

"Sure."

The next day she told me her story. She began with her American father arriving in Haiti in the early years of the Great Depression. He had begun his business in Haiti importing rice and sugar from America. He was a business man and his business thrived. He met his wife Theresa in Santo Domingo. She came from a wealthy family who owned commercial real estate in Santo Domingo. They married and she moved to Haiti. Helena was their only child. When Francois "Papa Doc" Duvalier, the ruthless President of Haiti came to power, Helena's parents decided to quit the country. One year later, they settled in Israel. Helena was just fourteen years old when they arrived.

She ended the story about herself and the difficulties she encountered making the transition to Israeli life and learning Hebrew. But she was an excellent, hard-working student, and soon she was speaking and writing Hebrew like a Sabra—a person who was born in Israel, but with a noticeable Caribbean accent. She was also fluent in French and Spanish.

I was surprised by her story and sleepy by the time she finished. She helped me up for the short walk to the bathroom, and kissed me after she tucked me into my bed. Was I a lucky guy or what?

CHAPTER 43

Dr. Kaplan, a Tel Aviv psychiatrist friend of my doctor, flew up to Ein Gev to see me. He has a license to practice medicine in America, which made him uniquely qualified to be my doctor since his diagnosis and all my records needed to be sent to the American draft board. Dr. Kaplan agreed to see me because an unidentified Israeli government agency had demanded for him to attend to my needs. Of course, he would be well compensated. As for me, I had no idea what was behind my V.I.P. status.

After evaluating me for two days, Dr. Kaplan had completed his report. He told my doctor about my serious issues. "He's a nice kid, fearless to say the least, but I can't rule out that he wasn't mentally deranged for walking through a minefield a second time. Let's go speak with him."

The two doctors sat down with me. I waited expectantly on what Dr. Kaplan would tell me. "My first diagnosis, Adam, is depression. You left America depressed for various reasons including the deaths of your parents and the Vietnam War. The next is concussion from head injuries you experienced this summer before and perhaps after the mine explosion. Next, and don't be upset when I share this with you, is schizophrenia, not based on angels you saw on top of the mountain easily explained as delirium, but because of your guardian angel issue. And the last diagnosis is post-traumatic stress disorder resulting from your fall and the explosion."

I couldn't believe the diagnosis. "A concussion I can understand, but schizophrenia? Post-traumatic stress disorder? Are you sure about those?"

"Consider those working diagnoses, not final ones. They are my professional opinions based on where you are today. In time, diagnoses often change. Patients progress. I have treated many PTSD cases here in Israel, but only a handful of schizophrenic ones. Collectively, the hospital physician staff and I have the expertise to treat and evaluate schizophrenia. My plan is for you to go into therapy treatment for further evaluation and treatment in a Tel Aviv hospital after you have recovered from your physical injuries, heatstroke and dehydration. But let me tell you some good news. Those diagnoses will weigh heavily on your draft board back in your state of New Jersey. When they eventually receive my final report regarding your medical fitness for military service, there is a strong chance they will reject you, and your miracle will happen. Speaking of miracles, it's a miracle you are alive today after your two military zone experiences. Your relationship with Helena could also be considered a miracle in my opinion. Now, you just get well. And it's not going to take a miracle. Mark my words."

I glanced at my doctor for reassurance. He said, "I am as confident as Dr. Kaplan: everything will work out fine for you. Give it time and adhere to Dr. Kaplan's treatment plan for you."

"Doctors, about Helena. I need to tell her about my health. What do you think I should tell her?"

Dr. Kaplan answered. "Tell her you have a concussion, along with buttock and rib injuries. Don't give her too much to worry about. In time, tell her more if you want. Now, are we all on the same page? If so, I will see you in Tel Aviv. Adam, it was a pleasure meeting you." We shook hands and he left us.

My doctor told me, "The nurses will continue to care for you. When are you moving in with Helena, or do you have a different plan?"

"The kibbutz has a place for me to stay. Helena thinks we shouldn't move in too soon, but she winked after she said that. It won't be long before I will move in with her. The kibbutz director already gave his permission. It's curious, but she thinks I'm getting special treatment from the kibbutz director, but she doesn't know why."

"I don't know why either. But I do know you are a lucky guy."

"Not luck, sir. I believe a *miracle*."

CHAPTER 44

Three weeks later, Helena and I were together in our room. I moved in two weeks ago. Our relationship was as good as we had hoped for.

I will be traveling to Tel Aviv in the morning to see Dr. Kaplan and become his patient in a Tel Aviv hospital. My remaining symptoms were bad headaches. Thankfully, they responded to medication. Helena was shaken by my diagnosis of depression and post-traumatic stress disorder at first, but now she had no doubts: she had fallen for the right man.

"Adam, I want to get married in Tel Aviv one year from now. In six months, we will be able to set the date, because in six months we will know if we should be married. By then, you will be speaking Hebrew and some Spanish. In my family's house we speak Spanish. Also, we need to be married before you join the Israeli Defense Force. I don't want you away from me and be single. Israeli girl soldiers are cute in uniform."

"But it's a small country. I will never be far from you."

"It isn't so small when you are stationed in an isolated place or somewhere very dangerous. Take for example the Suez Canal. You can't have visitors anywhere near there."

"I get it."

"Adam, I want an engagement ring, with a nice diamond with a beautiful gold setting. My mother has diamonds I can choose from. You my love, will pay for the gold setting. Agreed?"

"I'll say yes if you say yes to this: Helena, will you marry me?"

"Yes, I will."

We held each other tight and kissed. "Wonderful. But you need to know this: I can afford the ring's gold setting, and a nice diamond. My father made a lot of money, much more than my family could spend. My mother wisely invested money in real estate in Manhattan. She bought brownstone apartment buildings. She was a good real estate investor."

"I won't hold it against you. But right now, I need a kiss and a shower." We kissed and showered together.

I finished my shower first and entered the bedroom with a towel wrapped around my waist. Helena stayed behind to relax as the warm water beat down on her neck and upper back.

I pulled back the bedding so most of the bottom sheet was exposed, then unwrapped my towel and dried my hair some more. I turned on our brand new soft-light lamp, our first purchase we made together. It sat on the vanity. I turned off the bright overhead light. I relaxed and listened to the "music" of running water coming from the shower room. *There is no finer music than listening to your woman taking a shower. Not Barbara Streisand, Johnny Mathis, or Percy Sledge could compete with it.*

She returned from the shower with a towel wrapped around her waist. She used a second towel to dry her hair. She was gorgeous without a touch of make-up. She was a huge part of my life.

I had once been captivated by the young goddess Colette. But Helena was beautiful like Helen of Troy, the daughter of Zeus and Leda, who, according to Greek Mythology, was the most beautiful woman in the world. So beautiful in fact, a bloody war was fought over her.

She turned her back to me and bent over the sink to brush her teeth. When she was done brushing and rinsing, she removed her towel. I wetted my lips and softly made a two-note glissando whistle, also known as a wolf whistle. I could see her smile in the mirror.

She laid the towel on the vanity, turned around, and stood there, hiding her nakedness from me with the new lamp light directly behind her and the overhead light turned off. I immediately sat up and went pale. My pulse rate sped up and my heart starting pounding in my chest. I mumbled.

She said, "What did you say?"

Was my guardian angel standing before me?

"What is it? You've seen me naked before."

"Come here," I finally said.

She walked toward the bed. "What?"

I had to be sure. I said, "I didn't mean to frighten you. You know every time I see you naked, I react the same as if it were the first time. You are so beautiful. Please, sit down here, put your feet up, and lean back against the headboard." She did. I laid across the bed and put my head on her lap. I peered up and saw past her breasts that framed her beautiful face. *It was her.* How did I miss it? I was so excited. I sat up and faced her.

"And?" said Helena. She knew her secret was out, but said no more.

"Helena. When I was on top of the mountain, you came to me as my Greek Guardian Angel. You shouted to me. You were magical down there. I tried to get a better look. Then I was pushed.

"Who pushed you?"

"An angel, I suppose. Who else could have?"

She paused, then ignored what I said. "You fell seconds after I called up to you."

I raised my voice. "Why didn't you tell me?"

"How could I? I didn't want you to be angry at me. I felt terrible about it. And I still do. Because of me, you fell and got blown up, and could have died in my arms. I almost killed you. Will you ever forgive me?"

"Helena, there is nothing to forgive. You were never told."

"Told what?"

"I was dying on that mountain from heatstroke and dehydration. At the infirmary, I had a high fever, my blood pressure was extremely low, and my heart rate was dangerously fast. I didn't know I was dying. And then you appeared. Down I came. You are the miracle who saved my life. You, and I must include an angel, got me off that mountain just in time.

Something else I need to tell you. Dr. Kaplan believes I have a mental issue because I strongly believe I saw my guardian angel. Now I know it was you. It explains everything. But I think it's best not to tell Dr. Kaplan right away. Since it might matter, let's not tell him until after Selective Service decides what they want to do with me."

"If you think it's best."

"I think it's best. I can always change my mind." I got up and turned off the new lamp. It was a priceless purchase. Helena turned away and backed up to me. I reached around and gently held her. "I want to be with you forever. I have no doubt we were meant to be together. I owe my life to you. And I am very much in love with you." Helena squeezed my hand. Her eyes were filled with tears.

CHAPTER 45

I returned to the library and pulled out an artbook of Rembrandt paintings from a bottom shelf. Rembrandt was a favorite of mine, right up there with Leonardo da Vinci and Vincent van Gogh. I drew Rembrandt's "The Man with the Golden Helmet" with the man's face replaced with my doctor's face. I can't wait for him to visit tonight, so I can show it to him. Hopefully, he'll examine it and not ask for a pair of scissors or a box of matches.

Most of my sketches were of Helena. Yesterday, I portrayed her in my sketch as the goddess Flora in a painting simply called "Flora." Rembrandt painted his wife posing as the goddess Flora in his 1634 painting. But Helena's face was so much lovelier than Rembrandt's wife's face.

I did the same with the mythical character of Danae in a painting of the same name, where she welcomes Zeus into her bed. In the original painting, he used his first wife as the model. Later, he replaced her face with his mistress' face. I now replaced the mistress's face with Helena's, and then I replaced Danae's body with Helena's. Finally, I replaced Zeus' face with my own. Why not? It turned out to be the finest picture I ever drew.

Helena is so beautiful, and she is in love with me. Maybe I should destroy this painting since it might upset her. After all, who would want a picture of themself naked? Where could it be displayed? I need to give this more thought.

I am a resident in a Tel Aviv hospital, one of several men being treated for post-traumatic stress disorder. Twenty days have painfully passed. A determined snail could glide much faster than the passage of time in this place. How does it feel being here? It feels as if I'm driving my car five miles per hour on an interstate highway and all the other vehicles are zooming past mine. *And* I'm now late to meet Helena.

Helena is desperately waiting for my return to Ein Gev. I am concerned about her parents who want me to visit them before I leave Tel Aviv. I assume they have some serious doubts about me.

My sister wants me home. My uncle is happy for me, and is very supportive. "It's your life. You decide what comes next. Tell me how I can help with anything," he said. I am certain Uncle Rick has helped plenty already. How he did it, I don't know.

I no longer dream about fighting in Vietnam. Unfortunately, it has been replaced with one where I am dressed as a soldier, weapon in hand, standing guard on a catwalk above a tall closed gate. In front of me, children are playing at the edge of a pond. I sketched Dr. Kaplan a picture of it. I imagine it implies I'm protective, dependable, and trustworthy. He hasn't told me what he thinks, and I haven't asked. I'll give him some more time.

My doctor stops by almost every day. He works in a nearby hospital and passes here on his walk home. "You are healing nicely. Trust Dr. Kaplan.

He will help you," my doctor says. "Just keep it in mind that he sent your medical records to selective service people in the United States to determine your fitness for service. I'm sure it will all work-out for the best. So, don't worry."

"From your mouth to God's ear. I can only hope."

I still haven't told Dr. Kaplan or my doctor about Helena being my guardian angel. I will inform them after selective service notifies me that I am exempt from military service. When I think back to that moment, looking down on that magnificent miracle…

EPILOGUE

September, 1973 — 5 years later

Adam is working long days for his Uncle Rick in Paris. He is working with furniture designers in Paris and Milan, and textile mills in Italy and America. He works furniture conventions and shows throughout Europe, and is developing strong social and working relationships with the company's best customers. His Uncle Rick is extremely proud to have him with his firm. Adam misses his sister, but loves Europe and his professional life. He is both mentally and physically fit, and plans to divide his time between Israel and Europe once Helena finishes her studies.

His Uncle Rick doesn't believe his plan is workable. He wants Adam to spend most of his time in Europe, and other times in America. He wants him to take over his business someday. Rick's business extends far beyond the textile and furniture industry. Would Adam ever truly discover the extent of his uncle's influence? He knows his treatment in Israel was out of the ordinary and opines that Uncle Rick had something to do with it, but he never asks him. "If Uncle Rick wants me to know, he will tell me," he always tells himself.

Helena is a law student in Paris. She and her carefully selected study group are among the top of their class. She is competitive, determined, and has the problem-solving mind of a lawyer. She misses Israel and her parents, but loves Paris, her studies, and the university community. She plans to move back to Israel after she gets her law degree. Her plan is not negotiable.

The two of them don't have as much time together as they would like, but they love each other dearly, and the time they do spend together is quality time. Their television set is a dust collector.

Adam is the love of her life. She has no doubts after five years. They have been married for four happy years.

Helena is the love of Adam's life. It didn't take long for him to fall inescapably in love with her. Though learning Hebrew might take longer to win his heart!

Manufactured by Amazon.ca
Bolton, ON